NABEN RUTHNUM

THE GRIMMER

Published by ECW Press
665 Gerrard Street East
Toronto, Ontario, Canada M4M 1Y2
416-694-3348 / info@ecwpress.com

Editor for the Press: Jen R. Albert
Copy editor: Shannon Parr
Cover design: Lisa Marie Pompilio / Von Brooklyn Design

This is a work of fiction. Names, characters,
places, and incidents either are the product of the
author's imagination or are used fictitiously, and
any resemblance to actual persons, living or dead,
business establishments, events, or locales is entirely
coincidental.

LIBRARY AND ARCHIVES CANADA CATALOGUING
IN PUBLICATION

Title: The grimmer / Naben Ruthnum.

Names: Ruthnum, Naben, author.

Identifiers: Canadiana (print) 20230439357 |
Canadiana (ebook) 20230439365

ISBN 978-1-77041-704-5 (softcover)
ISBN 978-1-77852-193-5 (Kindle)
ISBN 978-1-77852-192-8 (PDF)
ISBN 978-1-77852-191-1 (ePub)

Classification: LCC PS8635.I65 G75 2023 | DDC
jC813/.6—dc23

This book is funded in part by the Government of Canada. *Ce livre est financé en partie par le gouvernement du Canada.* We
acknowledge the support of the Canada Council for the Arts. *Nous remercions le Conseil des arts du Canada de son soutien.*
We acknowledge the funding support of the Ontario Arts Council (OAC), an agency of the Government of Ontario. We
also acknowledge the support of the Government of Ontario through the Ontario Book Publishing Tax Credit, and
through Ontario Creates.

PRINTED AND BOUND IN CANADA

PRINTING: MARQUIS   5   4   3   2   1

To Rudrapriya Rathore and Robert Inch

CHAPTER 1

"**C**an I get a ride to the bookstore?"

Vish Maurya was in boxer shorts, standing on the desk in his room, and yelling through the vent cover in his ceiling. The footsteps above him stopped. The TV weatherman's voice drifted through the vent, as he let everyone know what they knew already: it was cooler today in Kelowna than in hell, but only slightly. And it was probably drier here.

Waiting for his mother to answer, Vish coughed and scratched his arm. A new patch of eczema had arrived, some dark shading under the forearm hairs that he was beginning to think were too thick, too noticeable.

"Come upstairs if you want to talk. I'm not a prison guard," his mom said, managing to get every word through the vent clearly. Anji Maurya could project without screaming. They used to talk like this all the time, through the vent. Always with the same conclusion, this exasperated invitation upstairs. It was one of the many things Vish had missed in his two years at the boarding school on Vancouver Island.

Vish considered just pulling on pants and one of the t-shirts from the floor of his closet, but he did a pit check with his nose and knew that a quick shower would be necessary.

"Just twenty minutes," he called up through the vent to no reply.

He got down from the desk by jumping onto the bed and bouncing to the floor, but the phone receiver made part of the trip with him. It was an ancient touch-tone with tiny plastic buttons, the number stickers on them peeling off, that his dad had gotten for free with a subscription to *Time Magazine*. It was cheap and brittle, but was precious to Vish, back when he had friends to call. It landed in the thick carpeting and didn't break. Vish nestled it back into its cradle on the desk. The familiar things in this room were important to him: they reminded him that he was back, back for good.

In the years he was gone, there'd been holidays, of course. Time that the other kids spent going on vacation with their parents or doing the turkey-carving-present-trading thing. Vish just came back to Kelowna and, like his parents, pretended things were okay. But never normal. Before they had sent him away, Vish told his parents that if they ever wanted him to pretend things were normal again, they'd have to wait until he was living at home again for real. And now he was. So he was keeping his promise and pretending he could live with his family again, and that they could live with him.

The water pressure in the shower was strong, and best of all, Vish was the only one in it: sharing bathrooms with eleven other boys who didn't want to be his friend and that he didn't want to talk to had not been his idea of fun. He turned the water cold for the final minute, hating the feeling, but knowing that cooling down in here would help him face the summer heat.

Vish started getting dressed from the empty apple crate he kept his underwear and socks in. It hadn't been in his old bedroom when he'd made the move back, but he tracked it down in the garage, where his dad had filled it up with old Canadian Psychiatric Association magazines. Vish had dumped them on the cement floor of the garage. His mom must have found them and cleaned them up before his dad saw, or there would have been a fight.

The apple crate was now tucked into the closet of his new digs, the former downstairs where Vish used to practice guitar, that he'd now swapped out for his upstairs bedroom. He wanted to make the move because it was bigger, he'd explained, and his parents had accepted that. It was another chance for the three of them to pretend. Vish was fifteen and wanted to be as far away from his parents' bedroom as possible, especially after a couple of years of having his own cell-like room at the school, where he could be completely alone for every hour he wasn't in the classroom or the shared bathroom. His dad had helped carry the bed, desk, and dresser, and Vish had done the rest. Most of the posters he'd collected as a kid didn't make it. Just *The Crow* and a collage he'd made of players from guitar magazines.

"Should ditch that poster," he muttered. Danny and Matt Pearson, his old best friends, used to watch *The Crow* at least once every weekend and would have loved to take it off his hands. But to give them the poster, he'd have to see them, and that was something he didn't plan to do until school started. Vish didn't want to see anyone he used to know until he really, really had to.

In his former room, he had a few photos of Danny, Matt, and himself goofing off at the mini-golf course at Scandia and on their cousin's boat pinned up next to the guitarist collage, above Eddie Van Halen's head. These photos now lived in a drawer.

Through the vent, Vish could smell coffee, eggs with the kinds of spices his dad liked, and the blender making one of the two smoothies a day his mother drank. Vish still hated breakfast, and now that he was back home, Anji was starting up again with her requests for him to eat something proper to start the day. But just like at the boarding school, where they couldn't force him to eat anything he didn't want to, Vish intended to keep eating an apple each morning, at most. He put on pants and grabbed a Megadeth shirt that his mother hoped he would lose someday soon.

As he pulled the shirt on over his head, Vish looked into the mirror over his dresser. Outside his window, just at the level of the sill where a potted plant would be if Vish had plants in his room, was a human head. Vish whirled around, too scared to yell, and the head was soon joined by shoulders and two hands held up in a gesture that was supposed to look calming but just looked panicked.

It was Matt Pearson, sweaty, his curly hair hanging lank around his face. He was wearing a dark grey t-shirt, which was a mistake on such a hot day. He looked like he'd walked through a car wash before getting to Vish's house. Vish cranked open the window. Matt spoke into the screen.

"You got taller, but not much."

"What are you doing here, man? Watching me change?"

"How could I see you changing with how dirty this window is, dude?" Matt asked. He usually insulted before apologizing, a habit that Vish had picked up too, according to his mom. "Sorry I snuck up on you. I went to your old window and you weren't there, so I was just —"

"Spying? It's weird, Matt."

"What's weird is you ignoring Danny and me."

"Keep it down," Vish said. "And where is Danny? He better not be bugging my mom."

"Yeah, I decided to sneak down here and crawl in your window to make sure not to bother your parents, while Danny knocked on the front door."

Vish stared through the screen. If Matt was waiting for a laugh, Vish wasn't going to provide it.

"He's not here. He's home practising drums. And I didn't come here to 'bug' you. You want me to go away and leave you alone, just tell me. I'll let Danny know. Anyway, can we talk for five minutes without the screen here? It smells like rust."

Vish hooked his fingers into the little plastic tabs on the inside of the screen, using them to pull the springs that kept it lodged in the window frame flat. The screen gently popped off and came inward. Vish waved Matt in. The window was low to the ground, but Vish still had to help pull Matt over the ledge. Matt had one leg shorter than the other, not by much, but that and a few other what he called "skeleton things" made it uncomfortable for him to stand around or run, and made it a bit more difficult to climb in an open window. Soon, Matt was sitting in a sweaty pile on the desk. His baggy black t-shirt and cargo shorts made him look like a heap of laundry with a small human lost inside of it.

"I'm getting a ride downtown soon," Vish said. "I don't really have time."

"Good. Maybe now you're in a rush you can finally tell me the truth." Matt took off his glasses and tried to polish them with his t-shirt before putting them back on.

"About what?"

"Just say that you're pissed at us. Say it. Because Danny and me know you are. We've always known. And it's because Danny told Mrs. Gulliver about your dad. So just say it." Matt pushed his curly hair up and back, but it flopped back down and seemed to stick to his forehead even more permanently. "It was my idea to tell her. We didn't know you'd be going away for so long, or we wouldn't have said anything."

Vish hadn't expected Matt to come out with this right away. He would have pushed him back out the window if he thought he could do it quickly enough and that Matt wouldn't be right back on his feet, yelling at him.

"Yeah, Matt, I didn't really expect my two best friends to tell the band teacher that my dad was a drug addict and that I was getting sent away until he was clean and my mom could stand being around me again. I didn't think you guys would do that."

CHAPTER 2

A great clanging sound from the vent shut both the boys up. It was Anji's Birkenstocked foot, thumping out a summons. Vish put a finger to his lips as his mother spoke down through the vent.

"Time to get going, Vish, if you're going at all."

"Five minutes," Vish called up.

"Five minutes?" whispered Matt.

"Hurry up." Vish waved Matt farther into the room, away from the vent. Matt took a seat on the unmade bed, while Vish sat with his back to the door.

"Look. Danny and me both apologized, Vish. In like fifty letters."

"So it's my fault you humiliated me and my family to everyone we know, because I didn't answer your stupid letters?"

Matt rearranged himself on the bed, sitting cross-legged, staring at Vish.

"No. That's me and my brother's fault. And we're sorry. I'm saying you never answered when we asked if you were mad. You didn't answer us at all, not about anything important."

"I didn't want to talk about it. I still don't, not with you. Not now or any other time. Because look what happened last time I talked to you about something important, right?"

Matt leaned back against the window. He opened his mouth, then closed it. They were both remembering that day in the middle of the seventh grade.

The three of them had been hanging out in the band room after class, free from the restrictions of the musical charts that they repeated endlessly. In the period they'd just finished, it had been *The Muppet Show Theme*, over and over because the French horn and flute players kept messing up. Vish played the flute part on his guitar, while Danny made Animal faces behind the drum kit while he pounded out the simple rhythm. Mrs. Gulliver had to shoot a look at them every few minutes to get Danny to quiet down enough so the other eighteen kids in the concert band could be heard.

Matt was one of two bass players, and he was concentrating on getting the intonation exactly right on every note because he'd been able to play the piece almost perfectly from his first try. Mrs. Gulliver was a former hippie, as she told everyone all the time, only she looked exactly like a hippie still, maybe with neater clothes. Wild, curly hair and a lot of purple, and she wanted to be everyone's friend, except when it was time to actually play a chart, when she tried to shift into military mode, threatening any kid making stray noises on a horn or tympani with suspension if that happened just one more time.

But she was always up for letting Vish, Matt, and Danny stick around and play music after class was over, as long as it was the end of the day. She would go to her upstairs office and do whatever it is teachers did after class. Vish knew that the math and history ones had papers to grade and lessons to prepare, but he genuinely had no idea what Mrs. Gulliver did up there. He asked once and she looked pretty mad.

That afternoon in the band room, only Vish knew that it was going to be their last jam for a long time. So he did his best to forget about what was happening to his dad, and what was coming for him in the next months or years, and to just have fun. Vish was pretty sure they sounded bad, and Matt would have confirmed they did, but drawing out the riff from "Enter Sandman" into a twenty-minute blues and noise jam, cranking the volume on the school-owned Fender Twin Reverb amp until the speaker crackled and the air between the three boys got thick with sound and excitement, felt better than almost anything Vish had ever done. He could tell he felt good because he wasn't thinking; he wasn't trying to forget anymore, his mind was in his hands and in the music they were making. That day, the janitor literally had to pull the plug on Vish's amp to snap the three of them out of it.

Afterwards, Danny, lanky and sweating in the spring air, took his t-shirt off and hung from one of the hoops on the basketball court to stretch out his arms. The hoops weren't standard NBA height, not even close, but it was still impressive. He and Matt were the kind of twins who looked nothing alike, and Danny was already almost a foot taller. While his brother swung from the hoop, Matt asked Vish the question that would lead to spending less, and eventually no, time with his former best friends.

"Do you want to finally get serious and do a band with us or what?"

Vish started to cry, something he hadn't done in front of anyone up until that day, not even his mother, certainly not his father, whose fault all of this was. His father and those little orange plastic bottles. It wasn't a full sob, but the tears came, and he walked off the court and back into the band room. The brothers came in to see Vish facing one of the corners. The walls had sound-baffling foam and carpet glued and stapled onto them, and as Matt and Danny walked up behind him Vish remembered staring at the grey foam, all the chunks torn out over the years by kids before him.

And then Vish told them everything. That there would be no band because he was leaving town, for how long he didn't know. His dad, the pill addiction, detoxing, the plan to send Vish away until everything at home calmed down. And the two brothers listened, each with a hand on one of his shoulders, neither of them asking Vish to turn away from the wall, because they knew he didn't want to. And then he'd run out of the room and gone home. By the time he got to school on Monday, every kid he knew had heard the story. And by that night, his mom was getting phone calls asking if the rumour was true.

"I trusted you that day," Vish said, as Matt stared at the desk he was sitting on, both of them snapped out of the memory. "I trusted you and the first thing you did was run to tell Mrs. Gulliver like she was your mommy."

"Vish, we had to. Her office door was open and she heard some of it. She asked us if you were dealing drugs and made Danny —"

"I know Danny's stupid but you're not, Matt. She didn't hear it all so she asked a question that would get you to tell her everything so she could tell all the other teachers, so they could all gossip about my family while they pretended to care about me. And about ten seconds after that every kid in school knew. You know what this town is like."

Matt stood up from the bed and looked like he was considering walking over to Vish. Instead, he went back to the desk and paused before boosting himself up on it.

"You're right. Gulliver probably did trick us, and we were stupid to talk. Stupid, but that's all, man. We let you down because we were trying to help you out, and we were wrong. But it's because we didn't want you getting in trouble. We're sorry, and Danny and me both think that if you came over, if we just jammed some and —"

Vish walked over to his still-open closet, pushed the hanging sweaters aside, and pointed at the dusty red Stratocaster guitar that rested there, abandoned in the shadows.

"I don't play anymore, Matt. Just because it was fun to play forty seconds of 'Leper Messiah' over and over after band class doesn't mean that I want to actually spend hours wasting time with you and Danny. It was stupid."

While Vish spoke, Matt stopped looking so much like a pile of laundry. He stopped staring at the floor and straightened his back out. By the time Vish was saying "stupid waste of time," Matt had turned and was edging out the window. He replied when he was outside.

"I don't think it's stupid to try to get better at something, Vish. Neither does my brother. And we did get way better over the past couple years, and it would be cool to see you do the same. Or we can just watch movies, or hang out. Just know that we're really sorry, and give us a shot again. If you want."

"No," Vish said. Matt stared back at him for a second, then started walking away, just as Anji thumped on the vent grating above Vish's head again. Vish put the screen back in place and ran upstairs. When he got to the kitchen, he filled a glass of

17

water at the sink. Out the kitchen window, he saw Matt walking away down the street. He thought for a second about running out to stop him, at least asking if he needed a ride.

"Vish, can you stop staring at nothing and focus for five seconds?" Vish's father spoke, and as Vish was taking the words in, he also tapped his coffee cup with his fork. Vish turned, nodding an apology, and sat down at the kitchen table with his half-finished glass of water.

Since starting up his practice again, Dr. Munish Maurya saw patients seven days a week. Today was a Friday, which he used to take off, working Sundays instead. But now, with so many patients having moved on, he took any booking he could get. He was wearing a shirt with a tie under a light cardigan as he finished his coffee over the near-empty plate. A square of paper towel protected his tie and shirtfront. Dr. Maurya didn't shave very effectively. He pushed his electric razor in a sort of winding stroll around his cheeks, chin, and neck. The result was a daily changing pattern of small triangles or patches of stubble in addition to the moustache he kept on purpose.

Anji was reading the *Daily Courier*, more particularly the real estate listings. Her hair was wrapped in a towel, but she was otherwise armoured for the day, in a light green pantsuit that had a few flecks of water on the shoulders. She pointed to the fruit bowl on the kitchen table, and Vish walked over to pick out a Honeycrisp apple. His dad was mopping up the last of the scrambled eggs with half an English muffin, and Vish was surprised by a quick flood of salivating hunger for the rich cumin-and-coriander-laced protein. But if he showed a willingness to eat eggs today, it could become an unavoidable routine enforced by his parents.

"I can give you a ride to my office, and you can walk to the bookshop," Dr. Maurya said. Neither of his parents had an accent, except in the imitations other kids did of them, which Vish used to join in on when he was tired of being defensive.

"Mom, can you drive me right there?"

"No. I want to finish cleaning and then do nothing for an hour. And it's only a few blocks' walk, Vish. That's a good deal." Vish had found his mother's clove cigarettes in a Ziploc bag in a planter around the side of the house last winter. He still hadn't said anything about them to her, but he now knew that part of her "doing nothing" involved smoking, while sitting on the plastic deck chair on the cement paving by the side door. Vish had found ashes there and scattered them away with his sneaker toe in a gesture of quiet solidarity. And to prevent the prospect of his parents having another fight about secrets.

Dr. Maurya rose, making his usual getting-up groan, pushing the chair out from behind him with the backs of his knees. Vish pushed it back in for him so his mom wouldn't have to.

"This is your first time going downtown since coming back, isn't it?" Anji asked. She set the paper down and circled four listings.

"Does the grocery store count?" Vish asked. "Or scrubbing floors at the office?" The allowance Vish's parents had doled out while he was at the boarding school had stopped, and he now earned his cash with chores at Dr. Maurya's new rental office: fifteen dollars a week sweeping it out, wiping down the chairs and surfaces, and Windexing the frosted glass with "Psychiatrist" and his name on it.

"Don't be sarcastic." Anji carefully drew an X through the photograph of Marissa Bingham, Kelowna's #1 real estate agent, who had twice interviewed Anji for a job at her firm and both times explained to her why she would never be a success in the business. Dr. Maurya's time in rehab and the long months of recovery had forced Anji to make the big decision to start working for herself. She'd become Kelowna's #16 real estate agent over the past two years.

Dr. Maurya walked into the hallway. Vish could hear the jingle of him transferring his wallet and keys from his weekday blazer into his weekend pants.

"Sorry, Mom. Yeah. First time back downtown for real."

"Are you meeting anyone down there? Anyone meaning Danny and Matt?" Anji asked. Vish hadn't come out and told her it was his friends who had let the family's secret out, but she had guessed immediately, and he hadn't lied to her when she asked. So she wasn't a big fan of the brothers.

"No, Mom. No one." The front door opened, the seal making its familiar peeling sound, blessing Vish with the chance to stop this conversation. He was in the driveway, calling "Bye!" over his shoulder, in seconds.

"You didn't bring a CD, I hope, because I'm not in the mood to cope with any of your noise," Dr. Maurya muttered as he hit the unlock button after opening the driver's side door. Even if he'd abandoned the guitar while he was out at the school, he was listening to more music than ever. That and reading were all he had done in his free hours at boarding school: after class, and after his forced counselling appointments, where a rotation of therapists, teachers, and administrators begged him to make friends, to talk to anyone, and he politely refused, Vish went to his room alone with music and novels.

Vish got into the passenger seat of his dad's Camry. They drove in silence for the ten minutes it took to get downtown. "Downtown" meant about six blocks of slightly taller buildings and clothing stores. Usually Vish would have reached for the radio to turn it to 104.7, where there would be the chance of Led Zeppelin or Pink Floyd and the risk of Green Day. But there was something fragile about the silence on this ride. Munish Maurya was thinking, which could mean that he was going to say something harshly critical to Vish, ask him something uncomfortable about his life, or just if he wanted to go to the German bakery on the way home for a secret strudel. Dr. Maurya's neck seemed to sink into his shoulders when he was deep in thought, which made him look old and wise, like a turtle stripped of its shell in favour of a grey Brooks Brothers shirt.

Danny and Matt were probably the only kids who hadn't made fun of the age gap between Munish Maurya and his wife. "Arranged marriage" was the top joke on the list, followed by "mail-order bride." Some of the more fanciful and complimentary but still cruel kids said Anji Maurya was a kidnapped princess because there was no way someone that beautiful would willingly end up with someone who looked like his dad. It was mostly girls who made this last joke; girls with parents who told Vish how much they loved samosas and butter chicken at school socials, girls who wanted to prove they weren't racist but still wanted to make it clear that while they considered Vish an interesting creature to talk to, they would never actually hang out with him. Calling someone a beautiful princess can't be racist, Geena Barnes told Vish when he'd gotten sick of her jokes in math before the end of term. Vish didn't know exactly how to explain that it was, and felt that anything he did say would just get him made fun of more, so he swore to himself loudly enough for the teacher to hear and accepted the refuge of the principal's office waiting room. He knew there was little chance of a detention in June, and indeed a written apology was all the vice principal asked for when the bell rang.

At least the jokes would have shifted to your-dad-is-a-junkie ones when school started up again in September. The variety would be nice.

"I want you to know, I wish you'd reconsider what you're doing," Dr. Maurya said, just as they were pulling into his parking space. He was reaching into his pocket for his wallet, which Vish had been hoping for, if not expecting.

"What?"

Dr. Maurya extracted the wallet, and from it, a ten-dollar bill.

"Do the weeding in the front garden before dinner."

"Okay," Vish said, tucking the bill into the pocket of his jeans. He hated sitting too long in the Megadeth shirt; he should have gotten a small, because the medium draped out like a dress when he sat in it. Vic Rattlehead, the Megadeth mascot, wasn't meant to billow, he was supposed to fit tightly over a sculpted chest or honourable beer gut. Vish felt caved-in, like an orphan, not like a biker with a thick presence. "And what should I reconsider?"

Dr. Maurya was halfway out of the car but still heard his son. Vish joined him outside.

"Eh?" his dad said. Vish wondered if asking to have something he had already heard repeated was a technique Dad used on his patients, and if so, exactly how much it annoyed them.

"You were saying that you think —"

"Matt and Danny Pearson. You've been moping around alone since you got back, not returning their calls, never walking over to their house. I know you got used to being alone out at the school, but your mother and I are worried. You used to like playing your guitar, spending time with those two. I think maybe a bit more of that and a bit less reading would be a good idea."

"I thought you were supposed to know things about people," Vish said. He felt the sharp edge of one of his nails in his right palm and had the stray thought that he hadn't clipped it evenly. Then he started to realize how angry he was.

"What?" Dr. Maurya said.

"You can pretend to do Dad stuff all you want, and Mom and I will pretend right back, but you know what you did and how much I hated being in the middle of nowhere with a bunch of strangers for two years. You did that. And everyone here knows you became a drug addict and ruined my life. Including Danny and Matt. No one wants to hang out with me."

Dr. Maurya looked at the ground while Vish spoke. Vish was whispering, not screaming. He wouldn't remember exactly what he said as soon as the words were out: he was so angry that his brain felt like it was sweating in his skull, like the sentences were coming out of him automatically. Dr. Maurya raised a hand, put it on his son's shoulder, and then dropped it back to his side.

"I'm sorry," he said. "Nothing you've said is unfair. I'm sorry."

"I didn't mean it," Vish said. He couldn't remember if he'd sworn at his dad in his anger, but he knew that he'd been honest, which meant he was very brutal.

"We'll talk about it later. I have to work, and I don't want to ruin your day. Go have your shop, read in the park, and meet me back here in four hours." Dr. Maurya pulled another ten dollars from his wallet and handed it to Vish, who wanted to refuse it for a second before realizing that the rejection would hurt his father worse than what he'd said. He nodded, and started to walk past his dad before he felt that hand on his shoulder again.

"Vish. I want you to know that I do feel strange playing the father after what I put you and your mother through. You got it right. It does feel a bit like we're all pretending. Understand that it means a lot that you still — that you still let me try." The hand on Vish's shoulder tightened, almost painfully, then let go. Munish Maurya started walking away quickly. Vish was relieved, because he didn't think he would be able to take his father crying without crying himself.

Dr. Maurya vanished into his office building. Two young women, one named Candice who used to babysit Vish when he was in kindergarten, came out of the dry cleaners next door with their arms full of plastic-sheathed dresses and suit jackets. They rustled past Vish as he stared at the door his dad had just walked through.

Vish stood by the car for a moment after he snapped back to reality. He transferred the ten-dollar bill to his wallet, which contained a library card, Metallica Club membership card, Tekno-Comix Fan Club patch, and a swatch of green felt from the bottom of an antique jewellery box that made him feel comfortable when he stroked it. He tucked the wallet into his back pocket and fastened the button.

CHAPTER 3

The walk from office to bookstore was so short Vish felt embarrassed he'd complained about not having a ride the whole way. In the two years he'd been away from Kelowna, distances seemed to have shifted, and not just because his legs were a few inches longer. It was because he'd forgotten what was where, and the familiar wasn't familiar anymore.

On the sidewalk, he got some looks, but those were expected. And they weren't looks of recognition. A t-shirt adorned with skulls and nails overtop a pair of black Marks & Spencer dress pants did not mesh with the early July look of Kelowna tourists and locals: white shorts, board shorts, sports tees with the sleeves cut off, golf shirts, tank tops with cotton spaghetti straps. And while the skin he saw was all tanned, none was as brown as his. In the last stretch of the walk, he spotted a familiar face: Mr. Clarke, the science teacher he and Danny had bugged with stupid questions for the whole of grade six, about tadpoles, pregnancy, and, whenever they could find a way to fit it to the lesson, poo. Mr. Clarke walked out of Towne Centre Mall and definitely recognized Vish, but just lowered his face into a huge croissant and started chewing it as he walked past him.

"Sorry, Mr. Clarke," Vish muttered to himself, about a block later.

Greycat Books was still where it was. Still familiar. Right on Pandosy, just off the main street. Vish accelerated his walk and entered. The air conditioning was on full, and Vish was immersed in coolness when he came in. Then he was immediately not in Kelowna any longer. He wasn't even in 1996. He was in the same place he went to when he was alone in his chamber at the boarding school for all those hours, walled in with books. As he walked his fingers along the spines of novels he'd vaguely heard of, he imagined a time when he'd know all of the writers by reputation and by name, and some personally. These would be the ones who wrote Vish respectful letters about his own future novels, which Vish would reply to with compliments of his own. All of this would be in a city, first just Vancouver, but then a huge one, one that was impossible to contain in his mind all at once: London, or New York. He would go from reading these books to creating them to inhabiting them.

Forty minutes passed. For about one of those, Vish was thinking about his conversation in the parking lot, remembering more of what he'd said to his father, but for the other thirty-nine, he was in the paper and spines of the books, pulling out the names that seemed familiar and the titles that felt like they should become familiar.

"So do we hang out in the Occult section because we wear metal shirts, or do we wear metal shirts because we hang out in the Occult section?"

"What?" Vish had heard the question perfectly: he just hadn't expected it and didn't want to answer it. He was wrapped up in his deep browse, and had a Sherlock Holmes book and a green-and-black edition of Franz Kafka's diaries in his left hand. He was kneeling in the miniature Occult section, which was right across from the till, and had just opened a copy of the Necronomicon that was a cruddy mass-market paperback, not an ancient skin-bound Arab text.

"It's not a mean question, I'm asking to figure it out for myself." The clerk, who Vish guessed might be the store owner, because he remembered him being here two years ago, pointed at the Motörhead shirt he was wearing, which fit absolutely right.

"Don't you do that? Ask yourself questions to figure out what you think of things?" the clerk continued. Vish nodded.

"Good. I didn't want to think I was alone on that. And that book is not what you think it is. Just something published on the quick and dirty to pull in Lovecraft fans. Stick to the stories." *Ace of Spades*, the clerk's t-shirt read, under the metallic dog door-knocker thing that was on so many Motörhead shirts. Vish had only heard the man speak a few words at a time when he used to come in before the move. Probably not even words, just numbers. The prices of the books he'd brought to the till, plus taxes.

Vish hadn't had a real conversation with a new person for a very long time. He'd devoted himself to avoiding conversation for two years. So he opened his mouth and just tried to reply to the question he'd been asked, without thinking about anything else.

"I don't know. I mean, if I got into heavy metal before ghost books, or if it was the other way," Vish said. "I guess I did start reading H.P. Lovecraft because of Metallica, though."

"'Call of Ktulu,' yeah. I hated that they changed the spelling. Lovecraft can get pretty old with the racism and the plastic characters, but he's the best at ancient evil and monstrosities and cool spellings. You have to give him that."

"Yeah," Vish said. He wanted to live up to this conversation. Not just because it was his first one with someone he didn't know for ages, but because it felt adult. The clerk/owner was also one of the only other brown guys in the city who seemed to have no connection to the gurdwara or the Hindu temple where Vish's mom sometimes participated in events in order to meet potential real estate clients. Kelowna wasn't tiny, but it was small, and the populations tended not to mix.

The kind of in-between brown guy that Vish believed he was hadn't otherwise existed at his junior high school. A cluster of Sikh boys had asked him on his first day if he spoke Punjabi, and when he'd answered no, the conversation had ended forever. And the boarding school on the island had been as white as it was small, with just Vish and one Korean Canadian kid, whose parents still lived and worked in Seoul, on campus.

The clerk brushed his hair back from his face. He looked tired and sick, but also cool, somehow. Maybe the three went together, Vish thought. He remembered a pale woman with long dark hair used to work at the store, always sorting, never behind the till. She had once stared at Vish with eyes so intent that he suspected himself of stealing something, and even started patting his jeans pockets for a small paperback he may have put in there by accident. Vish had the impulse to ask the man about her but realized that might be weird, and further realized he had no idea what to say next. So he didn't think, he just blurted.

"I haven't been in here for two years. Looks the same," Vish said. Realizing that he was still kneeling in front of the Occult section, he stood up.

"Some books have sold and some new ones have come in, but yeah. Why'd you stay away that long? Not a big reader?"

"I am a big reader," Vish said, trying not to sound offended. "I was just away. Moved to the island for a couple of years."

"Oh yeah? Why the hell did you come back?" the guy asked, then laughed. Vish laughed too.

He's about thirty-five, Vish thought, with a beard that seemed to have grown out of laziness instead of any conscious choice. He had the good taste to spend his life in a bookstore, and cool t-shirts — he was like Vish in at least a couple of important ways.

"What's your name?" the man asked.

"Vish. You?"

"Agastya. And I should make myself clear, about the *Necronomicon* etcetera: I'm not so much into the occult books, the non-fiction ones, that is. It gets too close to New Age, you know? The stuff that gets published, I mean. I don't think the big publishing houses exactly go deep when it comes to arcane knowledge."

"I dig that," Vish risked. He'd found a Jimi Hendrix documentary on Bravo while flicking channels in the boarding school commons one weekend when the rest of the kids had taken a shuttle into town. He'd harvested Jimi's speech for any language and vocal patterns he thought he could pull off.

"And I barely listen to metal anymore," said Agastya, rubbing two fingers against his temple, closing his black eyes, and breathing in through his nose. One or both of his nostrils whistled. "More just hard rock." Eyes still closed, Agastya pointed again at his own t-shirt and said "etcetera."

Vish didn't quite get that band yet, but most of his guitar heroes worshipped Motörhead and its forceful singer, Lemmy. Vish at least loved the lyrics to "Ace of Spades." Lemmy's wart unsettled Vish, but the words about gambling while knowing you're going to lose spoke to something he hoped was in him but suspected was not: a recklessness that wasn't stupid, a desire to make what was probably the wrong decision because it was also an interesting decision that had a chance of being right. So maybe he didn't love Motörhead, but he understood it a little bit.

"Vish, can you stay here and not steal anything or let anyone else who comes in steal anything while I go upstairs and do sad things in my bathroom before taking two Tylenol?"

Vish suddenly understood why this man had decided to talk to him for the first time. He needed a favour because he was hungover. When Dr. Maurya used to drink, before the pills had started, these morning headaches that introduced a chattier, breezier tone were common. The hangovers had been rare occasions, but memorable ones. Even as a little kid, Vish had recognized his father's false-casual tone for what it was: embarrassment.

"I can do that, okay," Vish said.

"Might be a discount for you. Dig?" asked Agastya, coming out from around the counter. "Sorry. I'm not making fun of you. I mean, I am, but not in a bad way. And the discount is going to happen." Agastya was just under six feet tall, with hair that looked almost Beatles-ish without being deliberately retro.

Vish wondered whether he should shake hands as Agastya approached, but the bookseller kept walking, heading for the door at the back of the store between the last Fiction shelf and the start of Travel. He pointed at the books in Vish's hands as he took the last couple of steps backwards, opening the door.

"Isn't it weird thinking all you have to do to get to read someone's diary guilt-free is hope they get famous and then wait till they die?" Vish looked down at the Kafka book as Agastya quietly shut the door behind him, meaning that Vish missed a chance to see even the staircase that Agastya was now ascending. He'd left a gentle jet trail of alcohol scents behind him in the bookstore, a sharp smell both human and chemical that the dusty musk of old books couldn't cover.

Vish left the Occult section and started to browse the biographies. He did this every time he came to this bookstore or any other one, even though he didn't really know whose life would be interesting enough to read 500 pages about. The door chimed open, and Vish perked his head up, wondering for a second if he should have installed himself behind the till when Agastya handed the store over.

"Hi!" he said, in a customer service voice he had cultivated when he worked a volunteer position at the Regatta the summer before he was sent away to the school, a disaster that had ended up with him dropping his wallet in the lake from a sailboat.

The person who'd come in was a young woman. Vish didn't recognize her: she wasn't the one who used to work at Greycat. This girl was older than Vish's fifteen, but not by much. He would have to get used to not recognizing people. Every face in town was a little familiar before he left, but after two years, things had changed, even here.

Vish would have remembered seeing this girl if she always dressed like this: black on black on black. No logos, and a bit too elegant to be metal, but not the lace and ruffly '80s goth that he'd seen on the back of CDs that he sometimes picked up and always put back. A faded black trench, black jeans, and a blank t-shirt. She had hazel eyes and a septum piercing. Vish immediately thought that his mother would hate that piercing, and was annoyed with himself for thinking of his mother at all.

"Yeah. Hi," she said. The Septum-Pierced Girl walked straight past him to the Literature section, and right to the Rare/Firsts shelf at the far end, where Vish couldn't see her. He felt compelled to follow her, or at least to add something that would cool off his overenthusiastic "Hi."

Vish stopped walking before he'd really started, thinking that if it was him who was being followed by a crazily cheerful store clerk, he would guess that they were watching him to make sure he didn't steal. The girl might think that, or just that he was an annoying creep looking for any excuse to talk to her. Vish turned back to the Biography shelf and took out *The Autobiography of Malcolm X*.

"Excuse me. Are you related to the owner of this shop?" Vish almost screamed when this question was whispered at the back of his neck, because he could feel the speaker's breath. It smelled chemical, like bleach or chlorine. And the voice wasn't the girl's, but an older man's. He hadn't heard the chime ring again, but there was someone else in the store.

Vish turned and saw another person he'd never seen before. Unlike the girl, this man looked like he was trying to blend in with the general Kelowna look, but had gotten it wrong. For one thing, he wasn't just untanned, he was as pale as the inside of a tree root. The knees and calves between his slightly too-short cargo shorts and black dress socks (another mistake) were so white they almost gave off a light of their own in the little bookshop. The t-shirt, with a snowboard company logo on it, was almost right, but it was sky blue and too young for the man, who was at least fifty. His hair was dyed blacker than Vish's, but there was a small, thin moustache with a few white strands in it that glistened like mucous. He had the thinnest eyebrows Vish had ever seen on a man, which made his forehead look enormous, a big tank for a brain that Vish thought he would be able to see if the man stood with direct sunlight beaming onto that paper-pale skin. If Agastya had looked a bit sick, this man looked like he should be in a hospital bed.

"The owner will be right back. And no, we're not related."

"You work here."

"No."

The man stopped asking questions, but kept staring. Something rippled under the snowboard logo on his shirt: the kind of movement a sleeping person's fingers might make under the sheet if they were having a bad dream. Vish stared at the spot, which went flat again.

"You just assumed he was related to the owner? Why?" The Septum-Pierced Girl had come around from the rare books corner holding a small hardcover in her right hand. She spoke with an accent, maybe German. Vish was glad she wasn't talking to him, because he wouldn't have been able to answer right away. The Thin-Eyebrowed Man turned to look at her, then spoke.

"The owner of this establishment is a man of subcontinental extraction. The young man I'm speaking to is of that race, as well. Virtually no-one else on these streets is. Hence my question. Should I apologize?" He said this last part to Vish.

"It's okay," Vish said. He was still staring at the now-inert snowboard logo. When the conversation didn't resume, and Vish looked up to see disappointment in the Septum-Pierced Girl's eyes, Vish looked for something else to say, this time with a bit more of an edge in his tone.

"What do you want?" he said. "From the owner, I mean. What should I tell him?"

Instead of answering, the man kept on staring at the girl.

"Yes," the girl said. "I know it's you. You look worn out, Mr. Farris. And not really holding together. The meat's starting to separate. Not long left for you, is there?"

At a speed that didn't seem quite real, the man crossed the floor and was in front of the Septum-Pierced Girl. He reached out and grabbed her hand, and pressed his thumb into her palm, hard. The girl pulled back, but he didn't let her hand go for another moment.

When he did, the Septum-Pierced Girl looked at her palm, and so did Vish. There was a print seared into it, as though in red ink: a puffy, perfect tracing of a thumb, blocking the lines and byroads of her palm.

The Thin-Eyebrowed Man had backed into his original position as Vish and the girl were distracted.

"Like my apparent feebleness, my coming-apartness, that marking is just an illusion," he said, smiling. "It will fade, and I will endure."

"So will this," said the Septum-Pierced Girl. And she spit at him. But not a gob of spit, nothing resembling a loogie hocked on the playground. This was a thin spear of clear fluid that jetted from a small gap between her front teeth. It crossed the few feet between the girl and her target and landed on the man's cheek. He flinched away violently and ended up facing Vish as he reached around in the pockets of his ridiculous cargo shorts.

Vish stared at the man's face, and no longer noticed the thin eyebrows. He was looking for the landing place of the girl's saliva missile, but didn't see what he'd expected. Instead, where the fluid should have been, he saw: nothing.

There was a gap in the man's face, a little smaller than a dime.

Through this opening, Vish could see nothing gory, nothing bloody. But what he did see made him feel dizzy. He could see the cash register and the book-lined wall behind it.

The Thin-Eyebrowed Man found the handkerchief in his inner breast pocket and wiped his face, but the girl's spit had made a hole in him. A definite gap. That there was something as boring as a cash register just on the other side of this tiny, round window in a human face convinced Vish that he had really seen what he saw. If he were hallucinating, it would have been way more creative and weird. There would not have been a cash register in it. He was sure of that.

"Very rude people around here," the man said, talking to Vish, but keeping his peripheral vision trained on the girl. "But they give away all of their secrets in their rush to be impolite. Tell Agastya that Mr. Farris has come round. Tell him we all know we're in the last fortnight."

Farris turned to Vish. "Fortnight means two weeks."

"I know," Vish said. Being mildly annoyed at Farris's presumptions about his vocabulary made Vish forget to be afraid for a moment. But he soon remembered.

"Agastya can give me the stolen names, or he can be killed like his arrogant wife. Tell him he still has time, before the decision is made for him."

Vish may have nodded. Farris turned to the girl.

"Isla wouldn't have been able to stop this. Her useless husband certainly can't, and neither will you, Gisela. Even after all this time, you're nothing but her little apprentice."

"Farris, you don't know anything about Isla. Or me. Or time," the girl said. She held up her palm. The thumbprint had vanished. The man's smile, thin and closed but pushed forward by his uneven teeth, vanished into a slightly sagging open mouth that he only remembered to close when the girl started speaking.

"Faded a bit quicker than you thought, didn't it? I'm protected. Just like Agastya. And you're getting weaker. You're barely here at all."

Farris spun to look at Vish, who was leaning against the bookshelf behind him — recoiling, really.

"This boy's protected as well," Farris said. "I can tell. He's Agastya's blood, no matter what your lies are or why you invent them."

Gisela just stared at him.

A book slipped off the shelf behind Vish's shoulder and landed on the floor in front of him. *The Quest for Corvo.* Vish found himself thinking that it didn't sound much like the title of a biography, and wondered if Agastya had put it in the wrong section. He realized he was having these thoughts because they were more comfortable than thinking about the hole in the face of Mr. Farris and that finger that had moved under his shirt.

"And you," she said to Farris. "Do you think you can make it 'a fortnight'? Looks like you're going to fall apart a lot sooner than that."

Farris rubbed the spot of new skin that had formed over the hole.

"I won't need this bag of skin for much longer," Farris said. "New homes for what is within me await. And frankly, I spend most of my time outside of this body. You'll both find that out when you fall asleep and I pay a visit."

Coming closer to Vish, Farris smiled, revealing gums a darker grey than his skin and a lack of back teeth. Vish instinctively raised his hands and was about to shove Farris back, gently, so as not to damage this delicate but scary man, but the girl yelled.

"Don't touch him. Never touch him."

The girl took a pack of spearmint gum out of the green army surplus bag she had on over her shoulder, the strap teeming with little circular band logo buttons. She started chewing, loudly and wetly. Mr. Farris reached up to his own face and touched the place where her spit had landed, then pulled his hand away quickly.

Mr. Farris extracted a Blue Jays 1993 Championship cap from one of his pockets and pulled it down hard over his huge forehead. He walked to the door, which did chime on his exit, and a second later, the sound of almost two hundred pounds falling down a set of stairs echoed through Greycat Books.

CHAPTER 4

"Is he gone?" Agastya said. He spoke from the base of the stairwell, his head upside down.

Vish had opened the door to the stairwell, and the girl — Gisela — first locked the store up, then came to help.

"Of course he's gone," Gisela said. "You can stop being scared."

Agastya walked his feet along the wall to swivel himself around, then accepted a hand up from the two teenagers.

"I wasn't scared. I just hate Farris. Did you hurt him?" Agastya asked.

"A little," Gisela answered.

"Too bad it wasn't more."

Vish swivelled and backed away from the two of them, brushing the marble pigeon bookend at the end of a row of French cookbooks, almost knocking it to the ground. Agastya's face when he'd asked Gisela if she had hurt the strange little man wore an expression that Vish had only seen in movies. And in movies, there was a screen between Vish and the killing rage in the actor's eyes. In this bookstore, which seemed hotter, smaller, and more crowded by the moment, there was nothing between Vish and the cold anger on Agastya's face. It was almost more frightening that the man's voice stayed calm and friendly as he spoke to Gisela.

Agastya shook each leg out, checking to see that the knees worked, then sat down again on the stairs. A shorthaired grey and white cat with an agile tail walked down the stairs, sidestepping the humans, and started to patrol the store. The cat had a round face and a small moustache spot below his left clump of whiskers. Vish now noticed that Agastya's clothing was covered with fur. And he understood why the bookstore was named Greycat, but it wasn't the time to discuss that. The cat sniffed the place where Mr. Farris had been standing behind Vish and pawed at the floor there, as though there were an invisible mouse to be toyed with.

"So," said Gisela. "Farris is truly falling apart."

"Probably starting to look like what he ate," Agastya said, pushing the heel of his hand into his lower back and wincing. Gisela nodded, while Vish didn't even understand if it was a joke, and if that joke was supposed to be funny.

"And by the way, I am fine," Agastya continued. "I stumbled avoiding Moby. Mostly caught myself and went down the steps on my ass, except at the end there."

"You're lying," Gisela said. She was smiling. "You were sneaking down to spy better and lost your footing while trying to tiptoe. Embarrassing."

Gisela moved a step closer to Agastya and whispered a question that Vish didn't catch, just the words "the grimmer?" which made no sense.

"Gisela, we're on a deadline," Agastya responded. He looked less angry than he had moments ago, but very tired. When he turned to face Vish, he put on a grin that looked unreal.

"Why are you looking at me like that?" Agastya asked.

"You were just talking about hurting somebody," Vish said.

"I wasn't talking about hurting anybody. Anybody means a person, and Farris isn't that, exactly. And Gisela and I certainly aren't going to hurt you." Agastya said. There was no trace of the fury of a moment ago; if anything, he looked burnt out and tired, the way Vish's dad used to look when the pill addiction was at its worst and he was still working full-time, when he and Anji were regularly getting into the fights that were the one thing Vish certainly didn't miss about home when he was at the school.

Now it was Agastya who was looking at Vish funny, and he didn't like it. Vish walked over to the spilled *Quest for Corvo* book and picked it up, suddenly angry. Vish slid the book, which was by a guy named Symons, back into its slot on the shelf.

"No one's hurting me. I know that. But either you guys tell me what I just saw in here, or I'm going to leave and tell everyone that something's going on here." He'd already set the two books he had intended to buy down on the Belles-Lettres shelf. He could come back for them another day. Or never, depending how he felt.

"'Everyone.' Okay. The police? Your mom? What'll you say?" Gisela asked, just as Agastya said, "No," and stood up, walking to stand next to Gisela.

Vish looked up the staircase, which had a rumpled plaid shirt on the top two stairs that Agastya might have slipped on. A framed *Conan the Barbarian* poster leaned against the wall of the landing. And as Vish's gaze tried to make its way around the corner, into where the staircase opened into a room, something appeared, just for a second. A foot, a calf, a knee. The foot was bare, its skin the light brown of coffee that had been spoiled by an overpour of milk. But the part of leg that Vish saw was more

fur than skin — not just hairy, but black-pelted, with little trac-
eries of visible skin showing through.

Gisela stepped between Vish and the stairwell. She reached in
and pulled the door shut.

"Who else is up there?" Vish asked.

"No one. Just me and the cat live up there," Agastya said.
"Look, we're going to tell you whatever you want to know. You
deserve that for staying calm in here, being patient with us.
Before I forget, and before we have a discussion, I should ring
you out. How's 30 percent off sound? For watching the store?"

"It's fine," Vish said. "I mean, thanks." He kept staring at the
closed door. Gisela lightly tapped a knuckle against it and smiled
at him.

Agastya grabbed Vish's two books from the shelf where
they'd been set down and walked, holding his right hip. Vish followed him to the register.

"I don't want to see you hung over every time I come here,"
Gisela said from behind Vish. Vish resisted the urge to turn.
Agastya didn't say anything back to her, just rang in the numbers
and asked Vish for $8.89.

"You're not going to answer me?" Gisela said. Vish thought
her accent definitely sounded German now, but also understood
that he only knew that accent from television and movies, and
didn't want to ask her where she was from, not yet. He was sick
enough of people asking him where he was from, and he didn't
think she'd appreciate it.

"Sure, I'll answer," said Agastya. "It's just that I'm wondering
why I should be comfortable talking about something you clearly
think I should be ashamed of in front of our new friend, when
you're clearly not comfortable talking to him about our recent

visit from Mr. Farris." Agastya walked out from around the counter to unlock the front door of the store. The cat was hiding behind the blue recycling bin just by the entrance. Gisela came over to heft him in her arms.

"You stay here, Moby," she said to the cat.

Agastya opened the door and poked his head into the street, looking down the sidewalk both ways before letting the door drift shut.

"That guy said he was going to murder you, and it didn't sound like he was joking," Vish said. "I want to know who Mr. Farris is, and why you were talking about hurting him, and why I shouldn't talk to the police about it. Or my Mom," Vish added, directing this last bit to Gisela.

"He's seen quite a bit and I think it's pretty likely he's going to see more, Gisela. There's no point in secrets right now," said Agastya.

Gisela lowered Moby to the floor, ignoring everything Vish and Agastya had said.

"Why don't you keep the cat down here?" Gisela asked.

"I don't know," Agastya said. "People have allergies."

"Bookstores are supposed to have cats. Isla even named the place after him. Let Moby roam," Gisela said.

"Who's Isla?" Vish asked.

"Isla was my wife," Agastya said, pushing the paper that the old till had slowly spit up down onto a green and brass receipt spike on the counter. "You probably saw her in here a couple times."

"Any other questions?" asked Gisela.

"I already told you! That Mr. Farris guy bruised your hand and you spat a hole into his face, and I want to know what's going on," Vish said. He sounded whiny, and he knew it. Stooping to pet the cat, he lowered his face to hide his expression and was thankful that he couldn't blush visibly unless he was straight-up humiliated, not just a bit embarrassed.

Gisela poked the cat's rump with the tip of an enormous Doc Marten lace-up boot, then lowered her recently injured hand into Vish's field of vision. The skin that had the thumbprint seared into it was pristine, just as it was when she silenced Mr. Farris with it. The only marks on her palm were the ones that were supposed to tell her future. Vish took her hand to look at it more closely, to make sure that there was nothing left of the raised red mark Farris had left, and only realized what he was doing when Gisela laughed. Vish dropped the hand.

"No need to get mad, Vish," Agastya said. "Gisela's used to keeping secrets because it's what we've been doing for a very long time. And we had to make sure that you really wanted to know. Because it wouldn't be fair for me to invite you into this unless it was your decision."

"What happened to being on a deadline?" Gisela asked. "I would think the time for polite invitations was over."

"Is this deadline the fortnight thing Farris was saying? The two weeks?" Vish asked. Gisela glanced at him and away without answering, which made Vish feel quite small.

"Yeah. The two weeks, Vish. Being on a schedule doesn't mean we're going to be forcing anyone to do anything, Gisela," Agastya said, but he didn't look at her when he said it. He nodded at Vish, trying to reassure.

A set of footsteps clicked by just above their heads, and Vish looked up. The sound stopped. It didn't sound like a cat, unless it was one with paws that were mostly claw. Moby brushed by Vish's calves and he leaned down to pet him for a second.

"Let's go for a chat," Agastya said.

CHAPTER 5

Agastya locked up the store again, this time with the three of them on the outside. Moby watched them through the glass door, posting indifferent guard while Agastya fooled with the keys.

"That cat's got almost as much white as grey in his fur," Vish said, then pointed at the store's sign.

"So we should call the store 'Greyandwhitepatchescat Books'? They teach marketing in junior high now?" Agastya said.

"I'm in high school. Well, I will be this year. The place I went to on the Island was a weird academy thing that taught all the grades."

"Vish was just making an observation. A correct one," Gisela said.

"Isla picked the name," Agastya said, finally getting the door locked.

"Aren't you worried that guy is still right here? Waiting for you?" Vish asked.

"He can't touch me," Agastya said. "Literally. Farris and everything he's carrying around would minus himself from existence if he tried anything more than his fingerprinting trick on Gisela or me, or so I think. So he thinks too, and he isn't going to risk seeing if it's bull."

"What do you mean, 'everything he's carrying around'?"

"We'll get to that, Vish. Come on, let's get ice cream and go to that park off Clement."

"You're too old for ice cream," Gisela said.

"You look too young to be judging me, but that does hurt my feelings," Agastya answered. Vish was legitimately no longer sure if the shared story these two were caught up in — death threats, spitting holes in people — was a coded explanation of some sort of crime ring, or if they were both just crazy. They seemed to banter like friends, not master criminals. In fact, they spoke to each other the way Vish wanted to speak to friends he didn't have yet. And since he'd seen a gap in reality open up in that creepy man's face in Greycat Books, he already had something in common with these two, even if it was just a loosening grip on sanity.

There was a miraculous break in the lineup traffic at Old Single's, the ice cream shop. Vish ordered chocolate chip cookie dough. Gisela got coffee and Agastya took vanilla, paying for it all. He also asked for a clear plastic cup, a big one, if they had it. The kid doing the scooping nodded and called the request to two older teenagers who were talking near the soda machine.

"I wouldn't be telling you anything if you'd ordered black cherry or tiger stripe or something like that," Agastya said. "Cookie dough is borderline."

"Too many flavours at once," Gisela said.

"It's not," Vish said. "Cookie dough is one flavour."

"Anything with chocolate chips in it is another flavour plus chocolate. Two, and two is too many," Gisela said. Vish didn't recognize the kid who had scooped their flavours, but the girl at the register, in her paper hat and apron, was Melissa Lyall, whose father had always tried to get Dr. Maurya to join the country club before the rumours started. Melissa had beaten him in the MathCounts local competition at the end of sixth grade, which was also the last year that Vish was better at math than he was at English. Melissa wasn't looking at Vish, but he had seen her notice him, recognize that this was someone she knew two years ago. He knew she was listening to him talk to Gisela. He imagined she was impressed.

"Did you know that girl?" Gisela asked outside.

"Kind of," Vish said. He did a perimeter lick of his cone with his tongue to seal off drips, then started pulling out chunks of cookie dough from the scoop with his teeth. Old Single's used high-quality stuff, and Vish could taste the bitterness of the dark chocolate before he dispelled it with a bite of dough. It really was two flavours, he had to admit.

"She was spying on you, clearly. Were you trying to show off that you had cool new friends?" Agastya said, striding in front of them toward the tiny park that wasn't far from KSS, the high school where Vish would be immured for the next three years. Vish knew that Agastya was making the kind of joke people make as friendly small talk — he'd seen it a thousand times on TV — but he was still embarrassed. Gisela had the kindness not to turn to face Vish as his body and face superheated to the point he was sure that not just the ice cream but the waffle cone was going to dissolve in his hand.

"Nah, she wasn't spying. Everyone here knows each other, so there is no privacy. That's how it works. And even if I'm cool and new, you're neither, especially in the ice cream place, Agastya," Gisela said. She had to put on an American accent for *nah* to sound right, and she did.

Agastya led them past a senior living building, a tall complex that had ads on television full of elderly white people having "the time of their lives" in pastel rooms full of pastel food. Their smiles did look authentic, and Vish's mom used to tell him that she wouldn't mind living there when it was time for him to abandon her. Dr. Maurya hadn't figured into Anji's conversations about the future, not in the last year or so that Vish was at home.

Agastya pointed to a small wooden bridge that went over a creek — the opening to the bridge was barely visible through an overgrown hedge, but the clear grassland was visible on the other side. Agastya stooped and they followed him.

"Here I thought you just wanted a prettier setting for story-time," Gisela said. She pushed a branch aside, letting it go as she passed. It whipped back and flicked Vish's ear. He winced, and Gisela turned and whispered an apology.

"Running water," Agastya said. "Any time you see Mr. Farris, that instinct you have to wash your hands is a good one to follow through on. And you want to go further than that. Unpleasant little beings like him hate crossing streams."

When they got across the bridge, Agastya walked down to the banks of the creek and filled the large plastic cup he'd gotten with water. He held it up to the sunlight, smiled, then showed it to Gisela. She didn't smile back.

"I've told you at least fifty times. That's a folk superstition," Gisela said. "Farris can't get into the lake, but that's different. There's logic to it."

"Isla liked the folk tale stuff. Said anything that wasn't disproven couldn't hurt when it comes to warding off a nachzehrer keeper," Agastya said.

"What?" Vish said. On that one strange word, Agastya had sounded more German than Gisela.

"Nach-zeh-rer. Sorry, you have to put on the accent for it to sound like anything at all. You're about to find out."

"This creek might protect us from Farris for another reason, anyway," Gisela said. "You should have seen his skin, Agastya. He probably can't even take a bath anymore, or stand in a hard wind. That shell is falling apart."

"Nachzehrer," Vish said. "Is Farris a nachzehrer?"

Agastya and Gisela turned to look at him.

"Good pronunciation for a first try," Gisela said. "No. Farris collects and, sort of, holds nachzehrers. Stores them."

Vish took an assertive lick of his ice cream and Agastya laughed. Vish hadn't meant to be funny, but felt the little thrill that comes from making an adult laugh. They walked farther into the little park, which was empty, save for some empty Capri Sun drink pouches and a few beer cans. Gisela *tsk*ed and started kicking all the trash together into a little pile, encouraging it closer to the garbage can in the centre of the circular patch of grass. Vish, not quite running, came up to her and picked the stuff up to throw it in the metal basket, holding the last of his ice cream cone well away from the dirty work. He walked over to the water fountain to rinse off his left hand.

"Heartwarming," said Agastya, eating the tip of his waffle cone. He set the plastic cup full of creek water carefully down on a flat part of the grass. "I knew you were a dutiful type, Vish. I remember when you started coming into the store. I've been waiting for you to come back for a while, you know. Did you feel a real urge to come this morning? Gisela and I have been hoping you'd pop up for all of last week."

"Not just hoping," Gisela said. "If you hadn't come in today, one of us would have had to come and get you."

Vish, still facing the trash can, kept looking into it as he thought about what he'd just heard. He wondered if he'd made an incredibly stupid decision walking to this park with these people, these near-strangers. In an episode of *Oprah* he'd seen with his mom a few years ago, a cop or FBI guy talking about the dangers lurking everywhere outside your house had said at least eight times that you *never* "go to the second location" with a kidnapper, that you do everything to stay put and scream and be heard. This park was beginning to feel a lot like the second location, even if it was technically less private than the locked bookstore had been.

"The kid's body language really screams," Agastya said. "Coiled terror, in this case."

"Shut up," Gisela said. She had walked the perimeter of the park and was now standing on the other side of the garbage can, a few feet away from Vish. "Hey. Look at me. No one's going to hurt you. You're fine. We just need help, from someone, and that someone could be you."

"Okay," Vish said. Turning, he saw that Agastya was looking up at the sun, shading his eyes. The jokey tone in his voice hadn't made it onto his face. The older man looked miserable and lost.

"Let's sit," Gisela said.

They all did, in a spaced-out triangle, cross-legged. Vish checked his Casio: he had an hour left before he had to meet his father. Agastya spoke.

"I was waiting for you because I knew you were going to be a part of this, Vish, from the moment I saw you. I knew that moment would come in the store, where Farris was going to encounter you and ask if you were my family. And I knew that no matter what you said, he was going to think we were related, and that is exactly what I need him to believe. My wife — Isla — she told me something like this would happen, that the brown kid who came into the store would return and be important, but she just couldn't see the exact shape of it," Agastya said. The sadness on his face had dissolved now that he was speaking with purpose, but there was some dried vanilla ice cream in the stubble to the left of his mouth.

There wasn't much cover from the sun in the park, and the heat was magnified by Vish's nervousness. Agastya was sweating, beads of it visible at his collarbones. Gisela brushed some of the glisten off her upper lip with the back of her hand. The back of Vish's shirt was completely soaked. He felt like he was inside one of the mossy terrariums Mrs. Schuyler had gotten them to make in the sixth grade, under an invisible dome that sharpened the light and raised the temperature.

"So you think the occult is bull, but you believe running water kills creepy men and that you and your wife are psychic," Vish said, grabbing a handful of grass and rolling it back and forth between his fingers. He couldn't say anything remotely tough while making eye contact and doing nothing with his hands; he knew this about himself.

"I said that occult *books* are bull. What is real is that we're at a place and time that is packed with more magical potential of the bad kind than any place or time for the past eight hundred years. If you hadn't come back from that fancy private school, you might have missed it."

"That might have been okay with me."

"This valley, this lake, in this dry and hot summer, is the place that Mr. Farris has been searching for since he did his first apprentice magic, a long time ago, when he was all human. It's what he promised every dying person that he collected over —"

"One thousand eight hundred and forty-three years," Gisela said, not too loudly, but very precisely. Vish ignored the number so he could keep concentrating on what Agastya was saying without his brain boiling over.

"Mr. Farris has been following my wife's trail, and since she died, my trail, for years. Isla knew he was getting close, to her and to what Farris knew she was guarding. But with her gone, the magic she put in place to keep what Farris was looking for obscured — it's gone."

"And I wasn't strong enough, or fast enough, to build those defences again," Gisela said, leaning into the circle.

Vish decided to put aside the disbelief portion of his reaction in order to continue the conversation.

"What is it that Farris is looking for?"

"Gisela?" Agastya said. "You want to take this one?"

"Wait," said Vish. "If you don't want to tell me that, Agastya, tell me about Isla. She's your wife?"

"Yes. And I'll get Gisela to tell you about her when I'm not around," Agastya said.

"Why?" Vish asked.

"Because she only died six months ago. She was hit by a car. It was a pointless and stupid death, and that's as much as I can tell you," Agastya said. "I'm not great with even saying her name out loud yet, okay? I can't handle this Farris situation without her, and pretending that I can is hard enough without talking about it." Agastya dug a thumb into the grass, scratching into the dirt and staring at a tree behind Vish.

"Okay," Vish said, embarrassed, thinking desperately of another question he could ask to get that terrible look off Agastya's face. Gisela did it for him.

"Isla's spells had staying power, all of them, but the one that protected the lake from Farris's vision was just too complex to keep up permanently. But she and I worked together on the magic that keeps Farris from hurting Agastya, anyone related to him, and me, and anyone related to me, if I had any living relatives. It works as long as Farris doesn't trick one of us into touching him by our own will. So I've been able to keep that magic strong."

Vish was going to ask about what happened to leave Gisela without any family, but he didn't want to make Agastya think of his dead wife again, so he kept his mouth shut. Gisela went on.

"So when Farris came in the store and saw you, Vish, he assumed you were related to Agastya. Even though you don't look alike at all, except for skin tone. So he thinks you're protected."

Gisela's combination of explaining and distracting had worked: Vish kind of understood a bit more, and the terrible dark look was off Agastya's face. Agastya got to his feet and gave Gisela a teacherly nod-and-point.

"Exact," Agastya said in a French accent that he couldn't do without smiling in a weird rictus-y way. "Which makes you, Vish, a major asset to us. Gisela immediately denying that you are any sort of relation to me makes Farris dead sure you are. Farris is not a creature who can believe that others aren't as dishonest as he is."

"How am I an 'asset'?" Vish asked.

"The magic Isla and Gisela put on me and anyone of my blood acts a little like a seven-thousand-volt electric fence on Mr. Farris in particular. If he tries any sort of major attack, anything beyond that bruise he tried to lay on Gisela, on me, he'll cease to exist. And then his nachzehrers will be homeless."

"Can someone *please* tell me what that word means?"

Gisela put a hand on Vish's arm. He turned to her, and she drew quick shapes in the air with her other hand: even though nothing appeared there, the air itself seemed to colour where her finger darted, taking on a light redness that Vish saw when he stared hard at it.

She was making a human figure out of flattish red shapes, dozens of them, then hundreds, piling them up on each other until there actually was something in the air in front of Vish. Two human legs, built out of these little red building blocks that looked more like steaks than bricks.

"Mr. Farris isn't one thing. He's a collection of 12,506 long-dead people, people who made a very wicked deal with Mr. Farris because they wanted to live forever. And now they do, trapped inside this body he made out of their bodies: he ate a little piece of each of these people to capture them, and now they live within him."

Gisela finished her drawing. There was no detail to it, but the shape was clear: it was a man, drawn blood-red against the sky, built out of the meat of other people. It was Mr. Farris.

CHAPTER 6

G isela leaned forward and picked up the plastic glass of water. Vish knew that something was about to happen with it, so he watched her hands carefully for any sleight-of-hand David Copperfield tricks. The human-steaks-made-of-coloured-air he had to admit were beyond his understanding, but he wasn't willing to completely surrender the idea that there was a trick behind everything he'd seen today.

"Vish, what would you call what happened to Mr. Farris in the store when you saw me spit on him?"

"Magic."

He'd tried to get good at card tricks for a month last winter at the school, but had given up in frustration when it became clear that he was no better at palming aces than playing guitar. But he'd gotten pretty good at studying the hands of real illusionists in a VHS instructional tape that had been in the library. If you really watched, you could feel time slow down, you could see the moment where they fooled you, even if you didn't quite know how they did it.

"Good. Yes. And what did it look like?"

Vish thought about this for a while, in the same way that he would fish for an answer in English class when he knew the teacher was looking for something in particular. What was literally true? What had real magic looked like when he'd seen it for the first time?

"A gap," Vish said.

"Perfect," Gisela said. She grinned, looking completely like a kid, and Vish felt both right and slightly less nervous. "That's what magic is. Gaps. Making gaps, finding gaps, widening gaps. In space, time, matter. Mr. Farris used to be a human, but he opened gaps in himself using some of the darkest, cruellest magic ever conceived. And in those gaps he crammed the dying essence of a lot of people."

While she was talking, Gisela shifted the cup of water to her left hand and made a series of darting movements with the fingers of her right hand in the air. It looked almost as if she was tracing the forms of numbers, before she flattened her hand as though she was setting up for a karate chop, and made a series of sharply angled slashes, as if she was drawing a triangle, or a rhombus, or a geometrical shape that Vish had never seen before.

The hand wasn't moving fast, but Vish was soon aware that he couldn't quite see it: that something was getting in the way, that there was something thickening the air inside this shape Gisela was carving.

Then Vish looked at her other hand: it was vibrating at an incredibly high speed. The plastic cup was shaking violently, but the water inside somehow stayed still in an unbroken column, and soon, the cup had shaken itself apart — not into splinters, but into atoms. But the water stayed, keeping its shape. It, too, had grown thick and opaque, like the air that was now shielding Gisela's face.

"There's something in the air and the water here, Vish. Right at this moment in time. Something that only needs a small suggestion to burst into existence. Mr. Farris needs an enormous amount of energy to accomplish what he promised those twelve thousand souls over the years: new lives in new bodies. And it's not the kind of power he can generate himself. It's the kind that boils out of the core of this planet and others, the heat that life came from a long time ago."

The column of water above Gisela's left hand glowed with every colour of the spectrum, then turned completely black, then sprang into the solidified shape in the air in front of Gisela's face.

"Shut your eyes," Gisela said. "Now."

Vish obeyed. So he only felt the light, he didn't see it: as though a tiny sun was born and supernovaed in twenty seconds, a few feet from his face.

When he opened his eyes, Gisela was smiling, but nervously.

"There's power here, Vish, waiting to be collected by a thing like Mr. Farris. What Isla wanted to do — what Agastya and me and hopefully you want to do — is to make sure Farris doesn't channel that power into bringing his dead souls back."

"What would they look like, if they came back? These people that Mr. Farris — ate?"

While Gisela had been doing her demonstration, Agastya had been standing to patrol the little park area, making sure that no one was approaching over the little bridge. Vish touched his eyelids to see if they felt scorched. They did feel warm, but then again, so did the rest of him. Agastya was pacing now, and he circled around to start talking to Vish.

"They'd need new bodies. And they'd find them right here. Twelve thousand people in this city would find themselves occupied, against their will, with a once-human creature that has been rotting and going insane inside of Mr. Farris for centuries."

"Like, possessed?" Vish asked.

"Replaced. It'd be slow at first, just a new voice in your skull, then a change in attitude, then, eventually, there'd be nothing of you left. Some nachzehrer, some Austrian count from 1688, would suck everything he needs to know about the modern world right out of your brain, and then he'd just make it his brain. That's what Farris wants to do in fourteen days, right here."

Vish must have looked as panicked as he felt.

"Don't get too freaked out. There's a practical logic to all of this," Gisela said. "Magic isn't incantations and chalk circles. It's physics and biology. It's finding flaws in reality, or creating them."

"If you want to understand actual magic any better, you'll need to put in about fifteen years of studying quantum physics, at the end of which you still probably won't actually get-it, get-it. I know I don't," Agastya said.

"Agastya definitely doesn't get it, he's right," Gisela said. "Everything explained as magic in proper fairy tales and myths, not the glossy-and-sweet versions they animate for you, comes down to math, time, and a deeper version of reality. That's all."

"If it makes it any easier to believe, keep in mind that we're not telling you you're special," Agastya said. "Like me, you're not. You're just the only other brown guy who's come into my store in months, and that means that you've fallen into the pattern of what's going on with Isla, me, Farris, and the thing that he's come to get off me. He thinks you're part of this, and we're going to use that.

"Isla being dead is real. The power she had to conceal what was hidden here was real, and now it's gone. Farris is here, and he's real. For just a little while longer, the valley and this lake, all the waters around here absolutely glowing with power that could wipe out most of what you think of as the modern world, that's real.

"Spells have a lot to do with arranging people and objects, and I think Isla knew you were needed from the first time you walked into the store. You being here is part of what she wanted, and it's part of what's going to keep Gisela and me alive. But if you want to help us, it has to be up to you."

"What was that animal in your apartment, Agastya? Not the cat. The other thing," Vish asked. It was a small question to ask while he was still taking in the enormous things that Agastya had told him.

"Nothing. A leftover. Something that Isla sends around. Are you going to help us or what?" Agastya said, bothered and thrown off. Gisela walked over to him and closed her hand on his shoulder. Vish saw that he was making sure he didn't say anything more.

"If you answer the questions that I have, then yeah, maybe. What's a 'grimmer'?" Vish asked, this time staring at Gisela. She looked at Agastya, a glance that Vish caught.

"You're a grimmer, Vish, you frowning jerk," Agastya said, trying to smile. "We're trying to offer you some important fun, here. And we need your help. We don't know what exactly we need you for, but we do."

"You're lying," Vish said. "You know exactly what you need me for. So tell me."

"There's a thing called maximum-information-capacity, Vish," Agastya said. "We are going to tell you more, but it can't be all at once. You just saw a girl spit a hole into reality and make a glass of water into a tiny atom bomb, man. Can you just chew over what we've told you and come back for more later?"

"I don't know," Vish said. He did feel the truth of this maximum-information-capacity thing, though, even if Agastya had made it up, as he suspected. He'd eaten the ice cream too fast, and the sugar was making his blood and thoughts feel thick and murky under the heat of the sun. Gisela was watching him, and he wanted to stare back to let her know she was being rude, but wasn't bold enough to do it.

"Just understand one last thing, Vish. My wife came here, and I stayed with her, because we can't let Farris get to the energy in that lake. And since Isla died while waiting around for him, I've sort of wanted to see him totally evaporated. Gone, deader than dead, more than I've wanted anything in my life. Do you get it?" The look was back on Agastya's face, and Vish understood that it wasn't the rage that scared him, it was the purpose. He didn't think he'd ever seen anyone *mean* something as much as Agastya meant this, right then. Vish was witnessing an emotion that was private, a level of honesty and nakedness he himself wouldn't be able to show to anyone, at least not yet.

"Are you getting *any* of this? Any of it?" Agastya said. "As far as he knows, he can't hurt you unless you reach out and touch him first, which you obviously aren't going to do. So that gives us another whole person we can use to distract and defeat him and keep him away from what he wants in that lake. Until it's sealed away from him for good, and he's dead."

Vish hadn't backed away with his feet, but he'd recoiled, his head and neck and shoulders leaning farther back. This was how his father sometimes spoke to him in the bad, drunken days, even in the sober mornings — not like he was talking to a kid, let alone to his son, but like he was talking to an adult he was very angry at. Once, Dr. Maurya had told Vish that he was really yelling at himself when he got like that.

"I get it," Vish said.

Agastya turned away from the garbage and shook his head — not at Vish, but at Gisela. They both turned again and Agastya spoke to her quietly, two or three sentences. Then he left, walking right past Vish, not stopping to say goodbye. Vish might have been more annoyed if Agastya's face wasn't suddenly blank and wet with tears. Vish didn't turn as he heard the thump of Agastya's departing boots on the bridge. He spoke to Gisela for another two minutes, absorbing her translation of what Agastya had to say.

"That's exactly it," Gisela said. "A job. Weekends. Details to be decided. We need you close in the next few days, and he could use the sleep-in time."

"You're sure?" he asked.

"That's what he said. I took out some swears, but that's all. We need you around, badly, this weekend, but assuming we get through this, he wants you around for longer." Gisela stooped and wiped her hands in the grass. "Still have some ice cream stickiness."

"I have to go," Vish said.

"Well, wait, are you saying yes or no?" Gisela said.

"I want to but I don't know. But I can't leave my dad waiting, and I'm already late." Vish waited until he was out of the park and back on cement to start running. He didn't want Gisela to see him run. Really, he didn't want anyone to see him run — it had been caught on camcorder once on Sports Day in seventh grade, and Vish couldn't quite understand how his arms and legs could all move forwards and outwards at the same time, like he was a panicking spider.

Vish saw a lot of tourist and local foot traffic on his way to meet his dad, but the only person he recognized before he came to a panting halt outside Dr. Maurya's office was Matt, sitting on the curb, drinking a Slurpee in front of the used CD store, Memories, wearing a loose white t-shirt and shapeless grey gym shorts.

Vish made sure Matt didn't see him by turning into the nearest alley and walking through it all the way to his dad's office.

That night at dinner, Vish asked his parents if they trusted him. Anji Maurya looked down at her plate. Vish could see her preparing herself for a bad dinner and evening.

"What did you do, Vish?"

"I got offered a job. And I really want to take it."

CHAPTER 7

"**N**o," said Dr. Maurya. "No, absolutely not. You're fifteen, you're not working a job outside of the family."

"That's right, I am fifteen. Most kids have a summer job at this age."

"Kids whose parents can't afford to give them a good life, maybe," Dr. Maurya said.

"Munish, you know that isn't true," Anji said.

Vish looked at his mother, who had her fork in a piece of salmon. She let go of the fork and it clattered onto the side of the plate. Salmon curry was Vish's favourite, especially when the salmon was fresh, not canned, and he hadn't realized that his mother had made it until it was on the table. Anji had made it the first night he was home each time he had a vacation from the school, but this was the first night she'd had time to cook since he'd arrived back home. They'd been eating out of the freezer. Usually Vish was immediately excited by the smell when he came in, but tonight he hadn't been thinking of food even for a second. He didn't realize it was possible to be so distracted that smells didn't get through, but apparently it was.

"Mom, it's a job at the bookstore, not someplace gross. At Greycat. Agastya wants me to open the store and just be there from 10 a.m. to 2 p.m.; Thursday, Friday, Saturday, Sunday. And just for the summer, so there's no way it'll stop me from studying or anything like that."

"Vish, one thing at a time," Anji said. She pinched the bridge of her nose and Vish thought of Mr. Farris rubbing the spot on his face. When he was little he used to tell his mother everything that had happened during the day, even if she'd been right beside him when it happened.

"You're not going to get your way by trying to get your mother to side against me," Dr. Maurya said. His beard grew in quickly; the few patches that he'd missed that morning were now comfortably nestled in a new crop of stubble.

"I'm not, I was just explaining."

"Explaining that you want to be used as cheap labour by that vagabond who runs the bookshop, yes." Dr. Maurya was trying to be gruff and smile at the same time, and it wasn't working.

"I know you don't want me to do this. But I really want this. He'll pay a dollar above minimum wage and I get to take two free books every week. And you're always talking about how all your old friends in Vancouver never let their teenagers get jobs and they end up having no idea about money or savings or any of that."

"I meant older teenagers," Dr. Maurya said.

"I am an 'older teenager.' I'm not thirteen anymore. Just because I wasn't here for two years doesn't mean I didn't age." This was a dangerous thing to say, so Vish quickly moved on. "I don't want to end up being lazy, or stupid about money. I'll save half of what I make."

He watched his mom instead of his dad when he said this, and she did indeed register the information with the raised eyebrow and head tilt she made when she'd heard a good deal. But she didn't say that.

"The timing might not be right, Vish. Munish, please, tell him."

Munish and Anji Maurya both looked down at the table before facing Vish again. They didn't seem mad, or exasperated — it took Vish a second to understand what he was reading in their faces. Fear. His parents were afraid to tell him something.

For the second time that day, Vish started to feel dizzy, dislocated. When he'd been peering through Mr. Farris's face to see the cash register behind him, his ankles had felt a little shaky in his Adidas high-tops. And now, he could feel his elbows going liquid. His arms would have been dangling if they hadn't been resting on the table. He spoke in a dead voice, maybe the kind of voice one of the nachzehrers inside of Mr. Farris would use.

"You're sending me away again. Okay. Okay. So just know that this is the last time. It's the last time I'm going to leave this house, because I'll never, ever come back."

"Vish, stop, please. Calm down," Anji said. "You've been put through a lot of stress these past two years, and heard a lot of things no child should have to, and —"

Vish was about to stop her, and Anji saw it coming. She flipped her hair out of her face, something she did a lot since getting it cut short with bangs just before the summer, the first time she'd had it short since before Vish was born.

"We get it, Vish. You're not a child now, but you were when this all started."

"I guess."

"Your father and I want you to see a therapist. I know you didn't want to do it when you were at the school, but we really think you have to do this. She's new in town, someone your father knows from — her name is Rita Goodis. We don't want you to think —"

Dr. Maurya interrupted. "We don't want you to think this is a punishment. My actions, my addiction, are what caused all of this. I know that, and I know that going away for so long hurt you. This is to help you, not hurt you. We just want you to go once a week for the rest of the summer, and see what you think. This is time for you, that you don't have to tell us anything about. You deserve a place to talk about how you feel and what you're scared of."

Anji put up a hand and took over. She and Vish used to make fun of Dr. Maurya's "psychiatry talk" when he wasn't around, and as sincere as Vish's dad was being, he was also starting to sound a bit bumper-stickerish. Maybe he couldn't help it.

"Vish," said Anji. "I know you barely talked to anyone for those years at the school. That scared me more than anything, almost. You were so social, so out there — I worry that if you don't start talking again, to someone, anyone, you'll forget how to do it. And it will be our fault if you're not where a boy your age should be, and if you start to miss things because of it —"

Vish had thought almost the same thing when he was talking to Gisela and Agastya today. The strangeness of it, speaking to other people. But he didn't want to help his mother tell him what to do, so he kept it to himself.

"What's she like, this doctor?"

"I'll tell you this," Dr. Maurya said. He stood up, walked a few paces from the table, and faced the line of books above the little built-in desk alcove in the wall, where Anji sat and did the monthly bills and other paperwork. He didn't turn around as he continued speaking.

"I won't ever talk about it again, and don't bring it up with her. I could have lost my licence to practise, I could have lost everything, because of the pills. Rita was the one who advocated for me to the board, who convinced them that I wasn't prescribing to myself, that I hadn't worked while under the influence, that I was suffering and needed time away, but would be able to practise again. While I got better, she made sure that I had work to come back to."

"Do I have a choice?" Vish asked.

Anji and Munish Maurya looked at each other.

"I wish you didn't put it that way," said Anji.

"Can I take the job at Greycat if I say yes to therapy? You said I haven't really talked to anyone for a couple years and you're right. This is a great way to get back into just talking to people and spending time around them, not just in a classroom or alone. I really want to feel normal again, Mom."

Dr. Maurya turned away from the bookshelf and sat back down. He took up a large forkful of cold curry.

"You really aren't a little boy anymore, are you? Bargaining like a market vendor. If your mom goes down to talk to the owner and she's okay with it, then yes. You can take this bookstore job. But don't get into the habit of bribery."

Vish had a hard time keeping his face happy instead of happy-and-smug during the rest of the meal. He could only tell he'd crossed over when one or both of his parents laughed. After dinner, Vish rinsed the dishes and loaded the dishwasher, gave the stove and counters a wipe, and then left the room while the older Mauryas watched *Friends*. Vish listened to most of *Master of Puppets* while reading a John Fowles book he'd taken from his dad's study. He could tell that it was the kind of book that his parents would have told him to wait a few years to read, and the shiver of possibility he got from that knowledge reminded him of the world that had opened up when Gisela spat a gap into a man's face in front of him earlier that day. Vish closed the book after fifteen pages and headbanged gently to the fifth track on the CD, "Disposable Heroes." He had his eyes closed, so didn't hear his dad come in.

"You are getting weirder by the day," Dr. Maurya said. For some reason, Vish's first reaction was to slam the volume knob on his stereo to zero. Dr. Maurya laughed.

"Come on," he said. "There's a Clint on TV."

When an Eastwood film was broadcast in the Maurya household, no other channels existed. Anji was a fan, if not quite to the degree of her husband and son, but she usually watched with them. Tonight she went to the little office that had taken over the space of Vish's old upstairs bedroom to do some work. Vish and his dad watched *For a Few Dollars More*, which Vish had never seen, even though he had watched the third movie in the trilogy, *The Good, the Bad, and the Ugly*, three times. The VHS tape of that one, a fat double-tape case, was in the downstairs cabinet where the family's small movie collection was kept.

Dr. Maurya sat on his reclining leather chair, wearing slippers without socks, the corduroy pants he usually put on as soon as he got home, even in summer, and a free Canucks t-shirt Anji had gotten at a community event. He was quiet, absolutely, sipping tea and occasionally glancing at Vish, who was on the couch just next to the chair. Twice, he gripped his son's arm when a good part was coming up.

"Dad?" he asked.

"Shhh," Dr. Maurya said. "I've talked too much today. And this is where Clint finds the money."

Vish stayed quiet.

CHAPTER 8

V ish knew he wouldn't be able to sleep that night. An official new bedtime hadn't been discussed since he'd returned home, but he didn't want to push it, so he usually went to his room and had the lights out by ten-thirty.

Tonight, he waited until the noises in the kitchen above him stopped. The last, reliable sounds of every evening were Anji filling a pint glass with water from the tap and her slippered footsteps moving across the floor (or Vish's bedroom ceiling) toward the hallway and the master bedroom. It was exactly eleven-thirty-two, according to the clock radio on the bedside table. Vish pulled the blankets off, slipped back into his jeans, and walked out into the darkened house, flicking on the TV in the downstairs den. He kept it quiet enough to be able to hear any sign of wakefulness from upstairs. He had every creaking board memorized and an escape plan from the den that would have the television off and him in bed in under twenty-five seconds. Thirty, if he took his jeans off before getting under the sheets.

Vish wasn't really supposed to be watching the independent and foreign films on channel 24's after-midnight Showcase Revue.

He had almost forgotten about them when he was at the school, where the television was shared property and everyone was in their own room by nine o'clock. But Vish had quickly come back to this weekend habit — not just for the Viewer Discretion Is Advised parts, but for the stories, the images, because even when the movies weren't good, they were unlike anything he'd seen before. And after what he'd seen and heard today, Vish wanted to see something that was unfamiliar but not scary.

Sitting on the maroon couch with the broken springs that his mother had exiled down here after buying a new living room suite at Leon's with part of the money from her first commission for a duplex sale, Vish kept the lights off. He knew the rubbery topography of the TV remote control by heart, could tell the volume from the channel control by the different wear on the buttons. His thumb smashed Mute whenever he heard a creak from upstairs, and hovered over Power until he was sure there was no sound. The movie tonight was apparently about a musician named Veronique who had two lives, but Vish had missed the first ten minutes and was worried he'd never understand it. But the colours were beautiful, and what he could hear of the music was too.

There were a few bad memories that Vish had tried to bury of his father coming home at about this time of night. Fumbling his keys, sitting down heavily to take his shoes off, cannoning them into the hall closet. Like his mother had, Vish pretended he didn't hear his dad's stumbling entrances. They came when Munish paired up the pills with drinking at the bar, and took a cab home, leaving his own car at the office. And on those evenings, Vish simply turned off the television and did a silent, carpeted run into the corner of the downstairs rec room, a dark patch where he could see his father sitting heavily on the chair in the entryway. And more importantly, where he could see him stand up and walk off to sleep, whether that was in his own bed or on the guest room cot.

Vish had to believe that would never happen again, and mostly, he did. He got up from his comfortable nest in the old couch to pull a sealed pack of After Eight from behind a loose brick behind the never-used fireplace in the corner of the room and settled down with the chocolates. He'd put the box there on spring break last year, thinking it was a bit childish to keep using this old hiding spot for no reason, but doing it anyway. They would have to be finished off tonight, now that the box was unsealed, or there was a risk of attracting ants. Really, it was his duty to finish what he started, so Vish put the first two mints into his mouth at the same time.

Behind the television was the great bay window that looked out onto the Mauryas' backyard, which was overseen by a tall maple tree and backed by a line of tall shrubs that had their heads trimmed off every May, so there would be a view of the lake from the upstairs balcony. Dr. Maurya used to hire a gardener to do it, but eventually invested in a tall folding ladder and a gas-powered trimmer, and did an uneven job of it himself. Vish never got to use the trimmer, which looked like a junior chainsaw with bigger, goofier teeth. But he did have to hold the ladder while his dad was up there.

The woman onscreen fainted while she was singing something operatic that Vish realized he hadn't been listening to. Because he was watching something move, outside, below the maple tree.

The branches of the trees started about six feet up from its base and expanded to cover almost half of the yard. In the daytime, the shadow was huge and cool. At night, it was a place of deeper darkness. The moonlight that made the leaves above this patch glisten couldn't penetrate beyond them.

There was something even darker in the blackness. Something that hunched, that moved very quickly. Then seemed to turn a very white face toward the window Vish was staring out of.

Vish hit the Power button on the remote and the room went dark. The dead springs in the couch creaked as he leaned forward. His eyes got used to the absence of light, and he moved closer to the sliding patio door that was next to the bay window. It was a glass door, with a simple lock that Vish thought he was checking, just to make sure it was in the right position. It was. But Vish found himself pushing it down, unlocking the door. He slid it open, just enough to fit through sideways.

There were crickets, and the sound of someone swimming in the Ackroyds' pool, six houses over. Just one person paddling around. Probably their son Mikey, who was back from college in Washington. Mikey, tall and pale with an Adam's apple that was truly as big as a crabapple. He'd stopped calling himself Mikey years ago, going for Mike instead, but when he was Mikey he was also the newspaper delivery boy who had taught Vish to ride his bike. They always waved at each other, but they hadn't talked for a few years.

Vish could hear each splash and stroke because the night was so quiet. He stepped out onto the cool, pale cement just outside the patio door, leaving it open, even though mosquitoes might make their way inside. He didn't know if it was bravery that was making him come out here, but he did know that he wouldn't be able to stand taking another step if that door was closed behind him. Mikey swam regular laps when he was home, and those made a very clear sound, nothing like what Vish had heard since he'd opened the door.

What he could hear was a gentle slurping, as though someone was trying to get out of the pool as slowly and quietly as possible.

Vish started walking toward the maple tree. He stared at the small, fat hump at its base that was new. Vish would have thought it was a little heap of earth if he hadn't seen it move when he was inside.

The crickets didn't go quiet all at once. And maybe Mike Ackroyd just got tired of swimming at around the same time as the bugs settled down. But by the time Vish stepped off the cement and his bare feet touched the springing green of the wet grass and the crisp yellow of one of the patches that the sprinklers never caught, there was no sound in the air except the air itself. Vish's breathing. And, quietly, from that hump by the roots of the tree, a sound somewhere between breathing and the puffing a kettle makes just before it whistles.

Vish's toenail touched a rock. He would have stubbed the toe badly if he'd been walking at his normal pace. He was barely five feet away from the patio, and it had been almost a full minute since he'd walked outside.

Vish knelt and picked up the rock. It was smooth and heavy. It fit his palm. On a beach, he would have tried to skip it across the water. It was dark grey or black in the moonlight, with little lines of mica that glistered when he moved his hand. Vish wasn't moving it on purpose: it was shaking. He looked again at the hump, and stopped his breathing to see if he could hear it.

But the thing had stopped breathing as well. It was moving. What seemed at first to be an arm unfolded from the cluster of dark. Except it kept folding out, getting longer, until Vish was sure it was a leg. But then it seemed even longer than that, and it began to rise into the air, until the end of it wrapped around one of the lowest branches of the tree.

The white face that Vish was sure he'd seen within the quivering black mound began to turn towards him. Vish knew that if it smiled at him he wouldn't be able to stop screaming.

Below the turning face, the figure was only one arm and one leg, with a darkness between the two. Farris's ghost limbs taking shape, stealing solidity from the trees around them, perhaps from Vish himself. If Farris stored people by making deals and eating them, perhaps he could nibble and bite on living folk who'd made no deal. Mosquitoes and blackflies did it, taking blood and skin that wasn't theirs: why not this man? Farris had burned Gisela's hand even though he knew she was protected; maybe he would try to go further with Vish.

Feeling a coldness at his back, Vish turned around. And there, he saw the other parts of the dark shadow that was under the tree. Half green-black and dripping the Ackroyds' poolwater on the light cement of his patio. The missing arm and leg, the ragged torso, all walking toward Vish, as the other half of the body approached from the tree.

Something else, forming above that scrappy torso, began to smile at Vish.

Vish wheeled around and threw the rock at the only thing he could see clearly in the darkness. He was bad at throwing balls in any sport, but apparently good at throwing rocks. The corner of the white face that was coming towards him was hit squarely, and the breathing hiss started again. The green blackness behind Vish rushed past to join the other half of its body, which was retreating back toward the maple.

The hissing stopped altogether as both long arms, lengthening into handless tentacles, tightened around the tree branch and pulled the mound of dark matter up into the air, swinging it over the fence into the next yard. Vish heard a lolloping thump and rise, the sound of a sticky limb gripping branches and eavestroughs and windowpanes in yards farther and farther away, until he could hear nothing at all. But while he listened to all of this, he watched something that was drifting like a leaf down from the upper reaches of the trees, where the creature's first swing had launched it.

The whiteness fluttered into the grass just in front of him. It looked like a mask, but it wasn't made of rubber or latex. It was paper. Vish knew that if he touched it, it would be rich and thick, like the expensive stuff at the stationery store in the mall, but with even more texture. There was a hole where the mouth should be, a torn gap that went up at one end and down at the other. In profile, it could smile or frown when whatever was wearing it turned aside.

There were holes for the eyes as well, but they weren't holes, just now. As Vish moved back and around the mask, letting more moonlight hit it, he saw what was in the holes. In a way, it made perfect sense.

It was a pair of eyes. Real, pale blue eyes, without eyelids, staring up stupidly. Vish opened his mouth to scream, and as he did, the eyes vanished, either melting into the grass or evaporating into the air.

Before the mask blew away in a wind that hadn't been there a moment before, Vish saw that the mask also had eyebrows. Thin, black eyebrows. The thinnest eyebrows Vish had ever seen.

CHAPTER 9

"If Vish heard me say a dollar above minimum wage, he heard wrong. Or maybe I was mistaken. I meant two dollars above minimum. That's pretty good for a fifteen-year-old."

Vish knew he wasn't dreaming because even his worst embarrassment dreams didn't involve his mom making deals with his new boss in front of him. He was pretending to page through a Ruth Rendell book and ignore the talk happening right in front of him, but he looked up at the wrong moment. Agastya was staring right at him, grinning.

Anji Maurya had woken Vish up at eight-thirty that morning to ask if he was sure, really sure, about taking the job. Vish had barely slept. After seeing Farris's face and its melting eyes blow into the upper darkness of the sky, he had run inside and slid the patio door shut with a whirr and slam that should have woken his parents up. He spent the next few hours awake, with his hand wrapped around the Swiss Army Knife his aunt had given him. When his mom came into his room, the knife had still been in bed with him, having rolled under his back, luckily with all the blades folded in. Anji told him to get ready. She was going to drive both of them to the store so she could meet this Agastya character and make sure it was a suitable environment.

"Wasn't Dad just kidding about that?" Vish said, his mouth thick with the stale popcorn taste of a brief, deep sleep.

"Your father was laughing, but you know he wasn't kidding," Anji said. "I think he's met your Agastya in the store before, but he still wanted me to have a chat with the man."

"Mom. I'm fifteen, not twelve. This is kind of embarrassing."

"If you think your boss is the kind of person who'll be turned off by a parent wanting to make sure her son is safe, then I guess we can both be sure that Greycat isn't a good environment for you, right? Which would mean that neither of us has to go there. This morning, or ever."

Matt or Danny would have argued back with their mom and won this fight, Vish knew. But there was no way he could win. Whether that was because his family was Indian and Matt and Danny's was white, or because Anji was even harder to convince of anything since she'd started negotiating bigger and bigger real estate deals, Vish was going to lose.

He got out of bed, and less than an hour later, he was standing in the store, tucking that Ruth Rendell book back onto its shelf.

Agastya, his hair combed and with a plain black t-shirt tucked into a pair of dark blue jeans without holes or stains, had been seated behind the till when Anji rapped on the glass door, Vish behind her. He sprang into view and smiled, looking genuinely happy. Vish was relieved. When he'd pictured beginning his morning shifts, he'd expected Agastya to roll downstairs to open the locked door for him at 9:59 a.m. before going back upstairs to sleep off his previous evening. Anji had come in first, reaching an embarrassing hand back for Vish's out of some unconscious instinct. Vish ignored the hand and walked in unassisted.

Anji had skipped politeness and started with the wage negotiation.

"Two above minimum sounds right," Anji said.

"Some would say generous," Agastya replied. He was back behind the till, watching Anji patrol the aisles of the shop. Vish knew she was looking for smut: boxes of *Playboy*, an erotica section.

"I should make it clear that we in no way need this money. Have you heard any rumours about our family?" Anji asked. Vish felt his hands and face blush even hotter.

"Rumours?" Agastya said. He punched a button on the till and the drawer slid out. He started counting quarters. "Nope. I'm not big on talking to people outside of the store, really."

Anji smiled at this. Vish watched her discipline the expression away in under a second.

"My husband was off work here and there in the past two years, so there was some talk. But I've been doing quite well in my own business."

"I can see why. And of course, no one wants to gossip about how well you're doing in —"

"Real estate. Residential, mostly, but more and more commercial."

"Great. Look, I'm happy to pay the wage because I think your son will be great for the store. Vish is responsible, he knows more about literature than most of our adult customers already, and he really loves books. I think he'll be an asset, and I want you to be assured that I'll value him and keep him safe. I'll be right upstairs during most of his shifts."

"That's good to hear," Anji Maurya said. She was standing in the morning light spilling through the front window, right in the spot where Mr. Farris had been the day before. Vish felt an unreasonable urge to push her aside, as though Farris had left a filth there that would mark his mother's shoes and be tracked back into their home. As if she sensed it herself, Anji moved aside, coming back to face Agastya at the counter.

"What if we decide, Munish and I, that we're going to Vancouver for the weekend? And that we want to take Vish along?"

"Would I get a say here?" Vish said, putting enough attitude into the question that it was indistinguishable from a whine.

"Any time off we could talk about and would be no problem," Agastya said. "I'd just need a bit of notice. You don't mean this weekend, do you?"

Vish forgot to be embarrassed about his accidental whine and looked past his mother at Agastya. He looked calm, but there had been a little crack of concern between "this" and "weekend," a tiny exhale that sounded almost like panic. Farris said there were two weeks to go, but now he was wondering if there was even less time.

"No, of course not," Anji said. "We're a little more organized than that, and I have a couple of new listings to check on. If it's a busy summer for me, like I hope, we won't be going anywhere, whether Vish wants to or not." She smiled back at Vish, then she and Agastya had a brief conversation about real estate that Vish found far too boring to listen to more than five words of. He spent the time in the Poetry section, browsing with a sense of anxiety that went beyond his usual sense of doubt and ignorance when he was looking at spines with the names of Keats, Stevie Smith, Maya Angelou, and James Schuyler on them. It was one thing being totally ignorant about poetry just for himself, but what if a customer asked him something about one of these authors, or if he could recommend something? He'd be completely lost.

As Vish was holding an illustrated volume of William Blake, realizing for the first time that the same man had written the poems and painted the paintings, he noticed the store had gone quiet. Looking up, he saw his mother and Agastya watching him. He must have had a worried look on his face, because they both started to laugh at him.

"You'll have plenty of time to learn anything you don't know yet," Agastya said.

"He reads almost too much as it is," Anji Maurya said. "Although less Hardy Boys means more time for Wordsworth, I suppose."

"I haven't read a Hardy Boys for like three years." He'd actually read one just before he'd left the boarding school, *Hardy Boys Casefiles #1*, but that had been because he was thinking about his dad buying it for him at Coles and wanted to spend just a few hours reminding himself that there was a time when he felt comfortable in his old house before he moved back.

"I'll be working alongside him today," Agastya went on. "Might be busy. These early Saturdays in summer tend to bring in a few people wanting to stock up for the cabins and vacations. We'll have fun."

"Mom, I'm fine. Can you please, please go?" Vish said. Agastya laughed. For a gross second, Vish thought he was flirting with Anji, but he just seemed genuinely happy to have her in the store.

Agastya was the kind of bookstore owner who seemed mainly to tolerate the presence of customers, not enjoy it, so this was new to Vish.

"You can stay as long as you'd like, Mrs. Maurya. Vish knows I'm good for a discount."

"I think I'll follow the boy's orders," Anji said, smiling. "It's nice to know — I don't know how to say it, but I like that you're Indian. It's nice to see one of our own running a business like this, right downtown."

"The town does need some colour, yes. It's just me and your husband's practice as far as the melanin content goes for about eight square blocks, isn't it?" Agastya said.

"What's melanin?" Vish asked.

"Skin pigment. Colour," his mom said, laughing. "And yes. I just don't see that Munish — my husband — would have agreed to let Vish take a job if you weren't in the, the same boat, so to speak." She made a tracing gesture at her cheek, gesturing at her skin in a way that Vish had only done when he was making fun of himself in a joke at school.

"Then we're all in luck," Agastya said.

Anji nodded and walked toward the door, turning back to tell Vish she'd be back to pick him up at two. "For your first appointment with Rita."

This was a surprise to Vish, but he figured there was nothing wrong with seeing the therapist sooner than later.

"Okay," Vish said. "Thanks, Mom."

The door chimed shut behind Anji. Agastya exhaled hard, slumped onto his stool, his shoulders taking on their familiar hunch. Vish immediately began to spill out the story of what had happened below the maple tree the night before.

Agastya nodded the whole time through, looking surprised by none of it. As he listened, he took a box of old-fashioned wooden matches out of a box beside the till and crossed his legs. Vish had seen this box before: it was enormous, with a dark blue sky and a turquoise lighthouse beaming orange and yellow across the design. He'd assumed it was empty, because matches and a room full of old books couldn't be a good mix. Agastya started striking matches against the sole of his boot, letting them burn down almost to his fingers, shaking them out and putting them on the glass counter in front of him. By the time Vish was finished the story of the split body, the pool, and the mask of skin, Agastya had lined up eight burnt matches.

"I thought something like that might happen," Agastya said. "Gisela wanted to follow you home and set up guard, but I told her not to."

"I could have used some help."

"What are you more afraid of, that thing you saw last night or your mom discovering Gisela hiding under your basement steps?"

This was a genuinely good question.

"And you did have help. Are you wearing the same jeans as yesterday?" Agastya asked.

"Yeah," Vish said, and didn't know whether he should be embarrassed or not.

"I wash my jeans maximum once every two months, kid, do not worry about it. Just check the change pocket."

Vish poked a finger into the small square pocket and fished out its contents, walking up to the till and letting them rattle down onto the glass next to Agastya's burnt matches. It was the change from his $8.89 book purchase the day before: four quarters, a dime, and —

"This isn't a penny," Vish said. Agastya picked up the small metal disc, which was a dull gold colour, the size of a penny, and completely smooth on one side. He put it in Vish's hand with the other side facing up.

On the disc was a raised etching, just as there would have been on a normal coin. But instead of a historical person or scene or national animal, there was a claw. Or a paw. Whatever it was, it had seven talons, all outstretched, with long, sharp tips that touched the rim of the coin. The back of the claw-paw didn't look like a bird's, or a wildcat's, but something in between. Vish was sure he recognized it.

"This is a griffin's claw," Vish said. Agastya laughed.

"There are no griffins. Not in real magic. The symbols are very different from what was allowed to surface in mythology."

Vish didn't have as much control over his face as his mother did over hers: the combination of anger and embarrassment at being laughed at caused the little muscles on either side of his nose to twitch. Agastya apologized.

"I'm not laughing at you. It's just ridiculous, trying to learn anything about real magic. Even a major event like what's bubbling up from under the lake — you could hunt through every library in the world and never find anything about it." Agastya came around the counter with more speed than Vish was used to seeing from him, and waved around the paperback *Necronomicon* that Vish had handled the other day.

"It's part of the whole millennia-old scheme of it. The fake books. All the other distractions from the overlaps between advanced science and old magic. No one who isn't actually involved knows how actual witches like Isla and nachzehrer-herders like Farris do what they do. But there are nuclear physicists who made 'discoveries' in 1951 that some young woman just like Gisela actually discovered before the pyramids were built. Every creature of Greek or Norse or Arabian or Indian or Celtic myth that made it into a poem or a book was made up by a witch trying to throw the rest of us mooks off the trail." Agastya put the cheap paperback *Necronomicon* down and walked back to the till.

"So what is it if it isn't a griffin's claw?"

"I dunno. Maybe Gisela does, but it was Isla who knew all the real stories. I just held on to the stuff. Now put it back in your pocket, and keep it there. No matter what you're wearing, keep it on you."

"What does it do?" Vish asked.

"It wards off things like what you saw last night. Farris, out for a stroll without his rotting body. When you picked up that rock, it absorbed a trace of what that medal has in it, and throwing it at the hunched thing was enough to send it on its way. It's a slice of meteor that's been charged with concentrated energy from this dimension and a couple of others. Now he'll be more convinced than ever that you're under the protection of Isla's magic."

"Are you sure — did your wife really die by accident? Farris didn't do it to her?" Vish asked, blurting out the words because he couldn't wait to find out any longer. "I'm — I don't want my mom dying. My dad. Me. I don't want whatever killed —"

"It was a Ford F-150 driven by a drunk teenager from Calgary. That's what killed my wife. The truck's sitting in the lot at Apple Valley Auto Recycling Service and the kid is in the Correctional Centre waiting to get a short sentence. So don't worry about Farris coming for your family."

Agastya's voice had gotten quieter as he spoke, as though someone were rolling a volume knob in his throat. "Family" came out as a whisper. His eyes looked empty, almost confused, like someone who had woken up in a room he didn't remember going to sleep in. Vish had never made someone feel so bad, so quickly.

"I'm really sorry," he said, matching Agastya's whisper. Somehow that echo brought Agastya back to his former state, or at least reminded him to fake it. He looked back at Vish, smiled, grabbed the box of matches and started playing with it again, striking a light on his boot.

"Anyway, Gisela's talk about magic being physics and biology is true, but that doesn't make it any easier for people like you and me to understand. I couldn't even get past page thirty of *A Brief History of Time*," Agastya said. Vish had also tried and failed to read Dr. Stephen Hawking's supposedly simplified quantum physics take on reality and the world, and the older man's confession made him feel a bit better. A bit less lost.

The talking and the burst of grief had left Agastya tired, even if he had recovered from the dead-eyed stare. He was sweaty, with a strong smell of Old Spice coming off him.

"So that thing in my backyard was Mr. Farris?" Vish asked. Before putting the coin in the empty photo window of his wallet, he wrapped it in the piece of blue felt he kept in there. He put the quarters back into his change pocket. Vish backed away from Agastya, just a couple of steps, but enough for the man to raise one of his arms and sniff.

"It wasn't *all* of Mr. Farris. But in a couple more minutes, it would have been," Agastya said.

Just then, the first customer of the day came in, a very small old woman in a large sun hat that she asked Vish to hold as she looked at the gardening books. Vish took the hat and waited in silence during the woman's twenty-minute browse, which ended with her buying fourteen enormous books that he carried out to her car for her in a cardboard box.

When Vish came back in, Agastya wasn't in the bookstore. The door to the apartment stairwell was open, and Vish stood at the base of it, calling out.

"Are you okay? And what do you mean, that thing 'would have been' Mr. Farris in a couple minutes?"

"I'm taking a second shower," Agastya called back down. "There's an old portable television behind the counter. Turn it on and don't switch the channel."

"What if there's a customer?"

"You don't know how to use the register yet, and traffic is light this time of day. We did enough business on those flower books to justify the day. You're good luck for this place."

"Do I have to watch TV?" Vish called.

"Yes," Agastya answered. "I can tell this is your first job. You don't say no to watching TV at work. In this case, you have to because I said so and I'm your boss, and because it will answer your question about Mr. Farris. Now my voice is getting tired, so please just shut up."

Vish wanted to take a couple of steps up to see if he could see the thing he'd gotten a glimpse of the day before, but was worried that would be a weird thing to do, especially if Agastya was walking around in a towel, or less. As if to confirm his doubts, Moby appeared at the head of the stairs. The white and grey cat then lay across the top step, a lazy sentry. Vish went back to his post.

The floor behind the till was dusty and cluttered, which made Vish notice that the rest of the place was very well swept. He decided to take a broom around himself without being asked, as soon as he discharged his strange TV duty.

CHAPTER 10

T he television was on a little shelf below the cash register. It looked like a clumsy raygun: a deep rectangular box with a screen about five inches wide. It was already plugged in, facing a maroon BC Growers fruit packing crate that Vish could sit on comfortably. He would be invisible to anyone coming into the store. When he turned on the television, which involved twisting a stiff dial until green electronic life began flickering onto the screen, he heard the rapid clicking rush of claws and fur. But it wasn't from the TV speakers: Moby had run down the stairs to join him in watching the screen. The cat's eyes were the same liquid jewel green as the light coming from the television, which soon resolved itself into a human shape.

It was a woman, a tall, pale woman with masses of hair that looked curly and black, but could have been brown. She was wearing a sweater with a strange woollen hood, a large one that she could have pulled down to cover her entire face. The hood shadowed part of her face, but Vish recognized her.

"Isla," he whispered. The last time he'd seen her was two years ago, and she'd been in this very room, shuffling books. But she'd been alive then. Vish didn't know exactly what he was looking at on that screen: a ghost or a recording.

The words that shimmered into place in front of her were white and bold, and passed by in a slow stream:

What You Don't Know Can Hurt You: Or, What Mr. Farris Wants

Vish absorbed this before the woman on the screen spoke, in an accent that was similar to Gisela's, but not exactly.

"Hello, Vish. I'm Isla. And I have to lay out some things that Agastya is being too slow to tell you himself."

Moby meowed and pawed at the screen. Vish closed his mouth and the woman on the screen kept speaking.

At some point while Vish was concentrating on the TV, the bookstore around him faded. Not in the way a room fades when you're staring at a screen, but the way everything turns soft when you put on a pair of someone else's thick prescription glasses. There was that same blur and queasy sense that the world looked wrong, a sense that was even stronger because the screen remained absolutely sharp with all this blurring around it. Vish focused on that, the green around the figure of Isla, and soon the room went from a blur to darkness. Even the floor beneath his crate seemed to have gone away, but Vish didn't dare look away from the screen.

The green on the little screen vanished to be replaced by colours more vivid than the ones he was used to in reality. Still afraid to look down, Vish felt around at his sides. Moby was still there, which was so reassuring that he almost squeezed the cat instead of patting him. The splintery surface and sides of the apple crate were still there too. A few feet in front of him, he could see that Isla's hair was indeed a dark brown, not black, and the hood that coiled around her shoulders was dark blue.

She had small, even gaps between all of her teeth, and her eyes were large and pale grey. She was standing in an extremely fake-looking graveyard, with tombstones and crosses that looked like they were made of wet styrofoam.

"I'm sorry about how this place looks, Vish. Very silly, I know. I built it as a joke, once, for a birthday party Gisela and I threw for Agastya. And I'm not exactly Isla — this is a version of me delivered to you by Gisela and a special preparation of alchemical iron and magnetic oxide, repurposed by two equations and three drops of blood."

Vish started to reach forward, to tap the glass of the television screen that he could no longer see. Isla, leaning on a tombstone, raised a hand of warning.

"Don't do that. We'll have to start again. If you break an illusion with touch, it doesn't have a chance to exist as reality. That's what you did with your rock, and the help of the amulet that Agastya called a 'medal,' like it's a bowling tournament prize. He can be such an idiot.

"The asteroid metal in your talon charm in your pocket comes from Stedlingerland in Northern Germany. That's where me and another witch were supposedly burned for witchcraft, after we spent two months before harvest season in 1229 spelling everyone's crops back to life."

As Isla started this story, the graveyard behind her faded, except for the tombstone she was leaning against. Vish saw two women in a field, maybe of barley, maybe of wheat. It was tall and yellow. A large black cat, almost the size of a dog, nuzzled between the women, winding through their legs in a pattern that looked choreographed. The witches muttered and passed a flat metal disc back and forth, sometimes from palm to palm, sometimes flicking it. It was the amulet Vish had in his pocket.

The two women wore dark blue hoods made of some material that didn't look like wool or cotton, but more like fresh, shining leather. There was a flash of orange light that illuminated the fields, a distant yell, and then a blue light that made it impossible for Vish to keep his eyes open. When he opened them, the two witches were kneeling next to the large cat. As hoofbeats sounded, the smaller witch, who was very young, almost looked right at Vish. The cat nudged at the dirt in front of her and came up with the amulet in its mouth. The claw design flashed in orange torchlight as it swallowed the coin and ran into the fields.

The kneeling witch smiled, and this time did look straight at Vish. It was the smile that made him see it. The absence of the piercing had thrown him, but it was her. Gisela. The taller witch pulled back her hood to listen for the sound of hooves that Vish had just picked up himself: it was Isla.

The scene blew away. Not in a flash of light or an explosion, but a motion as quick as the flip of a coin that left Vish staring back into the cemetery. Only this time, when he felt beneath himself, there was no apple crate, but a porous softness that was somewhere between stone and a marshmallow. Vish looked down and saw grass. Moby ran past his Adidas and toward Isla, who was stooping to pet him. She scooped up the cat that was clearly hers and Vish saw tears in her dark eyes.

"Sorry. I miss my boy, but he's safe with Agastya," Isla said. With Moby cradled in her right arm, she pulled her hood down slightly so the fabric pooled over her left shoulder. Familiar with the move, Moby twisted around and climbed over her arm and back to settle into the hood, immediately falling into a purring state of bliss that was just this side of sleep. Isla reached up to stroke him.

"You're dead," Vish said.

"As far as it matters in that world out there, yes," Isla said.

"But you're not really gone, so why is Agastya so —"

"I'm dead. I really am. This is just a fancy recording you're speaking to, one that is loaded with my knowledge, thanks to Gisela's grasp of the reanimating arts. But Agastya isn't interested in a photocopy of Isla, and he and the real Isla can't see each other, can't speak, can't touch until Mr. Farris is dealt with. And even then, he'll have to give up a lot to be with me again."

Isla paused. "I — the real I, that is — love Agastya so much that I wouldn't be able to stand looking at him when I can't really touch him. Even as a cheap copy, it would hurt me too much to see him.

"The illusion is solid enough now that there's no evaporating it. That's what happens in every moment between sleight-of-hand or illusionism and real magic, Vish. There's a slippage, a zone where reality can be changed. When you stared at Gisela in that vision, when you saw that it was her in that German field eight hundred years ago, there wasn't an atom of you that didn't believe it. That allowed you to step into this cemetery with me."

"Was it really an accident, that you died? Are you human? You can turn up in an old TV and you can make a coin that scares away nachzehrer, but a drunk kid in a truck killed you?"

Isla smiled and pinched the skin of her own forearm. "If the TV-me is solid, imagine how solid the real me was. I was a person, Vish. Older than I looked, moving through space and time differently than you and Agastya do, but I was a person.

Four tons of truck without headlights coming down Pandosy did to me what it would do to anyone, witch or not. I'm just a little better able to keep the electrical parts of myself tied to dimensions where Gisela can find me for a quick Q&A."

Vish was walking alongside Isla now. She was tall, almost six feet, and he felt childish next to her, even when he was standing as straight as possible. There was movie mist swirling around their feet, and all of the stones and crosses around them were unmarked and new-looking, except for some not especially convincing moss.

"Was it really Gisela that you showed me? She's — she's a ghost now, because she was burned at the stake back then? Or she's reincarnated?"

Isla laughed.

"No real witch burned in those days. The hunters and monsters only captured powerless women and murdered them. We all carry guilt for it, even though we saved more women than were killed. No, Gisela and I flung ourselves that night in the fields when we knew that the hunters were almost upon her. We left behind everything in our little house in the woods."

"Flung?"

"That's what you saw behind your house last night, Vish. That's how Gisela got here, to this small town in this huge year of 1996. It's how I arrived a few years before her. That's what I mean by moving differently through space and time. It's how Mr. Farris travels too."

Isla stooped in front of a crypt, a big vaulted one that could have fit a decent-sized family. In a second, she was on top of it, taking a delicate dancing leap and landing on the tips of her toes. Moby was deeply asleep by now and didn't twitch on either takeoff or landing. Vish stared up at her. She was wearing black ballet slippers that were now quite grimed with cemetery dirt.

"It's a leap, like what I just did, but one that passes between air and the space it fills, a jump taken at an angle only a witch who can navigate gaps can see. It takes you through the other side of time."

"And Mr. Farris can see these angles too?" Vish stared up at Isla.

"Back when he was entirely human, before he became a ferry for nachzehrers, a witch made the mistake of teaching Mr. Farris things someone like him should never have known. And he's used that knowledge to become what he is: a ghoul moving through time, stuffed with the insane spirits of centuries of men and women who wanted to live forever, at any price. Spirits that are waiting inside of him to emerge into bodies in this terribly normal little city, very soon."

The doors of the crypt Isla was standing on top of didn't exactly move, but they seemed to *breathe*. A small puff of dust came from a crack that hadn't been between the doors when Isla had first landed on top of the tomb.

"Isla, are you doing that?"

"Doing what?"

Moby's eyes opened, then widened entirely. He placed his paw on Isla's cheek and extended the claws. She gasped and leapt down from the tomb, and Moby leapt down from her.

The crypt doors opened and Mr. Farris, wearing his pale blue t-shirt and cargo shorts, was standing inside the tomb, with splinters from six broken coffins and a heap of very real-looking bones around him. The slim eyebrows crinkled. His body was fuller, stronger, the shirt clinging to muscles that Farris didn't have in the bookstore yesterday. His skin was a glowing pink, his eyes glowing jewelled chunks of rage.

"Don't try to teach the boy anything about magic, Isla. You don't know anything about it. Your coarse instincts only helped you blunder into my way, and now you're out of it."

Farris picked up a long bone — a femur, Vish thought, the longest bone in the human body — and came walking into the light, flourishing the bone as though he were conducting, not threatening.

"Let me show you the reality, little Vishnu, blood of Agastya, let me tell you exactly how you're going to die and how many dimensions your soul will be splintered across —"

If Vish hadn't seen Isla being so tender with Moby, he would have been sure that she'd thrown the cat. Because he'd never seen a cat jump so high and with such accuracy. Before Farris finished hissing the last syllable of "across," that cat had ten claws embedded deep in the face that Vish had seen as a disembodied mask the night before. Mr. Farris howled with such extreme and immediate pain that Vish clapped his hands on his ears and screamed himself.

And stopped when he saw Agastya's hand turning the dial on the small green television, and the concerned skateboard-clutching customer who was leaning over the counter.

"Did he faint? Looks like he fainted," the teenager said. He had shaggy blond hair and more acne than one face could fairly hold.

"He's fine," Agastya said. "Unless I fire him for sleeping on the job."

"You should turn on the AC," the skater kid said.

"Yeah. We have *Thrasher* back issues in a crate in Sports / Leisure back there, okay?"

"I was looking for some Lester Bangs, actually."

"That's not a surprise either," Agastya said, pointing the kid toward the two shelves that represented the small but well-stocked music section.

Vish started to protest as the customer moved away.

"I swear I wasn't asleep —"

"I know, Vish, shut up. If it were a dream you wouldn't need to hose your sneakers off out back."

"She told me that you wouldn't be able to —"

Agastya grabbed Vish's t-shirt, then let it go immediately.

"Sorry. But that wasn't her. So don't tell me anything you heard her say in that dream. Talk to Gisela about her. But clean yourself up for now."

Before Moby could click across the wooden floor and up to the apartment, Agastya took a paper towel to his forepaws, wiping off the blood.

"Cats are pretty useful in this game," Agastya muttered, possibly to himself. "More useful than I am."

Vish walked to the tap in the alley behind the store to wash the fake moss and cemetery dirt off his sneakers. He watched it rush down the cement and into a grate and hoped that Isla was okay.

CHAPTER 11

V ish swept for the last fifteen minutes of his shift. The gradual, repeated motion helped him feel calm again, and touching the floor again and again with the broom made him absolutely sure that he was in the world where he belonged. He was pushing a tiny pile of dirt, fur, and the little fragments of paper that are breathed into the air of any used bookstore into a green dustpan when Agastya put a Slayer tape on the stereo at low volume and started humming along. Vish stood and did an extended nod-not-quite-headbang of appreciation, even though he didn't exactly get Slayer. Not enough melody.

"You did really well today," Agastya said. "I mean, just as an employee. Something about having you here encourages business. Maybe I've been giving people the creeps this whole time."

The doorbell chimed, and Gisela answered the question she couldn't have heard.

"You do. Definitely. Give everyone the creeps." She looked shorter today — was shorter, without her enormous boots.

There was some sort of logo on her tank top, but Vish was too dazed to read it — for a moment, he really connected her with the vision he'd seen of that girl in a field 800 years ago.

"What?" Gisela asked.

"Last time I saw you, you were standing in a field of wheat with a huge cloak on."

"It was barley," Gisela said. Vish just stared. "I can guess what Isla showed you, and I know it probably left you with more questions than you had before."

"Isla was going to tell me exactly what's happening at the bottom of the lake, I know she was. She said that Agastya was being too slow. And I guess that means you are too."

"You're saying I'm slow? Maybe you should have a little flashback of your own to yesterday when you were totally overwhelmed by what we'd already told you about Mr. Farris," Gisela said, smiling, but with a feral glint in her right eye. The septum ring caught a glimmer from one of the ceiling bulbs just as she turned her head, creating the illusion of a snarl. Vish was already quite scared of her, and that didn't help.

"No. I'm not saying anything, just that I don't know what's going on, and I'm kinda sick of it."

Gisela, illusory snarl gone, nodded.

"I'll tell you the rest tonight. Agastya is in no shape to answer you, especially since he needs to get to his drinking in just a couple of hours."

Agastya stopped the tape and walked to the opposite side of the store, pausing in the bleedover shelf where fantasy became horror. He took down two small hardcover books, then waited. When he turned around, he was smiling.

"Don't talk about what I do alone, Gisela. It's none of your business. And Vish has a pill popper in his own family to worry about, so he doesn't need to be burdened with another loser."

Vish let the dustpan droop. The collected pile of detritus drifted down to the floor it had just been lifted from. Agastya made a fist with his right hand and slowly ground it into his own cheekbone.

"I'm sorry, man."

"How did you know?" Vish said. He stooped and started brushing the dustpan full again, focusing on the task so he wouldn't start crying. Gisela came over and put a hand on his shoulder. He was so upset he didn't quite notice that she had touched him, or he would have nervously flinched away.

"I used to see your father at McCulloch Station. The pub, a couple years ago. Not anymore. He was always at a table, alone. Like your mom said, there aren't exactly dozens of brown guys in this town, so I asked the waitress who he was. That's it. He was in there, not happy, a few times a week. Some of the other guys talked about what was going on with him."

"So you do get out," Vish said. His eyes were still closed, so hard that he could see veins threading through the red backing of his eyelids.

"What?"

"You told my mom you didn't get out much."

"It didn't seem like a situation that called for the whole truth, Vish," Agastya said.

"Okay, fine," Vish said. Just as he noticed it was there, Gisela's hand fell off his shoulder. His heart rate was up, but it was from the exchange with Agastya, not the hand, he thought. Even eighteen is an alien-distant age for a girl, and Gisela had a few hundred years on top of that. Being excited by her made no sense at all, so there was no point in thinking about it.

Vish swept up the last of what he'd let drop, then let go of the broom and dustpan.

"See you tomorrow. I don't really want to talk to either of you until then," Vish said, not waiting for a reply. Vish headed for the door and pushed it open, walking into the full brightness of the afternoon. A block later, he heard running footsteps behind him. He could tell from the lightness and quickness of the steps that it wasn't Agastya. Gisela had a dark blue windbreaker on over her tank top.

"I know Agastya is a complete jerk who talks before he thinks. It took me months to understand what Isla saw in him, why she loved him so much. We don't have months, Vish. We need you."

"But why?"

"Because you're a part of this. You've arrived at a moment in time and place in the world that Isla, Agastya, me, and a very bad force have converged upon. Isla's dead, Agastya's drunk half the time, and that means that you're the only person I can count on being fully with me when I need you. So *please*. You have to know more, and I can tell you. There's a punk and metal show at the French Cultural Centre at eight-thirty tonight. Were you going to go?"

"Yeah," Vish said, lying. He'd seen the flyers for the show, but had no one to go with and was slightly afraid of what these shows were like. Matt and Danny and he had discussed going when they were in the seventh grade, but they'd never quite been brave enough to do it. The brothers probably did go now. On most weekdays the centre was just an empty white building, with occasional gatherings and classes, and he couldn't imagine it full of people who wore the same t-shirts that he did.

"Great. We'll watch a couple of bands, then leave so I can explain what you saw in that graveyard."

"So it was just an illusion. It wasn't real."

"Everything you heard was real. And Isla was about, um, 30 percent real."

"How old are you?" Vish asked. It suddenly seemed essential that he have the answer to this question. Gisela smiled. The logo on her tank top was some sort of Celtic symbol, maybe. Vish didn't want to stare.

"I'm two ages. Sixteen and seven-hundred-and-eighty-three. So, seven-thirty. See you there." Gisela turned and started to walk off.

"Wait," Vish said. She did. "Are you sure — are you guys sure you need me for whatever it is that's happening?"

"We need someone, Vish. I'm not enough. And I don't think Agastya is dependable anymore. Losing Isla blew him apart, and he's just starting to reassemble now. You're helping with that too, you know. The way he gets to talk to you about music or books and all this craziness, it actually helps him. Makes him feel in control, like there are parts of the world he understands and still has a grip on."

"I bet that would be a pretty good feeling," Vish said. He hadn't meant to be funny, but Gisela laughed.

She made her way toward Bernard, the main street, crossing and turning into The Bean Scene, the coffee shop that Vish intended to hang out in when he started to drink coffee in September, when he could walk here from the high school. Vish retraced his steps and waited across the street from Greycat, getting slowly hotter and sweatier in the relentless sun as he leaned against the yellow-painted bricks of a sandwich shop. Anji didn't come until two-ten, and she stopped right in front of Greycat, not hearing Vish calling out to her. She went into the store.

"No way am I going back in," Vish muttered. He couldn't stop thinking of Agastya toasting beers or whisky or whatever else with his dad as they sat at neighbouring barstools. "Pathetic drunk."

He waited by the car door, and his mom emerged from Greycat in another moment, holding two small hardcover books.

"Boss said you forgot these," Anji said, opening the passenger door and pressing the books into Vish's chest. He sat down in the lingering remains of the air conditioning before his mom started the car. Glancing up, Vish saw Gisela in the rearview mirror, crossing the street and not looking toward him. He didn't bother waving. Anji started driving toward the bridge.

"Rita is in Lakeview Heights," Anji said. "Practises out of her home. I'm really glad your father doesn't do that. I wouldn't want a parade of crazies on our furniture."

Vish laughed and his mother looked at him, eyes widening.

"I was just joking, you know that," Anji said. "I do not think that you —"

"I like jokes, and I don't think I'm crazy, or that you think I am," Vish said, before going quiet and examining the books that Agastya had given him. *John the Balladeer* and *The Lost and the Lurking*, both by a writer with the absurd but cool name of Manly Wade Wellman. There was a note written on a piece of receipt paper that had been inserted into *John*.

Sorry. Swap these out if you don't like them. If my behaviour just now demonstrates anything, it's that we do need your help, Vish. You know when to shut up, which I clearly don't. Please stick around. — A

Vish opened the book and started to read as his mother drove, not even noticing when they crossed the bridge, only coming to an awareness of his surroundings when the car was parked on a sloped driveway in front of an open ivy-covered garage.

A mackerel tabby cat with a green collar who managed to be both long and chubby simultaneously walked past Vish's window on the low-sloping brick wall of the driveway before jumping onto the hood of the car and then down to vanish under a shelf in the garage. He looked tough, but then again Moby didn't look tough at all, and Vish had just seen that grey cat take a chunk out of a monster.

"She said it would be a very short one today, and that she just wants to meet you alone," Anji told Vish, taking out the chequebook-sized agenda she carried in her purse and flipping through the pages with the tip of a tiny, blunt pencil. Vish stayed put.

"Go, Vish," Anji said. She put down her agenda and squeezed his hand.

"I should knock at the front door?"

"Your father said that Dr. Goodis — actually, I'm not sure if she's a doctor — likes her patients to go through the garage and just open the door to the house there without knocking. Opens into the home office."

"If she's not really a doctor, am I really a patient?" Vish asked.

"Save the smart comments for her," his mother said, now looking intently at her agenda. "I'm going to drive off and find a phone. Marissa Bingham lost a listing right around the corner from here, and I want to see if I can get the homeowner to list with me instead."

Vish got out of the car and his mom was soon reversing back up the incline and out of sight. There were no vehicles in the garage, or hoses or benches or tools or anything like that. Just a table covered with unopened cans of house paint, and a Welcome sign on a white door with a golden knob up three wooden steps.

The tabby cat was sitting on the bottom step, and looked up at Vish — then past him, as the garage door started to descend. Vish gave it a nod of greeting. Cats can be useful in this game, he remembered. The cat ran past Vish's legs and was out before the door was all the way to the ground, the garage completely dark except for a bit of sunlight that came through a gap between the doorway and the wall, which made the golden doorknob glimmer. Vish made his way toward it, feeling with his toe for the bottom step. Instead, he felt something less solid. Something living. Vish reached forward with his hand and touched cool, wet skin in the darkness. And he saw that the glimmer of the knob had vanished, because someone was standing between him and the door.

"Tricked you," Mr. Farris said. "I assume they told you that touching me changes things." His breath filled the entire garage with a stench that reminded Vish of the secret beach near Danny and Matt's cabin, where the boys had once come across dozens of dead, rotting fish being devoured by birds. Mr. Farris leaned forward until the beam of sunlight caught his glimmering blue eyes, which floated barely an inch away from Vish.

"All you've done is allowed us to really communicate, Vish. Agastya and the witch want something from you, don't they? So how's that different from me wanting to share something with you? I'll tell you how. They want to take, and I want to give."

Farris wasn't wearing a shirt, just those ridiculous cargo shorts. They were fastened above his belly button with a black leather belt. The muscles he'd had in the graveyard vision were gone. Farris's chest and stomach were hairless and greenish-white, like the belly of an alligator. The white hairs in his moustache glistened in the dark.

"All I want is to be closer to you, Vish. I don't want to be weak and sick any longer. If you don't want to help me, I could choose someone else, and you can die tomorrow. Whichever is easiest. But since you've gone and touched me, let's try a quick bond."

Vish tried to move. His hand had already dropped to his side, tingling from its contact with Farris's not-quite skin. He managed to pull his foot back, away from Mr. Farris's leg. Farris grinned, raising his head so the beam of light caught his exposed teeth, and started to laugh. More light seemed to come from somewhere beyond his throat. As Mr. Farris laughed, Vish tried to back away more, but couldn't. Mr. Farris reached into his own mouth and started pulling out his top row of yellow teeth, slowly. The roots were white. White and red. Mr. Farris pulled out all six upper teeth.

"That should be enough." Farris laughed, his top lip sucking back over the grey gums, the sound a cackle from the deep pit of his body.

"Remember that possession is a privilege. The people who have joined me are part of an eternal energy, a piece of the universe that is closer to the infinite than any human could be. Binding with me across the centuries is the greatest gift that any human could ask for, next to the new body that I've promised each of my little morsels," Farris said, pinching the loose skin on his own bicep as though the withered muscle had the answer for him.

Too quickly for Vish to move away, if he could even move at all, Mr. Farris grabbed Vish's chin and pressed on his cheeks, forcing his mouth open. Vish finally felt capable of screaming, but Mr. Farris pushed the six teeth onto his tongue before he could, then pressed the boy's mouth closed. At some point, he had stopped laughing and started exhaling, one deep sustained breath that poisoned the air and filled it with a sound like wind in a canyon.

That's when the tabby cat reappeared, whipping around a stack of boxes to sink his teeth deep into Mr. Farris's ankle, right where the Achilles tendon was. Vish had seen Eddie Purdue rupture his during a soccer match in the seventh grade, and remembered the screaming. With Mr. Farris's hand clamped around his teeth, Vish had followed the cat with his eyes, from emergence to attack. Mr. Farris let Vish go and kicked his foot wildly, the wind sound that had been coming from his mouth replaced by a quiet, shrieking inhale. Farris limped fast into a hidden corner of the garage and all sound vanished.

Until the door to the house opened, filling the garage with normal, 60-watt light. Vish, coughing, couldn't spit the teeth out; he felt them in his throat, and worse, down in his stomach. He didn't know if he'd just swallowed a piece of Mr. Farris, or a piece of one of the ancient humans who lived inside the ghoul.

A small woman in jeans and a purple sweater was staring at him from the doorway.

"Have you seen my Buddy, and do you need a napkin?" Rita Goodis asked. Buddy the cat, licking his chops, ran up the three steps into the house as Rita said "napkin." Vish followed him.

CHAPTER 12

The first part of Rita Goodis's home office that Vish saw was the bathroom. He spent five minutes there, retching as quietly as possible. He'd seen episodes of sitcoms about eating disorders, and Erin Fenton had missed half of seventh grade because she had a bad one that she talked about when she got back from the hospital she'd been in, making it clear to anyone who wasn't a total idiot that there was nothing funny about feeling compelled to throw up every time you ate. He didn't know how much of this Dr. Goodis could hear, but he assumed there would be questions.

Vish did a last silent, long hack into the sink. No teeth came up. He found a half squeezed-out bottle of Crest below the sink and filled his mouth with toothpaste and hot water, doing his best to burn Mr. Farris out with fluoride. As a last step, he took the talon charm out of his wallet and rested it on his tongue, where it tingled with a glow that felt cleansing. Vish was thinking hard about swallowing it when there was a gentle knock at the door.

"You can take your time, I just wanted to know if you need anything in there."

"No!" Vish said. "Be right out."

And he was. Less than a minute later, he was seated in a small, bookless study, on a loveseat couch too short to lie down on. Rita Goodis was standing across from him, holding a cup of tea. She watched him without speaking. Vish was familiar with the tactic from his father.

"Quite hot outside for tea, but I can't figure out how to get the air conditioning down here to a normal level. I just moved in, you know," she said.

"Oh," Vish answered. The talon charm had definitely helped, but he didn't quite know how. He didn't like to think of it, but Mr. Farris's teeth had left an immediate, heavy weight in his body when they shook down his throat, and those hands clutching at his face had left a slow, under-the-skin burning. Neither feeling had stopped until Vish had put the charm in his mouth. It was still nestled in there, up against a back molar; he would have to be careful how he spoke, or it would definitely tumble out.

Rita Goodis didn't sit. She leaned against the empty desk behind her. She had a mass of curling grey-black hair, a small nose that almost vanished below the bridge of a pair of thick, round grey-rimmed glasses, and lips that didn't move much when she spoke, as though she were practising a slightly lazy type of ventriloquism. She was small, wide, and solid, and some-how looked immensely strong. Vish had a quick vision of her holding a medieval staff with a metal tip, before shaking the image off. He was still haunted by what Isla had shown him in the graveyard.

"Were you upset out there in the garage? I hope you know that's only normal. And if you were crying, I hope you know that's especially normal. Munish Maurya put you and your mother through hell for a couple of years, but the man I've known for thirty years wouldn't have raised his son to be ashamed of crying. Crying for no reason, maybe, but not crying because of the kind of pressure and confusion that you've been dealing with."

Vish almost let the charm drop out of his mouth, but he remembered to shut his mouth just as it started to roll loose. Maybe it wasn't doing anything, but it did help him concentrate on being here with Rita Goodis instead of panicking about what Farris had done to him.

"You've known my dad for that long?"

"We went to high school together in Vancouver. I was at your parents' wedding. Hunt up the pictures when you're at home."

"I will," Vish said.

"The reason I didn't make this a real session is because I want to tell you a few things first, Vish. Your father helped me out of a bad place I was in with drugs when I was in college. Hard drugs. I really could have died. And two years ago, I came up here and stayed in a motel for six weeks in that —"

"I remember when." Vish knew, suddenly. His mother had packed two suitcases for Munish and left them outside the front door. Vish was staying up late all the time back then, unable to sleep in the months before he was sent to the island school. Through his curtains, he'd watched his father walk up the driveway at three in the morning, pick up the suitcases, and walk right back into the taxi that had dropped him off.

"Yes. I don't know if your parents ever told you the specifics of what happened in that time."

"I asked Mom once and she couldn't talk about it. And a couple weeks later she drove me to the boarding school. Maybe I should have asked again."

"Don't bother. I'll tell you," Rita said. She went from leaning against the desk to perching on it. She was as direct and harsh as Agastya, almost, Vish thought.

"Your father didn't want to dry out in a hospital here in the city, where everyone would know him. Where everyone would talk about him. Where your friends' parents would see him. He thought there was a great chance that he'd lose his medical licence, and any chance at having patients trust him again, if he cleaned up in Kelowna. Because of how people talk, and how unwilling they are to give second chances."

This sounded about right to Vish.

"I'm a certified nurse, not just a counsellor, and I told him he was being a certified idiot not just flying to a facility in Vancouver, but he cried on the phone with me and said he was afraid that he wouldn't be able to do it anywhere but near his family. He said he needed to feel you near him and know what he stood to lose. I helped him through detox and then he started on his regular program. And I stuck around this little city long enough to love it."

"Why?" Vish said.

Rita laughed. "Most people hate where they're from. But you're probably at least a bit glad to be back, aren't you?"

Vish didn't answer. He put a hand to the middle of his chest, pressing in a bit, seeing if he could feel Farris's teeth in his esophagus. By the time he was ready to say anything back to Rita, it was too late.

"I'm going to be making you talk a lot in here, so it's okay if you're a little quiet today. I just wanted you to know that your father's mistakes are ones that he recognizes, and that it makes sense if part of you hates him right now for making you feel how you felt."

"How did I feel?" Vish asked, annoyed.

Rita Goodis did something that made Vish feel sightly ashamed. She smiled, and apologized.

"I don't know anything about you that you don't know better yourself, Vish. It's just the situation I've seen before. That's all. Having a parent suddenly become unreliable can make it feel like your world is falling apart. Getting cut off from everything you know for two years is really painful."

"Did you tell my parents to send me away?" Vish asked.

"No."

"Did you tell them not to?"

Rita hesitated for a second. Just a second, before slouching a bit and lowering down from her perch on the desk, walking over to a mini fridge in the corner, and pulling out a Cadbury Fruit & Nut bar, which she opened and started to eat.

"I won't eat in our real sessions," she said. "And of course I told them not to send you away. I understand why they did it. I understand how your father couldn't stand for you to be around him when he was unstable for another second. I understand that your mother had to pour everything she had into making sure you didn't lose the house and everything, but I told them you'd be better off in the house with them. That wasn't a professional opinion, it was just my opinion. Was I right?"

"Yes," Vish said. "I barely talked to anyone outside of the classroom for two years. I started to hate my dad so much I pictured — I can't even tell you what I pictured doing to him. And the only fun I could really have was hurting my mom's feelings by ignoring her. Because they sent me to that place."

"It wasn't where they sent you, it was that they sent you away. We can talk about that here, and I can help you find ways to talk about it with your parents. And if you want to spend a session crying alone in my garage, that's fine by me."

"I wasn't crying today. A ghoul spat his teeth into my mouth," Vish said.

Rita Goodis stared at Vish and smiled, widely enough that her glasses moved. He could tell she wanted to laugh.

"Telling stories is another thing we can do in here. That sounds like a good one."

"Just a joke," Vish said, and then started talking about how he hadn't been able to sleep all night after seeing his father leave with the suitcases Anji had packed for him, and how he'd used expired eyedrops to try to make his eyes look less bloodshot the next morning. Rita smiled, differently this time, and the conversation kept going for almost an hour.

Vish realized how good she was at making people talk right at the end, when he was in the middle of telling her something he'd never actually realized, let alone decided to talk about.

"When Mom and Dad sent me out there, just shipped me off without really asking me if I could handle staying at home, they made me get, really get, that I didn't have control over anything. Not even where I slept. Maybe what I ate, but really only who I talked to. So I decided not to make any new friends at that school, not to even try, to only talk to the teachers and counsellors and everybody as much as I had to. Not a word more."

"You're talking to me, now," Rita said. Not as though she was correcting him, just pointing it out. The cat, Buddy, jumped into her lap. The chair Rita was sitting on had felt pads on the legs so it didn't scratch the floor: they were the same colour as the swatch in Vish's wallet. Like everything else in the room, it made him feel comfortable, made him forget Mr. Farris.

"I guess I am. And I talked my parents into the job at the bookstore."

"You did. So what does that mean?"

"I don't know," Vish said. He searched around for the right answer, like he was in math class and his first guess had been wrong. Rita saw what he was doing and laughed.

"Not knowing is a fine thing, Vish. Not being sure. You weren't right when you decided there was no point in talking to anybody, but you were sure about that at the time, right?"

Buddy leapt off Rita's lap as she was talking.

"Yeah," Vish said. "And I was wrong."

"Not knowing is better than being wrong. We'll talk about other stuff neither of us know next time you're here."

Vish petted Buddy on his way out of the room, putting his thumb on the diamond pattern between the tabby's eyes, which blinked closed.

When he left Rita's house, it was through the front door, not the garage. Waiting for Anji to arrive in the car, Vish sat on the steps and read from one of the Manly Wade Wellman books, only glancing up once when he saw movement in the high fir trees across the street, in a big undeveloped lot.

It was something white, high on the incline, behind a tree. A face. Farris's mask? Farris? Vish clutched the book like a weapon. Then, just before it fully vanished behind the tree, he noticed that the face was framed with long dark hair — and in that face, there was the glint of the sun reflecting off a septum ring.

CHAPTER 13

V ish insisted on biking to the French Cultural Centre for the show after dinner, even though it was all the way downtown, and even though Munish Maurya promised to make sure that no one saw him being chauffeured. Vish did go out to his dad's car, but only because he thought his house key might have slipped out of his jeans there: he looked around the passenger seat for a few seconds, checked the floor, then felt dizzy for a second and closed his eyes.

Vish was shocked to wake up with his head drooping toward the floor on the driver's side, jerking up to smack the back of his head on the steering wheel. He'd felt a little dizzy on the ride back from Rita's, but this was the first time he'd ever fainted. It was Farris's teeth. He knew it. He had to talk to Gisela.

Vish sat up, remembered putting his house key in his desk drawer downstairs, and got out of the car. He made sure he looked relatively normal in the bathroom mirror before going upstairs again.

"I just want to go alone. No reason," Vish said, as he returned the car keys to his dad. His mind felt blank for most of the pedal downtown, except for a vague fear that Mr. Farris would appear before he could see Gisela again and ask what to do. He was using the blue ten-speed he'd gotten at a garage sale ages ago, even though it was too big for him back then, no matter how much he adjusted the seat. He fit it perfectly now, and it took downhills so well that Vish could feel the wheels starting to steer themselves, to lean into curves before he did.

Neither of his parents had asked about how the session with Rita had gone, and while Vish understood that he'd been tricked, on some level — the non-appointment had most definitely been an appointment — he felt too good about talking to Rita Goodis to want to spoil it with any sort of complaint or conflict with his parents. And if his dad was offering him driving services that came with a promise to stay out of sight, it meant Munish Maurya was very happy with him indeed.

Vish straightened up as he passed the baseball diamond after the big downslope curve on High Road, taking control back from the bike before passing over the railroad tracks. He stuck to quiet streets as soon as he could get off High. While he pedalled, Vish knew he was pushing any thoughts of the teeth away as soon as they came up. He knew that even if he couldn't feel their weight in his gut any longer, they were in him, and Mr. Farris had forced them in there. And he knew that not thinking about what had been done to him was a way to keep from falling apart completely before he could talk to Gisela.

Vish locked his bike up two blocks away from the French Cultural Centre, a blue-and-white converted church with three minivans parked illegally in front of it. He didn't know why he parked so far away — maybe to preserve some illusion that he could have driven there? Older kids — high school seniors

— were loading amplifiers, guitars, and drums up the steps, grunting and stretching their hands. Vish crossed the street casually, so he could look into the centre, which was almost empty. His Casio told him it was eight-thirty, right on time, but the brightly lit room contained only a few arguing band guys and one silent kid he recognized, Barry Montague, sitting behind a folding table with a beige money box in front of him. Barry had played third trombone in band class, but mostly he talked and was told to shut up in class. There was no sign of Gisela.

"Hi," Gisela said, from right behind him. Instead of jumping, Vish walked a few steps rapidly away from her, before turning around. Gisela was wearing a large black hoodie with *Meat Puppets* across the front, and both her hands were shoved into the pockets. She had done something different with her eye makeup that Vish couldn't come close to describing or understanding, but it looked cool. He thought about commenting on it but didn't know how.

"Sorry," she said.

"For spying on me from the woods?"

"Yeah."

"You followed me from the bookstore?" Vish asked.

"Of course I did," Gisela said. "Farris came to your house last night. I'm trying to make sure you're safe. Plus, wherever that was you went isn't far from my place."

"Your place?" Even though Vish knew that Agastya lived above the shop with Moby, and that was it, he'd somehow envisioned another apartment downtown where Gisela had a stack of books, clothes, and some sort of untidy sleeping area. Basically the kind of apartment he'd want for himself.

"I have a little cabin in the deeper woods on some property Isla bought. You can see it sometime," Gisela said, as though inviting him to her place was no big deal. She pointed expectantly to the entrance of the Cultural Centre. "I think we're too early, but I could use some water or a Coke or something. You want?"

"Let's go somewhere to talk before the show starts," Vish said. "More happened."

"What more?"

"More with Mr. Farris," Vish whispered. Behind one of the minivans, a snare drum case fell to the cement and burst open, cueing a lot of swearing.

"Did you lose the charm? If you did, you better find it," Gisela said. She walked past Vish and gestured with her head that he should follow her. Just as Vish started after her, he saw two guys run up the steps of the cultural centre enthusiastically and then stop dead when they saw how empty it was inside. It was Danny and Matt. It was Vish's first time seeing Danny in two years and he was shocked to see how different he was: taller, yeah, but he'd always been tall. His skin was clear and his bones were sharp, his always-greasy hair now looking messy in exactly the same way the guys' hair in the guitar magazines looked messy. His weird friend was now undeniably good-looking. And Vish couldn't help thinking of him as his friend. Him and Matt both.

Matt ran unevenly, but quickly, and Danny's run was really just a long stride that covered as much ground as a normal run. Looking into the empty hall, Danny laughed and then started coughing. Matt smacked him on the back. They did not see Vish behind them, and soon Vish was walking quickly after Gisela, who was jaywalking across the intersection.

"I don't know if this charm works at all," Vish said, trying to talk between breaths. Gisela walked fast when she wasn't slowed down by Agastya. "He was waiting for me in the dark. In a garage. I touched him by accident and he — he filled my mouth with his teeth, like he was pushing in pieces of gum."

"That didn't happen," Gisela said, stopping. "I watched you go into that place. You weren't followed."

"He was in there already," Vish said. "I've been trying not to think about it, because you said you're counting on me, and you can't count on me if I'm totally crazy, which is what I'll be if I think about being full of someone else's teeth. Him or one of his nachzehrers, filling my guts. Even saying that out loud makes me feel and sound crazy, doesn't it?" A laugh escaped Vish. He hadn't meant to laugh.

"Why are you closing your eyes? Vish? What are you doing?"

Shutting his eyelids was even less on-purpose than the laugh. They came down over his eyeballs like blinds, the string yanked by someone else. Vish could feel Gisela's arm on his shoulder, could hear her voice saying his name, but he suddenly wasn't with her.

He was with Mr. Farris. *In* Mr. Farris.

At the highest peak of a fir tree, Mr. Farris was looking down at his feet and the earth, a hundred feet below him. Vish was looking through Mr. Farris's eyes. He couldn't hear Gisela anymore: only the sound of the wind. It was cooler up here. Mr. Farris was now looking farther, to the lake, where a pale green light pulsed up into the dusk. Vish heard Mr. Farris's voice, but knew that it was his own lips that were moving.

You and me, Vish. Can you hear the rest of them?

"Vish!"

As a thousand, ten thousand, twelve thousand five hundred voices rose in a single scream in Vish's ears, coming from the guts of Farris, coming out of Vish's own centre, Gisela was standing above him, with her hand cocked back to slap him. He was kneeling, he realized, and got up just as Gisela's hand was swinging down. The slap got him in the arm.

"Ow!" Vish said.

They were in the Safeway parking lot. Vish saw a familiar face, the old Knox school librarian, Mrs. Herron. She was loading her groceries into the back of an old Tercel with a dog and her son in it. She was staring at Vish and Gisela.

Gisela started to laugh, as though Vish had made a joke so amazing she had just had to slap him on the arm.

"Ha! I know!" Vish said to Gisela, whose smile only made her look more terrified. He hoped the fear wasn't visible to Mrs. Herron. He waved to her.

Mrs. Herron waved back and made the kind of suggestive, cutesy smile adults make when they see two teenagers on what could possibly be interpreted as a date. Before Vish could think of what expression would be appropriate to beam back at the librarian, Gisela grabbed his arm and pulled him along with her down the sidewalk.

"We have to get to the lake, right now," Gisela said. "When did this happen?"

"Like, three, four hours ago."

"He can't hurt you, he knows that. Even if you touched him first, he must be too afraid of Isla's spell to really . . . I didn't think he'd be desperate enough to try something like this. He's trying to — to take you. To inhabit you. It's not hurting you, not hurting your body, so he must think he can get around the charm that way," Gisela was saying, walking even faster now, talking as though she didn't want an answer.

"I don't understand."

"He can't take a bite of you, but he made you take a bite of *him*. It's a huge risk: if he'd drawn a drop of your blood, the protection you carry would have burst him into atoms. But he was careful; he's trying to draw you *into* his body, leave your body out here as a shell, free for the taking for one of his nachzehrers. Did you see something through his eyes just now?"

"I think so."

Gisela grabbed his arm and started to hurry him along faster. It probably looked like they were late for a movie at the Paramount, like their date had moved on from the parking lot. Vish, stupidly, thought about that instead of what Gisela had just told him. Her hand on his arm just below the sleeve of his t-shirt, her cool palm on his sweating skin, seemed more important, for a second, than the teeth he swallowed that were basically eating him from the inside out, absorbing him into the body of a ghoul.

The restaurant patios on Bernard were crowded and noisy, the Kelly O'Bryan's overflowing with teenagers and college kids, even the wall outside the Willow, where the bikers hung out, crowded and social with older bearded men and some women covered in tattoos and denim. Greycat Books and Agastya's apartment were a block behind them. Gisela hadn't slowed down, taking Vish right through City Park, through the dark underpass that he used to be scared of when he was a kid, and finally onto a patch of beach that wasn't occupied by anyone. About fifty feet away, a family was packing up the end of a picnic dinner, paying no attention to them. Gisela led Vish across the white sand, littered with bottlecaps and Dubble Bubble wrappers, and stopped just at the shoreline.

"Keep walking," she said.

"What?" Vish asked.

"You can take your shirt and pants off, if you care, but you need to get into that lake, right away. Vish, how could you just hang around and have a casual evening after what happened? This could be too late."

"You said I was right not to overreact after seeing Farris in my own backyard. You said that he wouldn't try to hurt me, and you've shown me — you and Isla, if she's even real — illusions that seemed just as real as what happened in that garage. But you're saying this one is real. Real for real."

"We should have been even clearer about you not touching him. Never touching him," Gisela said.

"It wasn't on purpose. He was waiting for me in the dark, and I just reached ahead and my hand kind of —" For the first time, Vish remembered that his hand hadn't stopped when it had encountered Mr. Farris's chest. It had sunk in. Just as Farris's teeth were inside him, his hand had been inside of Mr. Farris.

I touched him first, Vish thought. I invited him into me.

"This isn't your fault. It's ours, mine and Agastya's. Is that clear?" Gisela seemed to have guessed exactly what he was thinking.

"Don't apologize," Gisela said. "You're not in trouble with me, you're just in trouble. Danger."

Gisela stepped back from Vish and stomped a booted foot into the shallow lapping of the lake. Water soaked into his pant leg, and she kept talking.

"You know that those teeth you swallowed were real. You could feel them in your mouth, in your throat."

The reminder was enough to make Vish gag, which he started to do. The beach was empty now, of anyone except him and Gisela. It was coming up to sunset, and dark clouds were moving across the western sky. No one could see Vish and Gisela as anything but obscure shapes considering a swim. As Vish was bent over, coughing, Gisela grabbed at his t-shirt and tugged it off him.

"Save the coughing until after you drink, Vish. Go. Take your pants off and get into that lake."

"I still don't understand!"

"You need to go out there, submerge yourself, and drink until all those teeth come out of you. All of them. You're going to find out what's at the bottom of the lake, you're going to see what we've been talking about, and you're going to get through this."

"I failed the Maroon level in swimming twice. I'm not good at getting deeper underwater," Vish said, starting to panic now, knowing that he wasn't talking much sense. He couldn't expect an ancient German witch to know how the Parkinson Rec Centre swimming lessons were graded.

"Don't forget to breathe, but drinking that water is more important than breathing for the next ten minutes. Don't ask questions, don't worry about bacteria or duck crap or anything like that, just do what I tell you and *go*."

Vish did it. He had seen couples on nighttime swims in movies on Showcase before this, but they were usually moonlit and exciting in an entirely different way. He didn't even stop to worry that Gisela was going to see how totally muscle-free his body was, or that he had a weird birthmark on his thigh. His shoes, shirt, and pants were off, and he barely had time to realize he was wearing his *Batman Forever* boxer shorts before his legs had led him into the lake, and his arms plunged into a swim until the water was above his head and he started to chug it down, rising every few seconds to suck air in through his nostrils.

He looked back and saw Gisela on the beach, kneeling and drawing in the sand with the fingers of her left hand, a bundle of sticks in her right. The sticks weren't on fire, not exactly, but each of them glowed with an elemental light, a deep orange and green pulse that looked both ghostly and entirely natural. She saw him watching her.

"I have to stay under?" Vish called out. He didn't even know if he'd spoken loudly enough to be heard.

"Yes! And DRINK," she yelled.

Vish swam out deeper and plunged again, drinking. He imagined himself chugging warm soda from a two-litre, the way he had on a dare from Matt in seventh grade — he'd thrown up after that, hot cola over his jeans and Danny's binder of hockey cards. It had hurt, a lot, and even worse because he couldn't stop laughing. Neither could the other two.

It was when Vish felt the water turn inside him, start to head up instead of down, that it started. What Gisela would call a vision. What Vish was starting to understand was another entirely real world poking its way into this one. Because the speed that he was being dragged down certainly felt real, even if he knew it couldn't be. It was real.

Vish was at the bottom of the lake, on black earth with enormous sturgeon swimming above him, great whipping bodies churning the heavy water, making the vegetation and creeping life at the bottom stir. These were the fish that divers had seen when they were building the great floating bridge that linked his part of the city to Lakeview Heights and beyond, the creatures whose rippling backs when they surfaced had led to the legend of the Ogopogo sea monster. There was more than a mythical monster down here. Vish could feel it as the water flowed out of him. There was a pressure in the water around him, as though the vibrations of thousands of screams were creating waves where they couldn't make sound. The orange and green light he'd seen beaming out of Gisela's bundle of sticks illuminated the scene. Vish started to throw up.

Literally *up*. A great stream of water left his body and started floating upwards incredibly rapidly. He felt a sharp, small lurching from deep in his body, then in his throat, then a sharp almost-bite on his tongue, and one of Mr. Farris's teeth, now much more red than white, came floating out in the torrent rising from his mouth. The feeling followed four more times, then Vish's mouth suddenly snapped shut. He looked up to see five teeth floating just above him, before they melted into something light and scummy that began to float higher, and into nothingness.

Then Vish looked straight ahead. The water wasn't churning any longer, and the green and orange light was even more vivid. It was bright enough for Vish to see — especially when he began to walk forward without wanting to, moving faster and faster ahead — that he wasn't at the bottom of the lake at all. Ahead of him was a drop into a darkness so deep and absolute he couldn't believe it could exist on this planet. It sucked the light in, physically, and Vish saw a twelve-foot sturgeon swimming into the hole, backwards. Only it wasn't swimming in. It was trying to resist being dragged in, without success. It was too close.

That was when all the light vanished, and the pull Vish was feeling on his legs began to feel inescapable when he tried to walk backwards. He was being pulled in too.

Vish looked up, and this time when he opened his mouth, water flooded in instead of flooding out. Into his stomach, and his lungs. With the last second he had to think before panic took over, Vish realized that he couldn't swim against the hole, as the fish had. But he could try swimming up. Up to the air, up away from this bottom without a bottom.

Vish Maurya had actually failed the Maroon badge level in swimming lessons three times running in the fifth grade. But he'd never had a reason to excel at the pool. Tonight, he had a reason. So he swam.

CHAPTER 14

G isela found Vish on the beach about a mile from where he'd first gone into the water. He wasn't shivering any longer. The air was warm and there was a breeze that had helped him to dry off. He stared at her as she walked toward him.

"I couldn't tell you how scary that was going to be, and I couldn't help you beyond giving you that light," Gisela said. "Did it work?"

"For a while," Vish said. His teeth chattered involuntarily before he put his hand over his mouth. Gisela and he both pretended it was cold, not fear, and she handed over his clothes along with her hoodie.

"Dry off with this. We can dump it off at Agastya's to get washed. Did you get the teeth out?"

"Five came out," Vish said, trying to use the hoodie as a towel and failing. It smelled a bit like sweat but mostly like dried flowers. "Can you turn around? I don't want to put my pants on over my soaked boxers, and —"

"Yeah, yeah." Gisela turned as Vish scanned the empty beach and started to do the complicated dance of getting his boxers off and his legs dried and into the pantlegs without bringing in a cargo of sand.

"How many did you say you swallowed?"

"Six."

"This isn't good," Gisela said, facing away. "It's not your fault, but this is very bad."

"Is there another way to get the last one out? Because I'm not going near that thing down there again," Vish admitted. Gisela stared at him.

"I don't know. Until I find a way, Farris has — he's going to be *with* you in a way that you won't like, but he won't be able to control you. You don't have a big enough —"

"Bite of him," Vish said.

"I guess so," Gisela said. "Each of those teeth carried an essence of Farris, if you'd like to put it that way. So a bit of him is still with you."

"That sounds creepy as hell." Vish, dressed, tapped Gisela on the shoulder and they faced each other again. She ignored his question.

"It is creepy, yes. It's not a vampire thing, but close enough." She said vampire *wampyr*, like Anthony Hopkins in the *Dracula* movie. She started to walk up the beach, and this time it was Vish grabbing her arm. He pointed to the sand.

"We're going to sit and you're going to tell me what happened down there."

Gisela sighed, then settled into the sand. Vish stared down at her face in the moonlight for a second too long, so she raised her eyebrows and made a gesture for him to follow his own orders and join her. He sat.

"Magic's biology and physics, like I told you," she continued.

"The whole lake is charged with magic now. Energy like that is as impossible to argue with as gravity, as light. The power all comes from deep in the Earth, it bleeds up to us. The science of magic lets us control it, but if a witch isn't using raw magic, it will use her, or him."

"What?" Vish stuck a pinky in his ear and tilted his head, trying to get water to trickle out. Enchanted or not, it was annoying.

"The energy sucked the magic out of you that hadn't quite soaked in. It pulled Farris's teeth out of you because they were magic, and you are not. But that sixth one must have been deep enough in you, digested, hiding, part of you. So you're stuck with it for now."

"What would happen if you or Mr. Farris jumped into that lake?"

"I'm a traveller to this time, which means every second I exist here is magic. It's unnatural. So me, Mr. Farris . . . if we took the plunge you did, we'd be torn apart. Atomized and combined with that energy. He can't confront the energy down there to do the work he needs to do, getting these nachzehrers into new bodies; he needs to pull the energy up to him."

"I didn't think I'd make it back up here. I just kept swimming and swimming. I don't think I'll be able to lift my arms tomorrow."

"You did amazing," Gisela said. "And now you understand what we're all here for, in this year, in this place, heading toward the hour and day that Mr. Farris wants to control."

"I don't understand anything because you and Agastya keep giving me *scraps*." Vish hissed the last word. Gisela held up her hands, the white palms flashing for a moment as they caught a bit of the moonlight that prevented this night from being the overwhelming dark that Vish now knew existed.

"This lake is one of the deepest on the continent," Gisela said. "That's what scientists know, what they've been allowed to see. But you've been to the bottom. You've seen the split."

"Split?"

"What you saw at the bottom isn't a cave, or a gorge, or a trench, anything like that. It's a gap. Not exactly a physical gap, not exactly a gap in time. But it's a leak, the most powerful leak of magic energy in centuries. It's incredibly dangerous and a magnet for creatures like Farris. Isla and I searched for this moment, this place, for centuries."

Gisela stooped, picked up a hollow white twig, and started to draw in the sand. The moonlight had gotten brighter, and made what she was drawing with an unnatural quickness visible, if not understandable. It looked like this:

$$c^2 d\tau^2 = \left(g_{tt} - \frac{g_{t\phi}^2}{g_{\phi\phi}} \right) dt^2 + g_{rr} dr^2 + g_{\theta\theta} d\theta^2 + g_{\phi\phi} \left(d\phi + \frac{g_{t\phi}}{g_{\phi\phi}} dt \right)^2$$

Vish stared at Gisela, who had gotten up and was brushing sand off the knees of her jeans.

"What the hell is that?"

"Do you know what the Kerr metric or a Killing horizon is?" Gisela asked.

"*No,*" Vish said.

"Don't get mad at me," Gisela said. With her boot, she swept away the formula she'd drawn in the sand. Annoyed, she didn't look sixteen anymore. She didn't look thirty or eighty, either.

She looked permanent, like a statue of some unbreakable element pulled from one of the impossibilities of physics she was describing. If Vish had wanted to get mad at her before, he wouldn't have been able to any longer. He was too afraid, and maybe too awed.

"Every century I've been in is full of people, usually men, being angry at me for things that they don't understand. Agastya has been an exception to that, and I thought you would be too —"

"Sorry, but —"

"No. I'm trying to show you, through physics that's decades old, some black hole concepts that have been a reality in magic for thousands of years. Forget it." Gisela started walking away from the shoreline toward the park. Vish pulled on his socks as quickly as he could with feet that were still slightly damp and sandy, then slipped into his sneakers and ran after her.

"Just be patient with me."

She turned around and started walking back toward Vish.

"I can't. Vish, we don't have two weeks like we were discussing yesterday. More like two days, which means there's now only one left," Gisela looked like she wanted to slap him, the nose ring quivering again. Vish remembered the hole she'd spat into Mr. Farris and backed off a step.

"Don't be afraid of me, you idiot, that pisses me off even more," Gisela said. Then she surprised Vish by laughing, and Vish surprised himself by laughing back. "I shouldn't have said that," Gisela added.

"What?"

"That it's only a day left before the rift at the leak closes up. Isla did the charts to the second. We've known this whole time."

"The more I know the better I can help."

Gisela didn't answer. She put her hand back against the trunk of the tree nearest to her. It was a willow with a thick trunk, but as Vish watched Gisela's hand, unable to look away, he saw it sink into the trunk, drift in until it disappeared. Her arm seemed to stop at the wrist. Then the fingers reappeared on the other side, but three feet up from her wrist: the hand kept emerging, at an impossible height and separation from the rest of her arm.

"We don't have time to tell you everything, but you can trust us. Trust me. I've trained for this. I can find those gaps in space and time we've been talking about. If you apply just the right amount of pressure, you can make a new reality," Gisela said.

"Show-off." Vish was staring at the impossible sight in front of him, his jaw moving automatically to say the words. Gisela added to the sight by taking her free hand and putting it in front of her face, then pressing it onto the skin — and then into it. Not quite able to understand what he was looking at, Vish watched Gisela's fingers vanish into her face, make pushing, twisting motions, careful, gentle ones, and then withdraw.

Gisela's face was totally changed when she dropped her hand. The nose was longer, the cheeks fuller, the shape of her eyes rounder. Vish could see it was her when he stared into those eyes, but he wasn't absolutely sure until she started speaking in her light German accent.

"I just thought that a demonstration would help the physics lesson stick. Especially with some biology thrown in."

Her disembodied hand waved at Vish, and he found himself waving back at it. Then Gisela made a quick motion from her waist, a twist, and her arm was out of the trunk, her hand back where it should be. She went to put it and her other hand in her hoodie pockets, before realizing that Vish was holding her damp hoodie rolled into a ball under his right arm.

"Give me that," Gisela said, and he handed the wadded bundle over. She turned around and put her hand up to her face again. When she turned back, it was the Gisela that Vish knew. Before he could ask her anything about how that particular trick worked, she was talking at full speed.

"Farris is here because the giant battery of that magic down there can get the people he's been carrying inside him into new bodies in an instant. He'll never find another chance like this again, especially because he's falling apart, and there's little chance a new rift will open up while he's still intact."

"So why doesn't he do it now?"

"Because he's lost their names."

"What?"

"Magicians keep very careful records. Farris too, but he didn't think to make copies: the names of all the people he's absorbed, and the incantations he uttered when he consumed them? Isla found them in his grimoire, his dirty book of magic, and took it from him, two hundred years ago on a different continent. And that's what Mr. Farris is trying to get out of the store."

"She hid the names in Greycat," Vish said.

"Yeah," Gisela said. "But she didn't tell Agastya or me where she wrote them down, and she even wiped it out of her own memory. So Mr. Farris would never be able to get them out of her if he or his — his 'tenants' ever got to her. And Isla's off the planet now, beyond any tortures that Mr. Farris might have thought of devising for her. Thanks to that stupid kid and his stupid truck, Isla left us, and she escaped Mr. Farris too. The names, the spells — they're lost."

"What are we supposed to do about it?" Vish asked, just as they emerged from the park's walkway near the sailboat sculpture at the top of Bernard Street. The restaurant and bar noise was loud, and outside the Paramount Cinema, older teenagers were just getting out of the early screening of *Kingpin*.

"We have to wait. We have to wait for Farris to try something again, and be ready for him this time. He's desperate, which makes him dangerous, but also stupid. We'll get him. Right now, we go back to the stupid Cultural Centre and watch the rest of that show. You need a cover story, and I need to see some bad indie rock. Are you going to be okay?"

"No," Vish said. "Not yet, no."

Vish had stopped walking without realizing it. Gisela pushed down on his shoulders and he sat on one of the many benches circling the sailboat sculpture near the park entrance. Old Single's was just closing up for the night, and Vish could see Melissa Lyall across the street, standing there while the manager locked up. A Toyota Supra pulled up at the curb and she got in. The sight somehow made Vish stop shaking, reminded him that the world could still be normal. Mostly because Melissa had stared right at Vish without seeing him.

"You don't have to say you're okay when you're not," Gisela said. "I'm glad you trust me with the truth. What can we do?"

"Can we just not talk about magic or nachzehrers for about twenty minutes somewhere before we have to be around people? I need to feel normal again."

"We can do that," Gisela said. "I have to drop this soaked hoodie off anyway. Let's go to the bookstore."

CHAPTER 15

T he lights in the apartment above Greycat weren't on when Vish and Gisela walked around the corner onto Pandosy. A few cars had passed them, but sidewalk traffic was mostly gone, except for people walking to and from the downtown steakhouse. If the bookstore was a place of calm during the day, it looked as peaceful as a crypt after nightfall. Gisela pulled a small key ring out of a deep pocket and opened the door.

Vish felt better already, much better. Dry, safe, relaxed. There was a skittering sound above their heads as Gisela locked the door behind them. Moby. As Gisela flicked the lights on, Vish could hear the skitter turn to a padding as Moby walked across the floor of the apartment upstairs.

"Is Agastya here?" Vish asked.

"No. He doesn't drink here. He promised Isla that he wouldn't drink in this place, whether she was around or not." Here, Gisela boosted herself up on the counter and threw the wet hoodie in a bundle onto the floor behind it. She sat, swinging her legs a little. The pants were tough and dark green, Dickies maybe, and her black t-shirt was blank and a contrast to her skin, which looked greenish-white under the dirty and dim lights of the bookstore. The sickly tone would have been more appropriate for Vish, after what he'd been through, and he thought about making a joke along those lines. He decided it would sound stupid, or worse, like flirting, so he just sat on the store's one tall stool, which had a printed DO NOT STAND ON THIS sign under a thick layering of clear tape on the seat.

"I'm kind of starting to wonder about the timing of things," Vish asked.

"Kind of? Timing of things? Please just say what you mean. And do you want tea or something warm? There's a kettle back here."

"No. I mean, no thanks. Thank you. And I mean how every-thing — I just came in here on Friday, and then Mr. Farris arrived, and tonight has been — well, things are just happening really quickly. And by 'things' I mean terrible events. Is that specific enough?"

Gisela laughed and blew hair off her face.

"If you're being sarcastic, I guess you're starting to feel better."

"Answer me."

"You said you didn't want to talk about magic stuff for twenty minutes. I'm going to respect that." Gisela leaned back and popped open the till after pressing a couple of buttons, then extracted a twenty-dollar bill.

"I'm not stealing this," she said. "But we might want to get some food, right? You need something with nutrition in it, soon. Fruit or vegetables or a roast chicken or some cheese, something like that."

"I'm not hungry. And not feeling like 'roast chicken or some cheese.' You really are from medieval times, aren't you?" Vish said. Gisela laughed, and looked nothing like the nearly torched witch that had been shown to him in Isla's dream movie. She looked as 1996 as possible, like she was from the future, if anything, not the past. She pocketed the twenty-dollar bill.

"I guess I never outgrew my tastes from back then, no. Not that it was easy to come by any of that stuff. Vegetables, sure, if you count parsnips and carrots, especially. But my parents sold everything they grew, practically, and I ate after my brothers. By the time I started showing the brain for magic and Isla was turning up to give me lessons that my father did not approve of one bit —"

"Wait. She just turned up? What had you been doing, scratching equations in the dirt in front of your house?"

"No talking magic," Gisela said. She trailed off as she was saying magic, looking not at Vish, but over his head: people were passing by on the sidewalk. Vish turned to watch as well. A young family, two parents and a little boy of about seven lagging behind them, walked past the bookstore. The boy looked in, seeing Vish and Gisela. He had black hair that his mother had probably cut: the bangs were too even, and stray clumps stuck up from his scalp. His blue eyes, in the second that Vish saw them, were intelligent: as though he understood that Vish and Gisela were in some sort of quiet conspiracy, he nodded at them and turned to face forward, walking on with his parents.

"We're talking about you, not magic," Vish said. "If some magic gets in there that's okay. As long as it's calm and un, un —"

"Farris-ish. Sure."

"You scared of him coming by the store again?" Vish said.

"He's not going to do that anymore. He only turned up here to see if he could scare Agastya or me into giving up the names. He won't bother working on us now that —" Gisela stopped.

"Now that there's me to work on. A weak point," Vish said.

"Stop sulking. No one called you weak." Gisela smiled, and Vish nodded, bothered that a sulk had crept into his voice, which it definitely had. He cleared his throat to get it out of there, but said nothing. The stool he was sitting on was parked next to the cookbook section, which got a lot of traffic when the store was open. Vish touched the spine of a couple of titles without looking at them, feeling the gentle crinkle of the dust jackets hovering a millimetre above the books they protected. Greycat felt different at night, quieter, more sacred. As though it were a room made specifically to protect books, not just house them.

"Anyway," Gisela said. Vish looked at her — she seemed very aware that she was snapping him out of some disconnected thoughts, but she probably thought he was dwelling on the nightmare at the bottom of the lake. Vish nodded, and she continued.

"The magic I was doing before Isla came was intuitive stuff. Arranging metal objects in patterns, using static electricity before I knew what static electricity was to generate little fields of — well, to kill plants. I killed my mother's flower patch with two copper statues and a buried rod of iron."

"How did you know how to do that?"

"I just knew. I could see the pattern before I made it, how to charge the metals, how to get them speaking to each other, how I could start to gently bake the living earth. I still feel bad about it. Those flowers were the last thing I killed. Pass me the amulet."

Vish, surprised at the request, took a second to fish the embossed coin out of his pocket. He flipped it over to her, praying desperately that it would follow the arc he aimed for and imagined and land right in Gisela's outstretched palm: it did. She made the moment even cooler by not making a big deal of it. She rubbed the design and pressed the cool coin into her right cheek.

"This thing really makes me feel closer to those days. That day, in particular. My mother sold some of those flowers, sure, pretended to my father that they were a useful if small crop that they'd be foolish to just uproot, but really it was the only part of our entire household, our farm, that she controlled. And that she loved. She really cared about those flowers, and I killed them," Gisela said.

Vish returned Gisela's favour of a few moments earlier and snapped her out of her reverie, but without that abrupt "Anyway."

"And Isla came?"

Gisela flipped the coin back at Vish without looking at him. His hand reached for it and caught it in the air. It was probably the most athletic moment of his life, other than tonight's swim — and that didn't really count, because it was life-or-death stuff, and it was a force that had dragged him down to the bottom, not his front crawl.

"Coming in down the market road, past our little house, Isla stopped dead. She looked at the dying flowers, at my mother bent over and tending to them, just as I walked out onto the porch. She was on a tiny chestnut pony, wearing leather and wool clothes that had no shape, but her face was that face you saw in the vision, even if she did travel with a little dirt smeared on it to keep the sun off and hoping that men wouldn't look at her with too much interest."

"I walked onto the porch while she was stopped there on her horse and she smiled at me. I'm not sure what she saw. I was little then, badly fed. Clean but sad would be the general impression. If I saw myself when I was a little girl, in any century, I'd give her spare change and turn the other way. But Isla came over to talk to my mother, asking if she could pay them for me. Said she needed an in-house serving girl, and that she'd throw in some weaving lessons for me, so I could have a trade if I didn't marry. My mother just stared at her. It was the end of summer, and the flowers my mother was trying to save would be dead anyway in a month. I looked at the shrivelled buds while my mother and Isla talked, trying to make myself feel better about my botanical mass murder. Isla waited for my father to come home, because my mother wasn't allowed to decide."

"Will Agastya come back soon, you think?" Vish asked.

"He doesn't drink for fun, he drinks because it helps him not think about his wife for a few hours. I don't know how to stop him and I'm pretty close to not feeling sorry for him anymore, especially since you're here and suffering more from Mr. Farris's plans than either of us have."

Vish didn't know what to say. Gisela tried to smile.

"Sorry, I just haven't talked about my past in a long time. Since Isla died. I know it's probably boring to hear about, and clearly I'm on my last nerve with Agastya —"

"It wasn't boring. It wasn't, I just didn't want Agastya to interrupt us." Vish didn't sound like he was lying, because he wasn't. Gisela looked at his face and Vish knew he'd watched the bright little kid outside the store with the same mix of generosity and interest. That's how she saw him: like a little kid, and he could understand why. Compared to her, he really was.

"One second," Gisela said. She slid down from the counter, her feet touching the floor lightly — Vish saw that she was wearing Keds, not her usual Doc Martens boots. She started tapping on floorboards in front of the counter with the toe of her sneaker, listening for something.

"Is this where Isla hid — is the list of names under the floor?"

"I told you, she didn't tell me where she hid that," Gisela said. "But this is important too."

Gisela knelt, pulled out the key ring from her pocket, and used the bulkiest key she had to wedge between two boards. A twist and a bit of pressure, and it popped up. Gisela pulled out a green and black tin.

"Bendicks Bittermints," she said, walking over to Vish with the extremely British-looking container. Popping it open, she revealed thick wrapped coins that, when unwrapped by a Vish who realized that he was feeling a little low on energy after all, were made of dark, slightly bitter chocolate and a tingling mint creme. They — Vish quickly moved from one to several — were good, and felt more like proper food than most candy. But they were still definitely candy.

"Isla has a few of these hidden around. She had to hide them because Agastya is such a sugar hog." Gisela was still working on her first Bendicks. She took another out of the tin before leaving it with Vish and returning to her perch on the counter.

"This is so weird," Vish said. "I have a — I hide chocolate mints too. Downstairs, near our fireplace. I have since I was a little kid."

Gisela looked at him with her head tilted slightly, then took another squirrel-sized nibble of her candy.

"I guess you're as weird as she was. Unless your parents are always raiding your chocolate supplies."

"They aren't. It just felt secret and cool to me to have this little trove when I was in elementary school, and I never got out of the habit. My mom would kill me and say that I'm inviting ants into the house if she —" Vish stopped. Gisela still had her head tilted, and it dawned on Vish that he was being very boring, but she was being kind to him after his traumatic dip in the lake.

It also occurred to Vish that this was the kind of situation where he might be supposed to try to take her hand, or kiss her. He was glad he was far from being able to attempt something like that, because he was sure that Gisela would just pull away and stare at him, confused.

"Forget about the After Eights. Tell me about the cheese and roast chicken in, um, thirteenth-century Germany," Vish said.

"Nothing I say can make it really seem real to you," Gisela said. "You could read your way there, maybe. Depends on how good your imagination is. How able you are to forget yourself. You want to be a writer, don't you? Part of writing is that, forgetting yourself."

"How do you know that I want to be a writer?"

"It was a guess," Gisela said, smiling. "You're fifteen, you're obsessed with books, so you're clearly thinking about it. And now you've confirmed it. Remind me not to commit a crime with you. You're a very easy interrogation."

"Fine." Vish unwrapped another mint chocolate, using just one hand. He wanted to put the whole thing in his mouth but settled for an elegant nibble, emulating one of Gisela's bites. The tin wasn't bottomless, and he wanted these things to last. "Tell me one thing about life then that was so different. The first thing that comes to —"

"The smallness of it," Gisela said, quietly. Her accent crept in more heavily. She bent her neck a little, and Vish could envision the dark hood from his vision of her in the field coming up to shadow her features.

"No one from our village travelled, except to market. Soldiers, yes, but we had a family farm and my brother wasn't going to be part of anyone's army. Just pushing that plow. My mother, my sister, and I boiling water, doing laundry, cooking. My world was smaller than Wernerus's, even —"

"Woah, 'Wernerus'?"

"My brother. He and my sister, Greta, stopped talking to me when I left with Isla. I would see him on roads, once even near my home in the woods with Isla, hunting. He had our father's bow with him. That time he nodded to me, but only because he was surprised. Greta I would see at market, and even bought some apples from her. She was only eleven, very small, but she was absolutely obedient and it was clear that my parents had forbidden her from really speaking to me. She was much prettier than I was too. That's why my mother was happy to let me go. Happy to see me and the cat go."

Vish had a clear thought, perhaps his clearest one since emerging from the lake: Gisela's story was so sad, that if it were his, he wouldn't really be able to tell it to anyone, let alone casually, like this. But Gisela didn't even look sad, just far away, as though some of her magic had drawn her back hundreds of years into the time she was speaking of.

"I saw that black cat. I mean, Isla showed me," Vish said. "Huge."

"That was Dammo. He was beautiful, wasn't he?" Gisela smiled, sounding more like her modern self. "Dammo was a great channel cat. They can't do the math, of course, but cats absorb. They can take in pockets of magic energy like almost no other animal. Certainly nothing else we've domesticated. They suck it in and retain it, from the earth and from people who handle magic. You saw what Moby did to Mr. Farris in that dimension. The little guy has enough of Isla in him to pose a serious problem to Farris. And Dammo, my big, beautiful black cat, he came to our house from the fields, from someone who had powerful magic, wearing that coin you have in your pocket in a locket hanging from his collar. Even Isla never figured out where he came from, but there's a good chance he came from a different time, a different place. People didn't put up Lost Pet posters back then, anyway. I just kept Dammo in the barn and my family left him alone as long as he kept up with the mouse-killing. What was I talking about?"

"The smallness of the world," Vish said.

"Are you making fun of me?" Gisela said. She didn't ask it in a perturbed way, but in a scientifically interested way. She unwrapped the bittermint she'd taken from the tin with both hands, her fingers peeling the foil off without breaking it. When she was finished, she set the perfect green rectangle next to her on the counter.

"I'm not, my mouth is just full. Sorry."

"Sure. Yeah. I'm sure you think Kelowna is tiny, and sure, in some ways, it is. You probably think everyone here is the same, into the same stuff, with the same history and the same future. Except for you and your few friends and maybe your parents when you're feeling good about them, right?"

This time Vish wanted to ask if he was being made fun of, but he also still felt a bit like Gisela had left mind-reading out of her explanation of magic, so he kept his mouth shut and nodded.

"I appreciate the honesty. You want to leave?"

"Go to the show? I mean, sure," Vish said. A streetlight outside flickered and his head whipped around in an instinctual search for Mr. Farris, but the movement just made his desperate answer seem funnier.

"No, I meant leave this town," Gisela said.

"I just got back, really. From boarding school. But I know what you mean, and the answer is yes. After I graduate, definitely yes."

"You live in one of the most beautiful places in the world, and you can't wait to leave," Gisela said.

"Yep," Vish said. He was starting to feel needled.

"I'm not making fun of you. I get it. I'm just saying, think of how much smaller and dimmer my world was. For the first thirteen years of my life, I don't think I saw more than eighty, maybe ninety different people. At church, sometimes at market, there would be a traveller, someone passing through. Otherwise it was the same people. The new people were the babies. That was it. That was how small it was for me. And when Isla rescued me from it, I only really saw her. We didn't mix with anyone until the drought came and we decided to help with the crops. Then instead of thanking us, the farmers —"

"I saw."

"Yes. They tried to burn us. They burnt poor Eberhardus Mulch's whole harvest, thinking we'd be caught in the flames. I wonder if they looked for our skeletons.

"Even though there was no one else there, I remember how big the world became when I was living with Isla in the forest, her and the books, her and the lessons. How she taught me that space and time weren't just limitations, weren't just facts, that they could be learned and navigated. Finding out you can negotiate with years and miles pushes any dreams — marriage, banquet balls, palaces, whatever it was I was supposed to be wishing for — totally out of mind. I wanted infinity, and Isla and I skipped around the next seven hundred years learning more about it together."

Vish unwrapped another mint. This one, he ate whole. There must have been something in the glazed way that he shoved the delicious disc in his mouth that alerted Gisela to the need for a subject change.

"Sorry. That was kind of remembering for me, not telling a story for you. No magic, right?"

"Limited magic, please."

"So I'll just tell you about where we lived. The house in the forest. First, Isla paid for me in gold, because while my father wanted me well away from the house with my cat-talking and math-puzzling ways, my mother was very reluctant to give up the hours of help I gave her in the house. And I think she loved me too, under all that tiredness. We just never had time to find out much about each other, not with working from before dawn, then serving my father and brother, then getting to sleep as soon as possible. She used to clean my nails for me and help me with my hair before church. She did both too hard and it hurt, but I didn't tell her. I liked that she was touching me at all."

"What was your mom's name?" Vish asked. Gisela had to think for a moment.

"Agnes," she said. "Agnes didn't want to let me go until Isla put down an extra few pieces of gold. Then she just turned away from the door and walked back into the house, to her other daughter. The one she wanted to keep."

Vish didn't hear the next few sentences that Gisela said. He was too consumed with the thought of what it would be like to forget your own mother's name. To be so far from her, and to have had so little connection to her before you left, that "Agnes" could become a couple of syllables with as much meaning as the name of an actor with a vaguely familiar face that you saw on television some afternoon. He felt, as strongly as though it were in his palm right now, the grip of Anji Maurya's hand on his when they used to walk through Orchard Park Mall together when he was very small, on his way to getting a haircut in The Bay.

"Isla, by that time, she'd existed in as many times as you've lived years. She could tell you what the air smelled like in Europe in eleven different centuries. She really took it easy on me at first: never let me know anything about the future, probably to fend off questions. Or panic, or —"

"Total brain shutdown," Vish said.

"Yeah." Gisela laughed. "Agastya and I are both bad at that. Overloading the information. I have no excuse, but with him, I think it's a bookstore owner thing. No offence."

"Why would I be offended?" Vish asked.

"Because you clearly love working here," Gisela said, thumping the counter. "Anyway, that first year in the woods, I learned English, how to survive outdoors, how to clean a house and when other things were more important than cleaning a house, how to dress for various occasions that we never actually went to, and all sorts of other skills outside of the hard numbers and, you know, emotional pain that go into magic."

Vish didn't know, but he didn't want to talk about it just then.

"What was she like? I've only met her ghost."

"That's her. There's nothing about what you saw in that vision that isn't the real her, but I do think she got a little nicer after she met Agastya and was only obsessing about destroying Farris and closing portals for half the time instead of all the time.

"But I missed the old her, and having her all to myself in that little house. It wasn't whatever gingerbread fantasy you have in your head, by the way. It was built of wood, and was one deep room with curtained-off chambers where we slept. Hers was at the front, near the door, and mine was at the very back. There was an enormous oven in the middle of the place, made of iron, that would radiate heat all day as long as we kept it fuelled, and when Isla woke up she made eggs and coffee and warmed bread on top of it. Dammo slept right in front of it. It's funny, he could sleep outside when it was freezing and be fine, but when he had the chance, he was right by the fire.

"She let me sleep in for a little longer because it was my job to keep the fire going at night, waking up to stoke it. It was easy for me because I can't stand the cold, and up until then, I'd been sleeping in the same bed as my sister and brother, stealing their heat. But I didn't miss it. I loved being alone, and that was the best thing about Isla. She understood how even in a world where there were barely any people around — maybe especially because I was always surrounded by the same people — being alone was the most valuable thing she could give me. I still love it. That's why I have my own cabin in the woods now."

Rita Goodis had reminded Vish of something he'd already learned from his father, but never really thought about doing himself. It was about listening. Like Munish, Rita didn't treat the pauses in a conversation as cues, as an invitation to speak that would be rude to reject. She had let those pauses sit in the little cluttered office in her house, and Vish had told her more about his feelings and his father than he'd told any other person in his life. So as Gisela stared into the air in front of her face, seeing a different time in a different country, Vish kept quiet. He waited for her to finish her story.

"We vanished from the field before they put the torch to it, those men who thought we were there to poison them and their children. But we didn't go straight to another time, or place — Isla just helped us, me and Dammo, slip with her through the miles back to our little house, so we could get ready to go, to leave forever.

"That didn't mean packing up, it meant burning. The men hadn't found the place yet, but they would. So we took every scrap of paper, every book — and a book two hundred years before the printing press was such a precious thing, written out by a scribe on animal skin, each letter and illumination a little piece of art — and put them into that enormous stove in the centre of the room. Because Farris would be with those men when they came, driving them, and Isla knew it. He already knew too much of our magic, and we couldn't risk him gaining anything else. Dammo vanished on his own, walking into a gap that Isla opened for all of us, but walking out at some different point from the one we chose. He may be in Mexico two hundred years ago, he may be living in 2360. I wish he had come with me, but you can't tell a cat what to do."

At some point during this story, Gisela had unwrapped a third mint that Vish hadn't seen her take, but she had forgotten to eat it. It was melted across her palm, a dark circle streaked with white.

"Alright," she said, staring at the chocolate goo. "Let's go to a bad rock show.

CHAPTER 16

When Vish and Gisela got back to the French Cultural Centre, the minivans that had been parked out front for loading in instruments were gone. Kids lined the stairway, leaving a narrow single-file space for people to enter. Across the street at the First United Church, some older teenagers leaned against the brick façade, smoking cigarettes and occasionally spitting on the mulch.

"I have to go to the washroom about five minutes ago," Gisela said when they got to the top of the steps. She threw a five-dollar bill next to Barry Montague's money box on the little table and ignored him when he called out to give her a stamp. Barry, who had either swapped out his glasses for contacts or for nothing at all — probably nothing, judging from how he was squinting at Vish — held out the stamp and an open palm to Vish, who dutifully extended his own hand.

"You gotta pay first, man," Barry said.

Vish was reaching into his back pocket when Danny and Matt appeared from behind Barry. Danny was holding a wallet that looked familiar.

"You owe us big," Danny said. A band started as Danny handed the wallet over, and Vish traded money for a stamp.

"We know you work at that bookstore now," Matt said, when they were around a pillar near the back of the room, speaking between the punk singer barking "Anarchy A.D." and about four people in the audience echoing it back to him when he held up the mic. There were about sixty kids in the room, which had a low ceiling that sort of blossomed over a stage that had a podium on it, pushed off to the side. The punk band had set up in the audience, but the singer kept climbing the stage and jumping back off it. The crowd was older, the people Vish would be seeing in the high school halls daily, except for the ones who had graduated and would leave town at the end of summer.

"You wouldn't even let me apologize," said Danny. "We were friends, dude. It was stupid of me to trust a teacher but it's even dumber to —"

"Where did you get my wallet?"

"Your mom came by and dropped it off," Matt said. "Don't worry, she didn't come in."

Vish had been worried about exactly that. His mom walking into the building in one of her power suits, ignoring Barry's request for money until she couldn't spot Vish and turned to ask the little man where her son was. Everyone seeing his mother, and later identifying the only brown kid in the room with the brown woman who needed to take care of even the most basic elements of his life, like he was still twelve years old. It would have been bad.

"I was outside. Told her you were in the bathroom and I'd get you the wallet right away," Matt said. Since crawling into Vish's window just yesterday, Matt had changed his look as well:

he'd dyed a stripe of lemonade-bright yellow into the middle of his mossy brown hair. Vish couldn't tell if it looked cool or really, really awful. Matt hadn't gotten taller like Danny had, but his face looked bonier, more grown up, almost strange on his skinny neck and chubby little kid's body. Vish wondered if his own growing looked this ugly, unnatural, and weird — he didn't notice vast differences in the mirror, but that may have been because he spent every day with himself.

"We saw you leave with that girl," Matt went on. "And we don't understand who she is or why she'd spend time with you."

"I thought you were apologizing to me, not insulting me," Vish said.

"I'm sick of saying sorry to you, Vish," Matt said. "I really am sorry. So is my brother. But if how good of friends we were to you isn't good enough for you to forgive us blabbing out your family problems that everyone would have known about when you disappeared to that school anyway, then okay. I'm not saying sorry again."

"That's just my brother talking. I will say sorry again if you want me to," Danny said.

Vish laughed, the sound coming out of him as uncontrollably as a sneeze. The brothers smiled back at him. Vish had to think about why he was mad at them; unlike the laugh, the feeling didn't come naturally anymore. Matt was right. Everyone in this city would have heard the gossip soon enough, about his dad, the pills, about him being sent away. It just didn't matter that Matt and Danny were the original leak. And next to the pulsing energy in the lake and the nachzehrer infestation, nothing that anyone said about Vish's family really mattered at all.

The three guys didn't say anything, just watched the band for a few seconds. But the fight was over, they all felt it. Vish knew they were friends again. Danny broke the silence.

"I never noticed that girl," Danny said. "I would have noticed her. So where did she come from?"

"Her name's Gisela, she's home-schooled, and I barely ever see her. She works at the bookstore too, that's all." He wondered if having Mr. Farris's remaining tooth inside him made lying easier. It certainly didn't make his lying any better, because the two brothers stared at him without an ounce of belief between them.

"No one thought you were dating her, don't worry," Matt said.

The punk band, incredibly, was finished their set. Maybe five songs, none longer than two minutes. As the applause started, the boys stopped talking and clapped as well.

"So you finally admit you're not hanging out with us, and there was no way you were going to actually call," Matt said.

"No. I didn't say that. I'm just not hanging out with anyone."

"Look how sweaty those dudes got," Danny said, awed. "Bass player almost dropped his guitar when he took off the strap just then because the neck slipped right through his hand. They went for it, man."

Vish took a moment to respect the sweat. Danny was right. The things Danny noticed often seemed stupid, and many of them actually were, but sometimes it was important stuff. That fifteen minutes of performance contained more energy than Vish expended in a normal week.

"We want to do that," Matt said. He was leaning against the pillar by now. "Me, Danny, you. We'll look for someone else if you're sure you don't want to, but we want you."

"Okay," Vish said, as though he were talking to himself. Even if he was, it was too late: Danny heard him and grinned, slapping him hard on his exhausted left shoulder, which ached from his long swim.

"That easy?" Danny said.

"As long as you get that I have two years of practising to catch up on," Vish said. This was something he could be in control of. No matter what his parents did, what Mr. Farris did, what happened at the bottom of the lake and whether it ever surfaced, Vish could put his fingers on the fretboard of the abandoned red Stratocaster in his closet. He could play music with these guys that he'd missed very much. On the guitar that he'd also missed very much. It was a good American Strat that one of his father's patients had given him after Dr. Maurya had treated him for free throughout a year when he'd been laid off. Vish wanted it in his hands again, even if it had made him feel incompetent when he really pushed himself to play the way he dreamed of playing.

"That's so cool," Matt said. "I mean, not cool that you're going to suck now compared to us, but that you're in!"

"I —"

"Playing with us will make you better," Danny said. "Did you really not practise the whole time you were on the island?"

"Zilch." A new band was setting up, wheeling out small combo amps. This band was half guys and half girls. One of the girls picked up the mic that the punk singer had left on the ground and wiped it off on her light sweater before turning it on and saying, then singing, "Test test test." One of the guys strummed a bright chord out of a Rickenbacker, a guitar Vish had never seen in real life, only in the magazines.

"I think we can be a great band. We're really gonna try," Matt said.

"Try what?" Gisela spoke from behind Vish. He turned as she was walking up to stand beside him. The group of boys became a bit more visible to the rest of the room when she joined them; a few heads turned, and Vish felt people looking at him, not just in a noticing-way but in a considering-way. Like they were trying to figure out what the three friends were about, not just noticing the only kid in the room who wasn't white.

When Vish turned from Gisela and his scan of the room back to Matt and Danny, they were quiet. Danny was looking above everyone's heads, which he did because he could and because eye contact made him nervous. Danny looked right next to Gisela in a way Vish knew he didn't: they could be a couple, with their height and sharp-boned faces, the magazine-look they both would have if someone put different clothes on them. Vish didn't notice this in a jealous way, he just noticed. To get jealous he would have to imagine a possibility that he and Gisela could somehow not only look good together, but be together, and he definitely could not.

"We were talking about doing a band," Vish said. "Being a band." Matt looked at him like he couldn't believe he was being so direct.

"Cool. What do you all play?" Gisela said. Danny and Matt spoke the one word required of each of them. Vish said guitar.

"Who's going to write the songs and sing?" Gisela asked. "I'm Gisela, by the way. Also by the way, I can sing and play guitar."

"No, you can't," Vish said. Gisela turned to him, giving him a "shut up" look that he wouldn't have recognized if he hadn't spent time with her before. Taking her cue — the slight and millisecond-long widening of her eyes and a movement of her lips that could have been the beginning of either a frown or a smile — made him realize that he did know Gisela better than he thought, almost well enough to call her a friend.

"I mean, I didn't know that you played, just that you were into music," Vish said. He thought of Gisela in that barley field, and of all the time in between that moment and this one, and of all the things that he didn't know and had learned just in the past hour. If she could put her arm through a tree, she could probably strum a better G chord than he could.

"I can kind of sing," Matt said.

"But would anyone want to listen to you sing?" Gisela asked. "Not to be mean. Just think about it. Maybe I could try along with you guys."

"We don't really know you," Danny said, but he was clearly interested in the prospect. Vish could already see Matt sizing Gisela up, not in a creepy way, but imagining what she would look like behind a mic on the stage in this very room. Danny looked at Gisela's fingers, which were long, almost as though they had a fourth joint. Vish remembered that Danny approved of long fingers in musicians.

"Vish knows me," Gisela said. "We work together, so he knows that I don't suck to hang out with. Unless he's not telling me."

"You don't suck," Vish said. He wanted to add that she wasn't exactly talking in the way he was used to her talking, and her accent had completely vanished, and he hadn't seen her be so forceful with anyone since she'd spat in Mr. Farris's face, or maybe since she'd screamed at him to jump into the lake. But he didn't say anything. He waited.

"Danny, you want to get a Slurpee and talk about this?" Matt asked.

"We're talking about it right now, aren't we?"

"He means do you want to talk about it just you two, since we'll probably be practising at your house so it has to be your decision," Vish said. Gisela nodded, and eventually Danny did too. The brothers left.

"What are you doing?" Vish asked. "Are you trying to embarrass me? For no reason?"

"It's just an intuition at this point," Gisela said. "But we need more people we can call on. More hands. I have to trust my instincts right now. And we could use more hands. Loyal, trustworthy hands. Those guys are your friends, aren't they?"

"Is it, like, a magic intuition?" Vish asked. Even he couldn't tell if he was being sarcastic. Gisela just looked at him and back to the stage. A couple of KSS guys in black-rimmed glasses and tight denim jackets that must have been baking hot inside the room had started sidling closer to her, and Vish watched as Gisela turned to look at them, straight in the eyes. They stopped sidling and pretended they had been concentrating on the drummer's cymbal setup the whole time.

The new band started, with clean sustained chords over a shuffling beat on the snare and the kickdrum. The rhythm was frantic, but the reverby guitar overtop played relaxed, cool chords. The singers, one of the guys and one of the girls, took turns with the melody. Sometimes the guy screamed like he was in a hardcore band, a weird eruption that signalled a little instrumental break and the start of the next verse. Vish was pretty sure that they sucked, but he still liked watching it.

Vish had to lean closer to Gisela to make himself heard without yelling. He probably still smelled like lakeweed and sand, but she smelled like a mix of things — tea, vanilla, maybe sweat.

"I don't want Matt and Danny getting involved. I don't want Mr. Farris coming anywhere near them. Can you promise me that?"

Gisela, still watching the band, was able to speak out of the side of her mouth clearly and with just enough volume for him to hear every word.

"Everyone is involved already, Vish. Everyone in this little city. You, me, and Agastya, we're just the only ones who actually know about it — to know we're in danger. And if we let Matt and Danny know — they'll be better able to deal with the trouble. From Mr. Farris and all the things he wants to bring back. No one's safe."

One of the high school jean jacketers was suddenly right next to Gisela, hovering over her shoulder and staring at Vish. Gisela sensed him there and moved slightly away, bumping into Vish. He made room for her.

"Hey," said Jean Jacket.

"Yeah?" Gisela asked. "I'm watching this." She pointed to the band, then to her ears.

"Do you go to OKM? I think I saw you at one of Robbie Gordon's parties last —"

A shatteringly bright guitar chord: Vish saw it was a D, played high on the neck of the guitar without the reverb, announcing a long screaming and distorted passage that Gisela screamed her own answer to Jean Jacket under.

"I did home school and got my equivalency last year. I don't go to any high school or really talk to anyone or go to any parties. Sorry. Enjoy the show though."

Gisela turned her back on Jean Jacket to look directly at Vish. She leaned close to Vish to continue what she was saying before the guy, who had wandered off very quickly, had interrupted.

"When those things break through, they're not going to ask permission for a body. They're just going to take one. Everybody in this entire town is at risk of being chosen to host a Farris-creature of their own. I thought you'd understand that by now."

"Don't talk to me like I'm stupid," Vish said, loudly enough that a group of older kids, a mix of the clean-cut Young Life Christian kids and the stoners they often tried to recruit, turned around. Vish started to walk toward the bathroom at the side of the hall just as Gisela started to talk. He stopped, but didn't turn around.

"I can't be direct with you about what's going to happen with Farris, Vish. Not anymore."

Vish turned to her.

"What?"

"As long as that last tooth is inside you, as long as Mr. Farris might be able to look out from behind your eyes, I have to keep some secrets. I don't think you're stupid. I think you're smarter and quicker than almost anyone I've met in this place. But Mr. Farris wants to use you as his new body. He may be listening to me through you right now."

"But you told me all that stuff about magic on the beach, and about yourself in the bookstore —"

"What I told you about magic Farris already knows. And I don't care what he knows about me and my past, but I do care about him finding out any more about the next twenty-four hours."

Gisela didn't call out after Vish when he walked toward the bathroom.

It was empty. Empty and dark. Vish flicked on the lights, illuminating three stalls and two sinks. He was less angry already, calm enough that he was wondering why he got angry in the first place. He replayed what Gisela had just said, and when he got to "permission for a body," he saw the same picture in his head that had appeared when she'd spoken it: his mother, pulled into the darkness of the lake, her hair pulled out of its bun and sucked into the dark void at the bottom, the vacuum at the bottom of the lake pulling on Gisela's arms and legs until her body started to stretch in a way no human body could.

Vish started to retch into the sink, coughing then letting spit trail out. And, finally, a tooth: not his own, but a curved, jagged yellow one with a two-inch root. It spanged against the side of the sink. The bathroom door pushed open just then and a kid Vish knew from French class, Colt, shouldered past him to the stall. Luckily he and the rest of his friend group had been ignoring Vish since the third grade, and Colt didn't take a second look while Vish fished the tooth from the sink and put it in his pocket.

When Vish walked back out onto the floor, the two guitarists from the band were in the middle of a long dual solo, stomping on each other's effects pedals — reverb, delay, overdrive, making a huge and ugly soup of sound. Vish was still pretty sure it sucked, but the power of the sound made him forget everything he was worried about, just for a second. When Vish was next to Gisela again, he opened his hand and showed her the tooth. She quickly grabbed it and thrust it in her pocket.

"So you can trust me now," Vish said. He could still taste the thick, buttery smoothness of the tooth as it had come up. He shivered.

"What happened?" Gisela said.

"It just came up," Vish said. "I was hoping you could tell me why."

Gisela put the back of her hand on his forehead. If it wasn't warm when she first touched it, the enormous invisible blush that came with her touch — and the peripheral glances he got from people in the crowd who had been watching Gisela, and were now realizing that the brown shape beside her might be a human of interest as well — turned him baking hot. Gisela let her hand slip away.

"Biology and physics. The atoms in the lake did the separating work for the first five teeth, those fragments that Mr. Farris was trying to fuse with your flesh. But this last one, rejecting it had to be pure biology. And willpower. You don't want anything to do with him, and everything in your body pushed it up and out of you. If Mr. Farris wants you, he's going to have to take you." Gisela poked Vish in the chest.

"Is it true about your home-schooling stuff?" he said. "You have a certificate or something?"

Recognizing that Vish desperately needed the subject changed, Gisela nodded. Smiled.

"I do, in case some nosy person from the school board wants to try to stick me in a classroom. I learned quite a bit floating around a few centuries with Isla, and caught up with the rest in the bookstore the past couple years. Isla and I were going to try to fake a certificate together, but then I realized it would just be easier to take the stupid exam. You should try it," Gisela said.

They both watched the band finish its set, the guitarist casually undoing his strap with a thumb and catching his Rickenbacker by the neck as it began to pendulum loose. I'm going to do that too, Vish thought, banking the move for his first show.

CHAPTER 17

Vish got a ride home with Matt and Danny and their older sister, Cynthia, in the family's dirty Previa minivan. Matt pointed into the back, where Vish's bike was resting on the folded-down last row of seats.

"That's not all we can move in this thing."

"No sane girl would ever get in here with any of you losers," Cynthia said.

"Shut up," Danny said. Cynthia took a left turn onto High Road faster than she had to and Danny's seatbelt dug into his hip enough to make him squeak.

"What I meant, obviously," Matt went on, speaking to Vish, "is that we can move gear in this. When we get shows. Plenty of room."

"Are you guys playing the Mini-Pops Talent Show when school starts again?" Cynthia said. There was nothing mean in her tone, Vish noticed. Cynthia was a year away from finishing high school. She was lined up for a volleyball scholarship, had ideal blonde hair but usually wore her hoodies up unless she was specifically dressed up for something, and years ago Vish had seen her crying out of frustration while her dad tried to walk her through an algebra problem. Now, she had a fake California accent and colourful elastics on her braces, wore mostly Hilfiger, and despite the algebra thing, had won the Top Student of the Year award at KSS for three years running. She was also really nice, as evidenced by her coming to pick her brothers up. Mocking them seemed like more of a job she had to do — just like her brothers had to do it back.

"If we get in, I'll make sure to let you know so that can be one of the hundred days of school you skip next year," Matt said.

"I skipped maybe six periods tops. And my grades are literally double yours, so don't worry about it," Cynthia answered. "Who was that gothy-looking girl you were bothering, Vish? She's cute."

"Just someone I work with. She's going to jam with us, maybe." There was still warmth in Vish's chest in the spot that Gisela had poked. He brushed at the spot, and zoned out of the conversation until he was getting dropped off, when he agreed to come by Matt and Danny's house the next night, after he was done with the bookstore and supper.

Vish grabbed his bike from the back of the minivan and closed it up. He wheeled the bike toward the house, waving his thanks. The kitchen light in his house was on, and his dad's car wasn't in its spot.

"Bring Jay-Zilla too," Danny called from the front seat. He'd found a ballpoint pen in one of the cupholders, and was leaving some serious toothmarks in it. Cynthia had just noticed and was staring at her brother in disgust.

"I will. I mean, I think we work together tomorrow, and I'll see if she can make it."

Cynthia was already backing out as Vish got to the end of the sentence. He locked his bike up to the bit of fencing behind the garbage and recycling cans, then let himself in the front door.

Anji Maurya was watching television in the living room, some lawyer show. But she was really going through what looked like an exploded box of files, kneeling in front of the coffee table and arranging them.

"These are property listings for this neighbourhood, going back five years," Anji explained. "I'm just getting a grip on all the trends that they don't tell you about in the courses. And I think this neighbourhood is underserved. Marissa Bingham doesn't even bother with Glenmore, let alone North Glenmore, you know that?"

Vish took a closer look at the coffee table: there was an enormous cup of coffee in the middle of it. The rapid-fire talk made a bit more sense.

"I didn't ask."

"But you were going to. Two questions — did you have fun, and where is your father?"

Vish had forgotten to come up with a good excuse for the clothes swap, so he aimed for the closest lie.

"It was fun, yeah, Mom. And thanks for the wallet."

"You're welcome." Anji stood up and stretched.

"I think it's a great thing that you're hanging out with Matt and Danny again. Really." Anji stooped and started piling the papers on the table, putting them into the box in no specific order that Vish could see. She took a deep slug from the coffee, which was no longer steaming. Vish guessed there was more than just coffee in that mug.

"So where is Dad?" Vish asked.

"That was my question. I thought he might have gone out to pick you up."

"I got a ride back with Matt and Danny. If he was looking for me on my bike, he wouldn't have found me." Vish got a quick vision of his dad at the French Cultural Centre, asking the older kids and the bands loading gear whether they had seen his son. It would probably be a concert first for both parents of one kid to show up looking for him at different times.

Anji Maurya's eyes had gone dull. She walked past Vish, and if he hadn't gotten out of the way, she would have pushed him. She threw her coffee and whatever was in it down the kitchen sink, then walked back, this time sitting next to the box on the coffee table. She hid her face from her son.

"We got in a stupid fight. I can barely remember what it was about, Vish. Me working, him working, the example we were for you, never going on trips or anywhere as a family — I don't know, we talked about everything. Then I said that if there was a problem with this family, he knew who to blame for that, because there wasn't anything wrong before he started drinking. Next thing I knew, he'd left in the car."

Vish sat down on the couch, facing his mother. He hadn't meant to sit, but his legs had done it for him.

"Mom. Do you think he went out to — do you think he went out to do something bad?"

Anji Maurya didn't answer him. She looked past Vish to the front window: strobing red and blue lights were coming through the open blinds. Vish jumped up and ran to the window.

There was a police car sitting in the driveway. Parked in his father's spot.

CHAPTER 18

V ish hadn't spent this long in the hospital since the week of his birth. It was coming up on 8 a.m., Sunday morning. A part of him tried to do the math for how long was left in the forty-eight hours until the rift in the lake sealed up. The rest of him couldn't figure out if he cared at all about magic or twelve thousand dead souls waiting for new bodies, or anything other than what was going to happen to his dad.

Anji was finally asleep, and Vish had passed out for a few hours sometime after midnight, but now he was standing at his father's bedside, staring at the thick bandages around his head, at his clean, unmarked face and the respirator tubes coming out of his nose.

"Geena Barnes would make a turban joke about this," Vish said. He was holding it together, acting like he was in a movie to avoid collapsing into a total sobbing panic. He would have to tell Gisela about Geena Barnes after Mr. Farris was out of the picture, see if Gisela was willing to help him with his day-to-day issues at school whenever it started up again.

But Vish's problems, which had already begun to seem tiny in the light of what Mr. Farris was trying to do, were now a total joke. Dr. Munish Maurya's car had crashed into a cement median at eighty kilometres per hour. He was in a medically induced coma.

Anji Maurya was sure the pills were back, that they'd find her husband's bloodstream full of chemicals. Vish didn't think so, but there was no way he could tell his mother why he didn't think so.

Vish was sure that his dad was in the hospital because Mr. Farris had put him there. And he'd used Vish's body to do it, taking control when Vish was unconscious in the car.

Vish turned around and leaned against his father's hospital bed. His mom was sleeping in a chair against the wall with her head balanced on her arms, which were wrapped around the big purse in her lap. When the cop in the driveway, a young man who introduced himself as Officer Ron Harrison and had as many zits as the singer in the last band that Vish had seen that night, told them what happened, Anji Maurya had two questions for him.

"Is my husband dead?"

"Mom!" Vish had yelled from behind her.

"No, absolutely not," Officer Harrison said. Vish could no longer see his face, because his mom had blocked the doorway. Officer Harrison was going to say more, but Anji interrupted him.

"Was he under the influence?"

"We don't know that."

"Okay." Anji backed away from the door, into Vish. Once her body made contact with his hands, she started to sag, and eventually Vish was trying to hold her up as Harrison ran into the house to help.

"Can I ask you to give us a ride?" Anji slurred before she fainted. It hadn't been necessary — Harrison called an ambulance, and Vish had ridden in the back with his mother, what seemed like a year ago. But it had only been about ten hours.

As Vish kept looking at his mother, she woke up, with a suddenness that made him flinch backward. Vish's hand brushed his dad's leg, and he pulled it back as though he'd burnt it. Anji Maurya got up from the chair and joined Vish at the bedside.

"They'll wake him up later today?" Vish asked.

"I'm still not sure if the doctor told us that to shut me up," his mom answered. The doctor, an old man called Cosgrove that Vish had seen in the mall often, because the doctor's wife owned the little craft gallery near Sears, told Anji the night before that Munish Maurya had the best chance of a quick recovery if his brain was allowed to recover in a state of unconsciousness. There had been details, but Anji couldn't remember them. Vish had been waiting in the corridor this whole time, only coming in with his mother's permission. Officer Harrison had given him a Coke and squeezed his shoulder before leaving for the night.

"Try to find out more today, Mom," Vish said.

"I will," Anji said. This time she sat on the bed. She reached out to Munish's hand and squeezed it. When she spoke again, Vish wasn't sure who she was talking to.

"I know I'm a terrible wife, but I can't decide whether or not I'm a terrible mother."

"Mom, don't —"

"It's not up to you to decide, Vish, honey. It will be someday, but right now, I'm just thinking about it for myself. Your dad is going to be okay, I know it. I really do, because I can't — I can't see the world continuing any other way. He has to be okay. Do you understand?"

Vish reached out for his mom's free hand and squeezed it so hard that she would have winced under normal circumstances. Instead, she squeezed back just as hard.

"I know. He'll be okay."

"Can you go now?" Anji said. She was still holding Vish's hand, but she wasn't looking at him.

"What?"

"It's nine-thirty. Could you go into work? I know you only slept a few hours, but — I'll call Agastya on your walk over, and it will give you something to do to keep your mind off of what's happening here, okay, Vish? Is that crazy?"

A nurse stood in the doorway for a moment, leaving when Anji Maurya held up a pleading hand.

"It's kind of crazy, Mom," Vish said. What was crazier was that he really, really wanted to leave. He wanted to be out of this room, and with Agastya and Gisela, thinking about a different huge problem. One that he might be able to do something about. "But I get it."

"I need to be alone with your dad and I can't — I can't let you see me the way I'm going to get," Anji said. Vish hugged her, hard, feeling her body tense up into just one huge sob that she didn't let out. Vish leaned back. Anji gave him a smile that was almost as scary as Mr. Farris's, but in a completely different way. Vish kissed his dad's forehead and left.

After a dazed walk in the cool, early sunlit day from the hospital through downtown, Vish found himself at the door of Greycat Books. He couldn't remember looking at anyone or anything on the walk over, just a blur of green around him and occasional lines in the pavement. There had been a crosswalk, and a car had honked. Yeah. But walking here had felt almost like time travel, like he'd closed his eyes in the hospital and opened them here, at his job.

Vish pushed the door open. Moby was sitting on top of the low bookshelf where the kids' books were kept. Without looking around the store for Agastya, Vish went straight for the cat, kneeling to press his face into the warm fur. Moby mrrowed, slightly perturbed, but was soon purring in sympathy. Vish had read that cats used the frequency of their purrs to heal their own fractured bones after accidents; he hoped that maybe the same could be true of the healing power of this purr on whatever was happening in his mind.

Munish Maurya hated one part of his job. He'd admitted this to Vish when they were out on a drive, a day or two after Vish had come back from boarding school for the last time. They drove an hour down the highway to Peachland, making the trip specially to get a pastry served at a diner in the little town. It was a coconut confection called a butterhorn. Vish had spent most of the way up there looking out the window and worrying that his dad was going to start talking to him about something uncomfortable. And he did, sort of, just as they got to the first traffic light in Peachland's tiny downtown.

"I've always hated giving advice," Dr. Maurya said. A young woman crossed in front of them, followed by a daycare's worth of little kids, their mittens dangling out of the coat sleeves on little strings.

"Isn't that your job?" Vish said.

"Patients think so. I have to tell them otherwise, straightaway. That is what people think therapists do: give solutions to problems. That's what the legal system is supposed to do, not psychiatry." Dr. Maurya was speaking quickly, but not in an irritated tone. The light changed and he drove forward.

"Oh."

"And it's a good thing. After what I've put you and your mother through the past while, I'm not qualified to tell anyone the right thing to do with their life. Even you, Vish. It's going to take me a long time to win back the right to be the father you should have."

"You are that, Dad," Vish said. It sounded lame, but he meant it. There was a diagonal parking space open right in front of the café, which had a tall neon sign from the fifties. The green glow of the letters flickered off the dark paintwork on the car's hood as Dr. Maurya parked.

"My job means getting people to talk about their pasts and their problems so they understand how to help themselves. I have to get better at doing that for myself. And I will, I promise."

"I know, Dad. Do you want to eat now?"

Dr. Maurya had stared into the reflected green neon in front of him. Vish fished changed out of the cupholder for the meter.

"I want you to try to forgive me for making you feel like your house wasn't a safe place. I want you to be able to trust me again."

"I do. I do forgive you," Vish had said, then gotten out of the car and fed the meter while his dad sat still in the car for another two minutes. Vish didn't turn back to look at him, but went into the café alone and asked for a table for two. His dad joined him and described Akira Kurosawa movies that Vish hadn't seen for the next half-hour. Vish thought that the car chat had left him too nervous to enjoy the pastry, but it was still delicious, sweet and rich with butter, with the light dissolving crunch of sugared coconut.

In the bookstore, Vish straightened up, petting Moby, who had fallen asleep. He spoke quietly.

"I didn't forgive him. And he's not stupid. He knows I didn't. He knows."

Vish looked around the store for the first time. There were no customers, yet, and the clock above the cash counter read nine-fifty-eight. Agastya, wearing an untucked blue plaid shirt and pale blue jeans that were so broken in they looked like pyjama pants, was sitting on the stool behind the register, holding the black phone handset and staring at Vish. It started sounding the off-hook tone, and Agastya quickly hung up.

"That was your mom. I'm so sorry, man. I'm sure your dad will be fine. And you really don't have to be here. I can get you a cab —"

"I did it."

"What?"

"Gisela must have told you about the teeth. Mr. Farris was inside me, Agastya. When I got home, right after it happened, those teeth in my guts — I went out to my dad's car. And I can't remember what happened in there, how long I was inside, but I know Farris must have made me do something, magic or not, do something to the car that made this accident happen."

Agastya looked at the phone instead of at Vish for a few long seconds. He got off of the stool, but instead of walking around the counter, he sank down behind it. Vish walked over to look at his boss, who was hugging his knees and sitting in the spot where Vish had been just the day before. Gisela's hoodie was still back there, and it hadn't been dried. A mild stink of mould and lake haunted the area.

"Are you going to say anything?" Vish asked. Agastya stayed quiet. "Farris thought he couldn't hurt me, so he got inside me to hurt my family. Kill my own dad, maybe."

"Less than twenty-four hours ago, Vish, I had you stare into a little TV screen back here that took you to a place somewhere not quite on this Earth, but just beside it. And you got to meet a Xerox of the person that I lost and that I can't really think or function without. I've asked you to see a lot, to understand a lot, to accept a lot," Agastya said.

Finally, he looked right into Vish's eyes, so serious that he almost seemed angry. Vish backed a half-step away, his right shoulder bumping into a shelf that was nailed into the wall, bearing a leatherbound set of Charles Dickens. The books rocked slightly but didn't fall.

"But I've never," Agastya went on, "I've never asked you to *believe* anything. You and I and Gisela are at the centre of a collapsing point in time and space. Because we happen to be here, and because of the knowledge that's ended up in our heads. I didn't have the power to choose you. You're just involved, because that's how it is. Like I am. And whether that means that things in our own lives are happening faster, or are going wrong — I don't know. I don't know everything. I know I lost the person I love, and I know your dad was in an accident but that he's on his way back, and I know that Gisela is —"

"You *did* choose me," Vish said.

"What?"

Vish grabbed the closest paperback — luckily for Agastya, it was a flimsy copy of *Jonathan Livingston Seagull* — and chucked it at his boss's chest, the way he and the other boys used to whip hockey cards in the knock-down game at lunch hour. He still had the accuracy and the wrist. The book thunked into the centre of Agastya's chest, right above his knees, knocking him out of his hugging posture. Agastya sprawled back.

"Maybe time or fate or god or whatever didn't choose me, but you and Gisela brought me into this, into this hell where I'm swallowing teeth and nearly killing my dad. You did this to me, you roped me in, you made it seem like it was going to be an adventure."

"You asked, kid," Agastya said, standing up to his full height. "You stood in this room and you said you wanted to know what was going on, that you weren't leaving until we told you. Gisela and I needed you, yeah. But you *asked*. You invited yourself. Remember that." Agastya pushed Vish's shoulder. Not a hard shove, but enough to rock him back.

"Agastya!" Vish and Agastya both turned. Gisela was standing at the door. She pushed it shut behind her, then flicked the overhead lights on. Vish hadn't noticed that the only light in the room had been daylight, and he flinched more from the bulbs than he had from Agastya's hand, which suddenly dropped to hang by his side.

"Sorry. Jesus, I'm really sorry," Agastya said, sinking back onto his stool. Vish walked out from behind the counter. Moby and Gisela were both staring at him.

"I guess I started it," Vish said.

"You get to act stupid," Gisela said. "Act however you want, Vish. A lot has happened."

"Did you hear about his father?" Agastya said, in a strange tone of voice. Vish looked at him — he was still keyed-up,

173

nervous. Gisela hesitated for a second, then said no. Vish didn't quite believe her, thought that she might have been following all night, but he decided not to argue. He was tired of arguing.

Vish told her what he knew, finding that the telling of the story calmed him down. He looked past Gisela, who was wearing the same clothes as last night, at the books behind her, imagining how this story would look written down. How the cheesy version would end with his father's eyes opening on that hospital bed and seeing his mom waiting, and Vish running down the hallway of the hospital. He'd groan and toss a book like that across the room, but would gladly accept the real-life version.

"It was one of those new medians they built for the bus loop. A witness told the cops Dad was going full-speed. Like, more than full-speed. The car's smashed. Because of whatever Farris had me do to the car, Dad couldn't control it." The same car they'd driven to Peachland in, that Vish sat in to be dropped off at school on his dad's way to work every morning. The car was dead, but his father wasn't. *Don't think "yet,"* Vish hissed in his brain. *Don't.*

"I've been in and out of the world for a long time," Gisela said. "And there's never been a better time to be in the hospital than now. They can actually fix people now. Just remember that. And if your mom is as shaken up as you say she is, there's no way she could be lying to you about what the doctors said to her. That means your dad is going to wake up, and the doctors will go from there. This is going to be okay," Gisela said.

"Farris just wanted to show us that he still has power. He wanted to hurt us and scare us," Agastya said, his head still hanging down as he sat on his stool. Vish noticed his extremely cool Slayer t-shirt for the first time, a faded *Hell Awaits* design, and didn't have anything to do with the information.

"I am scared," Vish said.

Greycat's first customer opened the door with a too-hard shove that clanged the chimes and nudged Gisela forward.

"Sorry," he said, but he didn't sound sorry. It was Mr. Clarke, Vish's old science teacher. Mr. Clarke saw Vish and looked like he wanted to turn around, but instead took off his glasses and polished them, something he used to do in class whenever Danny asked him a particularly annoying question.

"Hello, Vish," Mr. Clarke said.

"We have a few spy-adventure novels in the new arrivals, Mr. Clarke," said Agastyta, pointing to the trolley near the door. "New as in new-to-the-store, but of that sixties vintage you love."

"Ah! Thank you!" Mr. Clarke started rummaging through the titles, pulling out colourful paperbacks with photos of Berettas and illustrations of women on the covers, forgetting that Vish or anyone else was in the room. Vish felt bad for making fun of the old man, once again. As Mr. Clarke browsed, Gisela took Vish's arm and led him to the back of the store.

"I set something up for you last night. Sort of an illustration," she said. "Maybe it'll help you get your mind off the hospital for a few minutes."

Gisela opened the door up to Agastya's apartment. Mr. Clarke was chatting to the store owner, talking about how even knockoff James Bond novels were still better reading than anything being printed nowadays, and the gentle creak of the opening door didn't disturb the conversation. Vish looked up the stairs, remembered seeing that Conan the Barbarian poster, hearing that shuffling step, and spotting a hairy and impossible leg. There had been a half-dozen impossible sights and experiences since then, and Vish couldn't say any of them had been fun. Gisela was halfway up the stairs by the time he put his foot on the bottom step. She paused, turned back.

"I know," Gisela said. "I know you're right on the edge of just — closing up, stopping."

"Another magical guess?" Vish asked. This time he knew he was being sarcastic, and using a tone meaner than he'd ever used on a girl anywhere near his age. It was a voice he reserved for fights with his parents or times when he was needling Matt.

Gisela didn't respond in turn — she just looked sorry for him. She walked back down the steps, brushing past Vish, and pulled the door at the bottom of the stairs shut. With Vish standing on the step, he was a little taller than Gisela for the first time. She stayed where she was, letting him keep the height, leaning against the door behind her.

"Vish, I've lived in different centuries and in timeless spaces between this world and places that look something like the surface of Mars or a Dutch painting of Hell. A few years ago I had my entire essence absorbed into a collection of information that was more math than body, and I came out with Isla into this town I never wanted to live in, just like you never wanted to, looking the way I remember I did in the warped mirror my mother kept in her bedchamber eight hundred years ago. All I had to keep me sane was Isla, there for me through layers of reality and existence that you will never understand, and now she's dead too. She can't help me ever again."

Vish hadn't felt Gisela's finger settle on his chest again, but he certainly felt the pressure of it as she started to push. He started to back up the stairs.

"So, no, I didn't use magic to guess that you're close to giving up. I could tell because I've come close many times. But I didn't, and I don't think you're going to, either. Because you're right, this is all connected. Mr. Farris, one way or another, is responsible for your dad being in that hospital bed. And you are about to find out why you're so necessary to us, and why Mr. Farris is locked into you."

They were at the top of the stairs now, and beyond: Vish's back touched the wall, and he was pinned right next to that Conan poster. Gisela put her hand down and walked past him, turning on the tap in the small, dirty, green-tiled kitchen and clinking through the glasses on the counter and cupboards to find a clean one. Giving up, she washed two in the sink and filled them with cold water.

"Here," Gisela said. "This one's to drink now."

Because it was better than apologizing or really talking to Gisela at all while he thought about what she'd said, Vish drank. The apartment above Greycat Books was a studio, with no walls between the kitchen and the near-empty bedroom. There were no other posters. No bookshelves, either, just various books and comics stacked on the round, too-high bedside table next to the mattress where Agastya apparently slept. Vish reached the end of the glass and Gisela took it from him.

"This used to look a lot more like a place someone could live when Isla lived here, of course. And not because she decorated it — she could live anywhere, a cave, a bad motel, as long as she had walls and privacy. Agastya used to keep a nice place."

"He's depressed?"

"Obviously," Gisela said, setting the empty glass among the other dirty dishes in the kitchen. She was still holding the other full one. "But he was also looking for the names. The 12,506 names. We went through every book in the store, and I tried every unravelling spell I could think of, and then Agastya took this place apart to the beams and pipes and joists. And we didn't find the names."

"So where did Isla hide them? I mean, do you know now?"

"You do," Gisela said. For a second, less than that, she flickered, vanished between the overhead light and the shadow cast by the fridge. Gisela was gone, and the tall woman Vish had met in the cemetery stood in front of him, patient and tired, her green dress dark with dirt, her eyes invisible behind thick, unbrushed hair that was drawn over the top half of her face.

"But shh," Isla said. And then she was Gisela again, using her big Doc Marten boot to toe open one of the kitchen cabinets. An impossible creature, a pair of short, thickly furred legs topped not by a torso but the round dome of a huge arachnid body, with one enormous questing tentacle reaching out for Vish as the legs ran across the room quicker than seemed possible. And then Vish was collapsed onto the bed, the tentacle sucking and moving up his jeans and under his t-shirt, the flesh of it glossy and soft and the fang that began to poke out of it and into his ribs so sharp it vanished into his body before he had a chance to scream. And by the time Vish did try to scream, Gisela's hand was clasped over his mouth.

CHAPTER 19

V ish woke to yellow light glowing through the dirty, shut blinds of the little apartment. He was on top of Agastya's unmade bed, which was comfortable for the three conscious seconds before he remembered what had happened and began to grasp his sides, looking for the gaping hole he was sure the creature had left. His skin was blank and smooth.

Gisela was in the kitchen, a dirty white marble mortar and pestle on the counter in front of her. Unconsciously, Vish backed away from her, worming along the mattress on the heels of his hands until he fell off, backwards. He leapt up and backed into the corner of the room.

"That was it, Vish," Gisela said. "That was the last surprise. From now on, we'll tell you about everything we know before it happens. Agastya and I swore to do that after I got back from the show last night. Then there was this thing with your dad, and we just had to be sure — to keep your mom and you safe, we had to know that Mr. Farris, every bit of him, was out of you. He was only going to get deeper and deeper in, until he was in your mind itself. And we found out that he's gone. Almost."

Gisela took the pestle out of the mortar and held up what she was in the process of grinding up. A little yellower than the marble, and much sharper, it was the Farris tooth Vish had given her at the concert. The unbroken half. She let it fall back into the bowl and started pounding and grinding it again.

"Where is that *thing*?" Vish asked.

"Back behind the veil."

"What?"

"It's where Isla is. Not in that graveyard illusion she conjured up, but something like what you saw on the other side of the hole in the lake. But brighter, different. That thing, as you call it, used to be three witches and is now one creature named Zerg. Zerg happened when these witches made a little transportation miscalculation and fused some of their body parts and lost others in a jump across time. Now Zerg is something like a helpful demon. Helpful to Isla, anyway. Checks in on Agastya for her, because demons have an easier time stepping into our world from the other one." Gisela finished grinding the tooth.

"Not okay. No. You — you held me while that thing mauled me, Gisela."

Gisela made a strange finger-snapping motion and Vish flinched, expecting the Zerg creature to be summoned by it for another attack. Instead, Moby ambled up the stairs, meowing plaintively. Vish hadn't heard the door downstairs opening, so Moby must have been let in while Vish was passed out.

"Vish, what you see when you see Zerg is just a version of what it, he, she, they, actually is — just what the light bouncing off the shape Zerg chose arrives to your eye as."

"That's what EVERYTHING ANYONE SEES is," Vish said, starting to scream without intending to. He was humiliated at losing control, humiliated that his voice had cracked twice on "Anyone," and humiliated that he was tearing up. Moby, who had hopped onto the counter by the mortar and pestle while Gisela was talking, had crouched at the scream and was staring at Vish, his ears standing straight and alert. Gisela started to laugh.

"You're absolutely right. Agastya was giving me a hard time when I got back about dumping all that math and physics on you, but I guess you do know something about light and reality, etcetera. What I meant was that Zerg has no actual form, just a series of surfaces and angles that your eyes and brain trick you into seeing as a leg or a fang or whatever it is you saw. What pierced your body was pure energy and light, looking for any evil scraps of Farris, burning them out. You're almost clean. Now —"

Gisela did something that made Vish forget his embarrassment about yelling. She rasped, a crackling, spawling, throat-emptying sound, and spit an immense loogie of phlegm into the mortar and pestle in front of her. Moby, who had stopped staring at Vish, soon started making a similar noise over the marble cup, coming up with a cylindrical, moist hairball. Gisela grimaced at what had landed and then started in on it with the pestle.

Vish said a few words that he usually never did. His mom had ejected and used her bare hands to break the Venom mixtape that Danny had made for him when she heard these same words barked in a Birmingham accent coming from his stereo. Gisela kept at it with the pestle.

"This is more of that biological magic I've been blathering about," Gisela said. "This cat was with Isla every day of its life. I've been with her for centuries. There's some pretty powerful channelling suppressors in our blood, and luckily our spit too, that can neutralize the feelers Mr. Farris has had snaking through you for the past however many hours. Here."

"I thought that when we got rid of the teeth, that would be it."

"We're close, Vish." Gisela crossed the room, holding the mortar in both hands. She jumped lightly onto the mattress and walked over it. Vish couldn't back up any further, and soon she was in front of him.

"I'm really sorry, but you have to."

"Have to what?"

Vish looked into the mortar and saw that it was exactly the colour that he had hoped it wouldn't be — black with an oil-slick shimmer of green. He gagged.

"You know. Drink this."

"No."

"Vish, Zerg did the light part of this cleansing, but this is the rest. We need to make sure that every part of this monster is neutralized. Just consider this a last dose of the cure."

Vish found himself reaching for the bowl with shaking hands. It was heavy, but his hands stopped shaking when he had the cool weight of the marble in them.

"Did it happen like I said? Mr. Farris used me to mess with my dad's car?"

Gisela looked at him. For a moment, her hazel eyes shone the way Vish's had when he nearly cried, and she bit her lip.

"I won't lie to you. Yes." Gisela closed her eyes but kept speaking. "If Mr. Farris gets his way, he'll fill the body of every person you know and love here with one of those nachzehrers. He'll make sure everyone you ever cared for is possessed, gone. And he'll take over your body, but let just enough of you live on to see what's happened to your mother, your father, Matt, Danny, all of them. That they've been erased, taken over. So let's stop him, okay?"

Vish drank from the bowl, tipping it deep, even getting some of the stuff on his nose. With his eyes closed, he held the bowl out in one hand, feeling Gisela take it. Then he swallowed. The mixture, still warm and terribly grainy, slid down his throat, slowly. He thought of cement pouring slowly out of a mixer. Vish staggered forward, turned away from the mattress, and vomited all over the floor.

"This is perfect!" Gisela yelled. Vish opened his eyes. On the splintery hardwood was a shallow pool of hardening liquid: but it wasn't black with a green shine to it. It was yellow-white, the shade of Mr. Farris's discoloured fangs. As Vish and Gisela watched, the liquid turned hard and began to crack. Moby, walking past Gisela's legs, stepped onto the new surface, and it immediately turned into a powder so fine and light it vanished into the cracks and the air in seconds.

"I'm sick of throwing up. I don't like how magic feels," Vish said.

"Looks pretty cool, though," Gisela said.

"There's a lot of spitting."

"Apologies for the exorcism of a vile spirit from your body not being quite ladylike, Vish. I am a bit sorry for the ambush part of it, but the spit — you have to think of it more as a conductive fluid. Word spells are just book stuff, sorry to say. Magic is atoms, blood, and sometimes spit."

"Shortcuts," Vish muttered.

"What? First, look, I think Agastya has soda in the fridge."

He did, and it was good stuff. Vish and Gisela each had a bottle of a key lime soda Vish had never seen before. It was crisp and not too sweet.

"What do you mean, shortcuts?" Gisela asked, when they were a few gulps in each. Vish hadn't understood how thirsty he was.

"I meant that a lot of magic seems to be finding a shortcut. Not a gap, a shortcut. A corridor between two pieces of reality, or space, or time, that other people can't see, and taking it. Mr. Farris is trying to use me as a shortcut to spying on you. That's mostly what I am to him, one of these shortcuts."

At first, Vish couldn't work out what the expression on Gisela's face meant. She was looking down, her mouth flat, her eyebrows raised a little. She was tapping the lip of her bottle against her chin.

"I've never really heard it put that way. That's the first really smart thing I've heard you say," Gisela said, looking back up at Vish and smiling. Vish decided to ignore the insulting part of this. At least he understood why he'd never seen that look on Gisela's face before.

"You say soda instead of pop, eh?" Vish said.

"Yeah. You too?"

They were both too tired to say anything more than that. Eventually Moby walked down the stairs and began to meow at the door. It opened. A few seconds later, Agastya's head rose into view, then the rest of him. He looked around the room, seeing the empty mortar and pestle on the bed. He nodded at Gisela.

"How about a nod for me?" Vish said. "I'm the one who threw all that stuff up."

"You get better than a nod. We can finally tell you why we let you get involved in this."

Gisela walked a couple of steps to stand next to Vish, and put her hand on his shoulder.

"Remember," she said. "All your shortcut talk makes sense, but I don't want you to think that we've been using you. That we chose you to take advantage of. It really, really wasn't like that."

Vish was scared again, and found that his hand had travelled to the space in his ribs where he'd felt Zerg poke in. For a moment, the taste of lime and sugar in his mouth vanished, replaced by the chalk and slurry of the tooth and spittle mixture he'd downed minutes before.

Agastya opened the fridge, noticed that there were no sodas left, and took out a beer instead. He opened the bottle with the edge of the counter.

"This isn't serious drinking," he said to Gisela.

"I didn't say anything," she answered.

Vish wasn't sure he was stalling until he saw that Agastya couldn't look at him, that he kept staring at the counter when he finally spoke.

"My wife Isla didn't hide those 12,506 names of nachzehrers in this apartment or in the store. It took Gisela forever to figure it out after we'd searched everything, and boy was she mad when I remembered that Isla had joked about it when I was drunk, only it wasn't a joke. One day, when you came into the store two years ago, Isla hid the names in your mind. She opened a gap in time and whispered almost thirteen thousand names into your ear. And each of those names is still in your brain, right now. All those names from Farris's grimoire, every incantation that he needs, is locked up in you."

CHAPTER 20

V ish refused a ride home. His mom called Greycat just as Vish was about to start walking to the hospital, and Agastya handed the phone over. Anji Maurya spoke as soon as the phone touched Vish's ear, as though she could hear the sound of his held breath.

"Honey, your dad is asleep, but they say his brain activity is normal. He woke up earlier — never mind that, he wasn't quite himself, but he did wake up."

"Did he say anything, Mom?"

Vish heard what his mother must have heard when he took the phone: silence that meant something.

"When you get home, Vish, call Matt and Danny — I talked to their mom and told her what's going on. I'm not sure if you're feeling all the way good about them these days —"

"We made up."

"Good. Mae is bringing the boys to sleep over, and she'll have dinner with her. I'm staying here again."

"Mom, I need to know if he said anything. Dad. It's important."

"It was just sleep talk, like he was dreaming, Vish." Anji Maurya's voice started to shake again — she was controlled when she was telling Vish what she'd organized, and that was probably why she'd spent time organizing this sleepover for Vish.

"Please, Mom."

"He said that there was a, a face on the glass. He said that a few times. There was a face on the glass, a 'peeled face and I crashed.'" Anji did a decent impression of her husband's voice, the rumbling low tone of it, the glint of emotion at the end of a sentence.

Vish remembered the face in the yard. Mr. Farris's peeled face, the mask of a beast. He saw a vision of it floating through the dry, hot air of downtown like an out-of-season alien leaf, until it landed squarely where it was aimed: on his father's windshield, just as he realized something was wrong with the car, that the brakes weren't working right or the accelerator was stuck. Mr. Farris wanted his dad to see the face of the creature that wanted his death.

"That does sound like sleep talk, Mom. I hope he sounds more normal in the morning. He's going to wake up in the morning and talk again, right?"

"They can't tell me that. They don't know. There's something else that matters, Vish. The doctor —" The windy sound of her breath came before the next, whispered sentence.

"There was nothing in his bloodstream. No drugs. I just want him to wake up. I know you do too, but it helps me to know that."

"I already knew, Mom," Vish said. He handed the phone back to Agastya, who had a questioning look on his face. Vish didn't ask what that question was, and he certainly didn't answer it.

He just turned around and left. The day had been long enough, and he had a very strange task waiting for him at home. He took the small suitcase that Gisela had packed for him upstairs. It was heavy, but not with clothing. Vish got a good grip on it and left the store without saying anything more to anyone.

It wasn't until he was passing Dr. Maurya's office that Vish started to regret rejecting a ride back home. He had his keys in his pants pocket, so getting in and passing out on his bed would be no problem once he actually got there, but it looked like he had a long walk ahead. Vish stopped in the parking lot where his dad had dropped him off just last week, when they'd had their conversation about moving on from Matt and Danny, about Dad "playing the father." Vish sat on a parking median in front of the dry cleaners and put ghosts, witches, and demons out of his mind. He had walked here automatically, toward a ride his feet were expecting from a car that was now totalled, from a father who might never wake up.

"Hello, Vish."

Vish looked around to see where the woman's voice had come from. It was familiar, but he couldn't place it. Turning, he saw a head sticking out of the door of the vet's office that was just next to the dry cleaners. It was Rita Goodis. The rest of her emerged. She was wearing a purple summer dress in some light fabric, and a heavy cardigan buttoned all the way up over it. Just looking at it made Vish feel dizzy with the heat. Rita Goodis was holding a cat carrier with an annoyed-looking Buddy within. And Vish realized that there was something in this world that could make him feel a bit safer in his empty house.

"Hi, Dr. Goodis —"

"Rita, even if your dad was always strictly against letting patients cross the boundary into first-name territory," Rita Goodis said. Buddy licked the cage wiring with what looked like distinct impatience, and his mood didn't improve when the carrier was set down as Rita began to massage her wrist. He started to gnaw at the gate.

"I was supposed to meet your parents today, Vish. For a social coffee, nothing to do with — you know I'd never discuss anything you told me in a session, right?"

"Dad's in the hospital." Vish stooped and reached fingers into Buddy's carrier, rubbing between his eyes and the diamond patterning in the tabby crisscross. Having just seen Moby, Vish noticed now Buddy was frailer and older than the bookstore cat, his ribs a bit more visible. He hadn't looked frail when he was wandering outside the Goodis house and scuttling around the darkened garage where Farris had manifested, when he'd seemed like a miniature, decorated panther. From his limited experience with cats, Vish knew that they tended to expand when they got violent: arching, puffing, and making ominous noises that seemed to come out of a collective feline throat.

Vish told Rita Goodis everything about the car crash, including the recent news about his dad having been sober. He could tell Rita was trying to keep her professional face on, the one that didn't admit any emotion, just understanding and kindness. But fear came through. Fear that Vish recognized because it vibrated in sympathy with his own terror that his father was going to die.

"Thank you for telling me," Rita said. "I'm so sorry, Vish. This is more than anyone, let alone any kid — young man —

should have to cope with. And it must seem like it's all happening at once."

"You have no idea," Vish said, staring into Buddy's green, slitted eyes. He almost looked like a serpent, in his coiled, paranoid discomfort in the carrier. Vish managed to hook his middle finger around Buddy's right ear for a deep skritch that made the cat loosen up, slightly.

Rita *ahem*ed. Vish withdrew his hand and Rita picked the carrier up.

"I'm going to drop this lummox off at home and then go right to the hospital before visiting hours are over," she said. "It's almost five."

Rita did that thing Vish always saw adults do when they hit the brakes at the beginning of a swear. Her lower lip curled under her front teeth to start forming a really hard F, then her eyes flicked over to his and she turned the sound into a sighing "ffff" of worry.

"I hope they'll let me in. I should give you a ride home too."

"No, then you'll miss visiting for sure. My mom will be there right now, she'll make sure you get in." Vish didn't add that Anji Maurya would be at the hospital all night, no matter what any doctor, nurse, or orderly said.

"Okay. Well, we need to book another appointment for you very soon, I think. Don't you?"

Vish agreed quickly so there was a better chance she'd say yes to his next request.

"Yeah. I guess I'll have a lot to talk about," he said, while wondering how he would find a way to disguise the war with Mr. Farris as something that wouldn't cause Rita Goodis to commit him to a psych hospital for a few months. "What's Buddy in at the vet for?"

"He's just old. Getting some upkeep for his heart and joints. And I picked up his special food and some litter and a new litterbox for him, though he mostly goes outside, thank god. And yes, you will have a lot to talk about when you come see me — more than you do today. I bet you're feeling numb, and like you're talking to me through cotton. And that nothing that has happened since you heard about your dad's accident has been quite real."

"That and even some of the stuff that happened before it doesn't seem real," Vish said. Rita squinted at this, which looked especially strange behind her thick glasses, but let it go.

"Your brain is helping you to cope with all of this by only letting in a bit of reality at a time. That means you may feel worse tomorrow. You may wake up gasping. Just remember, however you feel is however you feel. It's fine, it will pass, and you have me and your mother and soon, when he wakes up, your father."

"Mom said the doctor can't promise when he'll wake up," said Vish. As if cued by what Rita had said, a dart of panic came through his voice and then stuck in his mouth, expanding, feeling like it was going to engulf his brain. He saw his dad bleeding onto the steering wheel and saw, even though it made no sense, Mr. Farris laughing in the passenger seat beside him, as sparks flew out of the sodium streetlight that the car had just plowed into.

Rita took Vish softly, by both shoulders. "I'm not a doctor, and I'm not in my office, so I won't be professional. I'll just tell you what I know about your dad: he will be fine. Soon."

"Okay."

"Is there anything more I can do for you, right now? Are you sure you won't take a ride home?"

Vish thought of Moby flying right at Mr. Farris, at the claws tearing through the soft white flesh of his mask as though it were soft cheese. And Buddy's teeth at his ankle in Rita's garage. Buddy looked a lot less gentle than Moby, and what Vish needed right now was something very ungentle around the house. So he asked.

"Can I take Buddy for a little bit? I'll take really good care of him. I just don't know if my mom is going to be home much, and I'm feeling pretty lonely, and if you've got all his food and stuff with you —"

Rita looked surprised but was also quick to cut Vish off.

"Vish. Of course you can take the cat. And you grabbing him would let me get to the hospital on time."

Buddy made an irritated meow from his carrier, indicating that whatever was being decided by the humans above him, he wanted it decided quickly.

"But if you're on foot —" Rita said.

"He's not." The voice came from over Vish's shoulder: he turned and saw Agastya standing there, leaning against an old blue Buick. "I'm Vish's boss at the bookstore. He ran out before I could insist that he take a ride home instead of walking in this heat."

"So you and this little goblin are in luck," Rita said to Vish. "As long as —"

"Agastya."

"As long as Agastya's vehicle isn't a pet-free zone." The sun was still hours away from setting, and it haloed her messy grey hair as she smiled at him. Rita made Vish feel calm, a sensation that just now felt as impossible as Gisela passing her forearm through a tree trunk. But if this week had taught him anything, it was that sometimes things happened even when they were impossible.

Agastya and Vish started loading Buddy and the Buddy-accompanying food and gear into the backseat of the Buick. It was a long bench seat, with lots of tears in the vinyl, but it was clean, and there were no wrappers or empty cans on the floor of the car. Like Greycat, it was surprisingly clean, a look that didn't seem to go with Agastya.

"Vish, can I say one thing before you go?" Rita said. Vish walked over to her as Agastya settled into the driver's seat.

"I'm sorry. I know I told you that I'd never give you advice, just that I'd listen to you and help you find your own advice, Vish. And I meant that. That's what our sessions are all about. But right now I'm just a family friend. And this is why family friends aren't usually good therapists."

"I —"

"Don't say anything, Vish. Don't tell me anything that I'll feel obligated to tell your mother about. We're not in session right now, so I can't keep any secrets you have to tell me. I can tell that you've got some sort of purpose, that you have something in mind that is keeping you distracted from what's happening with your dad. Maybe it's even distracting you from what you've been through as a family for the past many hard months. And that's good, that's positive. Your friends, books, music, that's good. But don't, and I mean don't, get obsessed with some sort of plan or mission or whatever it is that I see in your eyes. Because I do see it, Vish. There is no mission. Got that? You're just a young man who's dealing with more than anyone of any age should have to deal with. So just stay home and pet my cat and be nice to yourself. Can you do that?"

Vish nodded. Maybe he managed to say "yes," but he didn't think so.

Vish barely remembered the ride home. When they arrived and Vish opened up with his house key, Agastya helped him load Buddy and his supplies into the front hall, unlatched the gate to let the cat wander and get the feel of his new, temporary territory.

Buddy had stopped bumping at his ankles when Vish pulled the front door all the way shut and was currently looking up at Vish with a feline skepticism that made Vish feel ashamed for silently lying to this fine animal's owner about what he would be getting up to tonight.

Buddy walked to the top of the carpeted stairs, put a careful foot down on the first step, then took off at top speed, cornering like a Formula One racer when he got to the bottom. Vish set up the water and food bowls near the long kitchen cabinets that contained the family's pots and Tupperware, and decided to park the litterbox in the laundry room, which had a cement floor.

When he came upstairs Agastya was sitting at the kitchen table, smiling, a dreamy look on his face. Not even noticing that Vish was in the room, Agastya closed his eyes and took two deep breaths, taking in the smell of this room that was so familiar to Vish that he couldn't even really smell it anymore.

"Thanks for the ride," Vish said. "You meditating or something?"

Agastya's eyes snapped open.

"No, just tired. Cat okay?"

"He seems good. Wandering around."

"They do that." Agastya got up and started wandering around the kitchen and attached living room, examining the spines of books on tables and shelves, poking at a pile of envelopes on the little desk. Vish went to the sink and filled a glass of water for each of them. Agastya was staring out of the sliding glass doors at the view of the valley, with the few houses that had started to be built on the mountains, the elementary school that Vish used to go to ages ago, and a lot of other parts of the city that would have been visible if the hedges were properly trimmed. Vish handed Agastya the glass.

"Is Farris going to come for us?"

It took Agastya a second to answer.

"He's going to come for you. His invasion of you might not have tipped him off that you hold all the names, because you didn't know it yourself. But he's figured out you're important. That's why he had you — be a part of what happened to your dad. He was hoping the guilt of it would make you quit. To stop talking to me and Gisela. Leave yourself alone and unprotected."

Agastya sat down on one section of the L-shaped blue couch that had turned up in the house after Vish's first year away at the school. He still wasn't used to the way it looked in the room. Agastya gestured for him to sit down too.

"But you don't feel guilty, do you?" Agastya asked.

Vish thought about this, hard, and not only that, he searched for the feeling. All he found was worry for his father, some relief that he'd woken up, and a hot rage for Mr. Farris.

"I didn't do anything wrong. It was Mr. Farris. Not me."

Agastya lifted his right hand and pointed at Vish. He smiled lazily.

"That's what I mean. That's how I know Isla chose right. You're too smart to let Farris play with your emotions, and you're just dumb enough to keep fighting even when you're scared."

"Thanks, I guess," Vish said, getting up from the couch. "I should call my friends to come over. I'm guessing I'll be seeing you and Gisela again before the end of the night too? And Farris?"

"Wait," Agastya said, gesturing again for Vish to sit down. But Vish didn't want to, and resolutely stayed standing. Agastya leaned back into the cushion.

"I'm trying to say that you're brave. Braver than the rest of us, because you have even less idea of what's going on, and you're still willing to stick this battle out. That's a good way to be, and I think you should be proud of that. And stay this way."

Vish didn't know how to answer, but as Agastya put his hands on the table and creaked upright, standing like a much older man, he knew that he hoped what Agastya had said was true. And he also knew that even if it wasn't, Agastya believed it.

"You will be seeing us later, Vish. Farris has to make a move, tonight is his last chance. We'll be watching over you before we come back, but we'll be here soon enough."

"Thanks for saying that," Vish said. "The bravery part."

Agastya nodded, smiled, and walked past Vish to the kitchen door. From an instinct he didn't know he had, Vish came up behind his boss and gave him a quick hug, letting go almost as soon as his arms completed the circle. Agastya froze up, then looked at Vish for a moment.

"See you tonight," Vish said.

Agastya nodded and left.

CHAPTER 21

He checked the answering machine, then called Matt and Danny. Danny picked up.

"Yo," he said. "We heard —"

"I know you heard, my mom told me. Thanks for coming over later."

"We can come right now, man, it's no problem —"

"I gotta sleep, Danny. You have no idea how bad I gotta sleep."

Vish hung up, then walked into his room. Buddy was sitting at the foot of his bed, staring at Vish's open closet. Vish petted him, then switched his alarm from 7 a.m. to 7 p.m. and passed out almost as soon as he got into bed.

He saw just one thing before shutting his eyes: Zerg, the two legs topped by the spider body and resting tentacles, emerging from the closet, then using one of the tentacles to effortlessly pull itself up and sit peacefully on his desk. This must have been what Agastya meant by someone watching over Vish before he and Gisela got back. Buddy watched along with him, but Vish soon heard the cat snuffling in his sleep, and had to join him.

A fused witch-creature who was largely on his side was probably a good thing to have standing guard while he slept. Even though it didn't really seem to have eyes. Buddy had eyes, anyway, and he was probably a light sleeper. Vish could trust the cat, and Gisela had sent Zerg. He trusted her. Kinda.

Vish slept, and Farris found him almost immediately.

"There's no such thing as a dream anymore, Vish Maurya. Not for you. Not until we've finished with each other. We share one world, one set of rules, whether your eyes are open or not, until I've finished what I've come here to do. You're not dreaming. You're mine."

It was just a voice, and not even a real voice, Vish told himself. But he could feel the cool grass under his cheek where a pillow was supposed to be. He could smell the air, the stink of wet leaves and heaps of earth. All of that was real. And that meant Mr. Farris's voice was real too. Fighting against a deeper weariness than he'd ever felt, Vish opened his eyes. Farris was squatting above him on the crypt in the vision Isla had created for Vish on the little green television. But there was no television now, and no Isla. No Moby, no Buddy or Zerg, nothing but a sea of open graves and this creature in oversized jeans and a Fox Racing long-sleeve t-shirt in a horrible shade of purple squatting like a gargoyle above Vish.

Mr. Farris looked different — more like his peeled-off mask than like the man who had walked into the bookstore that day that seemed to be years ago. There were clawmarks in his face, empty white tears. The hole that Gisela had made was gone, but Farris's lips were now sucked inward, and not on purpose: all of his teeth were missing.

"I hope you're not thinking of insulting my appearance. It takes a lot of work to upkeep this human shell, old as it is, and I've gotten tired of doing it. Your father turned his windshield wipers on me, you know, and it utterly destroyed my eyelids."

Farris was staring at Vish through the cemetery mist. The creature pursed his lips and blew, and the air was instantly clear, dry, not a wisp of cloud in sight. Farris hadn't blinked because he couldn't: Vish could see the reddish rims of the torn curtains that were once eyelids.

"I have to devote all of my energies to my project here, Vish. You have been a great help, you know. And I don't mean just that business about nearly killing your father. I could have made it much more direct, you know. I could have walked into your home, in your body, and strangled both your parents with your own two hands. Perhaps I will, at that."

Vish noticed that he was still tired. He was cold, and he was tired — but he wasn't afraid. He'd gone to sleep in his boxers, the Harlem Globetrotters ones he'd gotten from an uncle who didn't know he had zero interest in sports, and that's all he was wearing now. Mr. Farris didn't jump down from the crypt: he unfolded his legs from their crouch, dangled them over the edge, and slithered down the mossy concrete. Vish sat, pulling his knees against his chest, leaning against the back of a tombstone. He looked over his shoulder for a second: the grave behind the stone was empty, dirt heaped up at both sides. These graves had all been full and flat when Isla had walked him through.

Vish's hand closed around a sharp, broken-off chunk of stone. Cold marble, maybe. Mr. Farris didn't see him do it.

"I haven't helped you with anything, and I had nothing to do with what you did to my dad's car when you were using my body. That was you. And you look really, really bad. Did those cat scratches get infected?"

"I don't have blood or organs, you stupid child. No, I did not get an infection."

"You screamed a lot," Vish said. He was doing an impression of someone tougher than himself — Clint Eastwood, Arnold, maybe even Danny — but using his own voice. Maybe that's what everyone who seemed tough was doing.

"Don't be irritating," Mr. Farris said. In two strides, he was at Vish's side, his foot on top of the hand that Vish was holding the rock in. Mr. Farris leaned his weight into it — more weight than Vish thought could exist in that ghostly, small body. Vish felt the stone cutting into his palm and grabbed at Mr. Farris's ankle with his other hand, but there was nothing in the jeans leg to grab, just air. Mr. Farris laughed.

"You tried to kill my father," Vish said.

"I absolutely did," Farris said. "I wanted to see if cowardice ran in the family. It does! You should have seen him staring and swerving, Vish. I've never seen such panic. I look forward to seeing it again when I've abandoned this body you find so grotesque and come into yours. Forever. I'm going to find a nice, slow way for Munish and Anji to die, a way that looks accidental. But I'll make sure they see your face, that they know it was you who killed them. Maybe a fire. Your parents in bed, your mother waking up to see the flames all around her, and her sweet son standing outside their bedroom window with a box of matches. That would be fun."

Farris pushed his foot down harder on Vish's hand. Vish could feel pressure, but no pain. Just rage.

"I'm going to be living inside you in just a few hours. I liked it in there. I'm coming back."

Farris suddenly released all the pressure he'd been bearing down with, stepping lightly off Vish's hand and leaning back into a tombstone.

Vish stared at his hand. The bones in his fingers ached, and there was a tiny tear in his palm.

"You really trust your new friends, don't you? I'm honest, Vish. I'm even honest about wanting to kill your family. You can't say I hide anything from you. But Gisela? Lying for hundreds of years. You're just the latest audience."

Mr. Farris leaned closer. The smell from his dying face was terrible. Vish closed his hand around the stone again, preparing to throw it. It pressed into his wound. Vish didn't care.

"That Zerg creature that sucked the last of me out of you, that's standing guard in your room? It's made from parts of stupid boys like you. Slaves tricked by Giselas and Islas for generations, used and lied to until they weren't human anymore, but little animal-energy entities, tools for a witch. That's where you're headed. That's what they're going to do to you."

"Gisela told me otherwise about Zerg. I know the truth, and I know she's my friend."

Farris laughed. "You don't know anything that I don't tell you. Know that I *can* hurt you. Now that I've been a part of you, whatever protection you had is gone, boy."

"I can hurt you too." Vish threw the rock at Mr. Farris. It only had a few feet in the air to travel, but the stone, rippling with a line of quartz through its centre, flew right into Mr. Farris's mouth.

Mr. Farris jerked back a foot. Then he swallowed the rock. And grinned.

"They're keeping you alive because they need you. And I'm keeping you alive because I'm tickled by the idea of living in that body of yours, and because I have a feeling they're keeping you around for a certain very good reason."

Farris sat down and leaned against the tomb, before slithering up it without moving his legs or arms. When he was back on its roof, he lay down himself. Vish couldn't see his face any longer.

"I'm sorry this nap hasn't been very restful for you. But I promise you'll get plenty of sleep when we're together again. I want you well-rested. I want a very relaxed new body to move into, Vish."

Vish didn't know if he fell out of bed and then woke up or woke up and then fell out of bed. He did know that his wrist got tangled in the cord of his clock-radio on his way down, and the heavy cube of plastic and electronics smacked into his face as he lay on the carpet, wrapped up in his sheets. He touched his nose to see if it was bleeding; it wasn't. There was no cut in his palm, but the ache was still there. Vish might have stayed on the floor for a little longer, maybe even fallen asleep properly to test Mr. Farris's threat, but the alarm went off, playing a Chili Peppers song he hated. Vish turned it off and unmummified himself. It was seven at night, he didn't feel at all rested, and he realized that he didn't have a phone number for Gisela to tell her about the Farris visitation.

Vish ordered two medium pizzas from Vern's, the loaded ones that Matt and Danny both loved and that Vish thought were slight overkill but admittedly delicious. Then he walked to the bathroom and stood under the hot stream of the shower. Vish switched the water to cool, and then cold, hoping to get a jolt of wakefulness from it.

There was a thunk against the shower door and Vish recoiled against the wall, reaching his arm out in a panicked sweep that knocked the soap, Head & Shoulders, and two loofahs that no one ever used to the floor of the shower.

"Muur," said Buddy, from the other side of the steamed-up glass door.

"Oh, man. I forgot about you," Vish said. "I could have used you in the cemetery."

Buddy didn't answer, because he was a cat.

Danny and Matt arrived seconds before the pizza did. They were both wearing Pantera t-shirts and talked with the delivery guy while Vish tried to remember which of the books on the small kitchen bookshelf his mother hid money in. It turned out to be *A Suitable Boy*, a 1500-page monster with four twenty-dollar bills tucked into it. Not really sure of how to ask for change without seeming cheap or rude, Vish overtipped the delivery guy, who was older than them but probably not twenty yet.

"Mark was at the show last night," Matt said. "I mean, he was —"

"You were in that second band," Vish said. "You had the Rickenbacker."

"Yeah," said Mark, smiling before he remembered not to. He had little blond wiry hairs poking straight out of his face in patches, like he'd had a beard and moustache once but they'd been burned off in a small fire.

"You guys were really good," Danny said. "Drummer slayed."

"She doesn't really," Mark said. "We're trying to replace her."

Danny and Matt traded a quick look, before Pizza Mark said his goodbyes and they closed the door.

"Are you okay, man?" Matt asked.

"Yeah. What was that look? You going to cancel our band and join that guy's, Danny?" Vish asked, sounding more annoyed than he was because he was exhausted.

Danny grabbed the pizzas from Vish and walked them into the kitchen, laughing.

"Dude," he called over his shoulder, "you're pretty attached to being in a band you didn't know existed until last night and we and your girlfriend had to strongarm you into."

"Don't worry, we definitely know she's not your girlfriend. That she would never, ever be your girlfriend," Matt said, as the three boys sat around the table and flipped open the first box. Danny was up immediately to the fridge, searching for —

"Tabasco," Danny said, bringing it over and liberally baptizing the whole pizza without any protest from Matt or Vish. Each Vern's slice looked like a crust with the contents of two Italian sandwiches on top of it, along with green peppers and melted cheese.

"And we were looking at each other because that girl drumming for those jerks was clearly the best part of the band. Not because we want to split off and ditch you. We would never ditch you," Matt said.

"Get it? Get it?" Danny said, then filled his mouth with a slice.

"Yeah, because I ditched you guys, I get it, I get it." Buddy jumped onto the kitchen table and picked up a fallen slice of ham as the brothers stared at him. Vish gently pushed him back down.

"The cat is a loan," Vish said.

"Is your dad gonna be —" Matt said.

"They don't know."

"You wanna talk about something else?" Danny asked. There was a long thread of cheese dangling from his bottom lip to the

T on his Pantera shirt. He clearly did want to talk about anything else, because Vish looked shaken up.

"I'm not going to cry. Don't worry. I've done a lot of that in the past few months, though. Mostly alone. I'm just exhausted. More tired than I've ever been."

"That's normal in a growth spurt," Matt said. "I tell Mom that if she doesn't let us sleep in until at least eleven on weekends she's stunting us —"

"No. It's deeper than that, weirder than that. I'm going to say stuff I'm not supposed to tell anyone, that is going to make me sound genuinely like a crazy person. By the time we get through this second pizza, you may want to call my mom or the cops."

"Damn," said Danny. "That sounds awesome."

"Please go ahead," said Matt, in the exact same thrilled tone of voice. Vish started talking after a second's pause when he remembered how much he liked being friends with these guys.

Twenty minutes of fevered monologuing later, one of the pizzas was completely demolished, and Vish finally looked up from his plate and his speech. Matt and Danny had never looked at him the way they were now. This was how his mother some-times looked at Vish, when she was afraid for him, or afraid of how he was going to react to what she was going to say. Some of the thrill he'd felt about being friends with these guys faded away as Vish waited for one of the brothers' mouths to unhinge.

"You remember how you said that your story was going to make you sound like a crazy person?" Matt asked. Danny tapped the back of his brother's hand with the pizza crust he was holding, to caution him. Matt nodded, still looking straight at Vish. Danny ate the pizza crust.

"I'm not crazy," Vish said.

"I wasn't going to say that," Matt said.

"No one thinks you're crazy. You've had a worse couple years than I could imagine," Danny added. Danny was extremely pale, and right now, his mouth was almost perfectly rimmed in sauce, liked he'd traced the tip of a lipstick around it.

"Then a really messed up two days. What I think is happening here," Matt continued, "and I'm your friend and I've known you for a long time, and I know you're smart — I think that you've trusted some people who are either totally nuts or after something you or your parents have. You're not the crazy one, but you have to understand, looking at me right here, that none of the stuff you're talking about could possibly have happened. That this Agastya guy and that Gisela girl found you because you've been totally rocked by your dad drinking, and then this crash happened —"

Before Vish could interrupt, Buddy did, jumping onto the kitchen table again and seizing, with rapidity and precision, a single piece of pepperoni before launching himself off the open pizza box lid and disappearing over the back of the couch.

"You gotta keep this cat," Danny said, delighted and obviously completely forgetting that he and his brother were trying to talk Vish down to sanity. "Super predator model."

"He belongs to my therapist."

Danny and Matt stared at Vish.

"I didn't steal him, I borrowed him, like I said. Farris was scared as hell of Moby, because he was bonded to Isla, sure, but I figure he might have a wariness of any cat in our circle. Gisela used to have this huge black jaguar-thing called Dammo. I thought a tabby couldn't hurt."

"Was it an actual jaguar?" Danny asked.

"Of course not," said Vish. "They didn't have jaguars in medieval Europe."

Danny was quiet and Matt didn't know how to answer either, so he took off his glasses and polished them on his t-shirt, getting a bit of mozzarella grease on the lenses during the voyage back to his face.

"What do you mean by 'our circle'?" said Matt. "Are they making you do cult stuff, Vish?"

Vish sat back in his chair, full of pizza and doubt. Not that what he'd been going through these past days was absolutely real, but that he'd ever be able to prove it to his friends. Buddy made his way back around the couch and toward the one empty chair at the kitchen table. As the boys watched him, he made a circle of himself and immediately fell asleep.

Vish had one last idea.

"What about Gisela?" he asked. "Why do you think someone like her — older, cooler, basically better in all the ways that matter — would want to hang out with me and be in a band together if none of the stuff I was talking about was real?"

"He just told you, dude," Danny said. "Cult stuff. Sacrifice. They're gonna eat you or something."

"No one's going to eat me." Vish sighed. "Look. Things are moving out there, under the lake and in town. Farris already came for my dad. I'm going to call Gisela so she can show you this stuff is real, and then we're going to find out exactly what we have to do."

CHAPTER 22

V ish caught Gisela at the store's number, just as she was
    about to leave.

"Glad I didn't miss you," he said.

"You wouldn't have," Gisela said. "I was on my way to your
house anyway."

The pizza boxes were in the recycling bin, the cat was still
sleeping on the kitchen chair, and Danny mimed the drum fills
from a Tool song while his brother and Vish washed the dishes.

Gisela met the boys in Vish's backyard. It was the peak of
summer, and the day had been long, but the sun couldn't stay up
forever. It was dipping behind the mountains that surrounded
the valley the town sat in. The bay windows of the mansions
on the hill behind Vish's yard glowed orange as they tried to
spit back the immense light of the sunset. Gisela was wearing
a hoodie with the sleeves cut off and the hood up, her arms tan
and face pale.

Matt and Danny looked at her doubtfully, and Vish apologized for the rude question but could she just . . . She felt along
the trunk of the maple tree, muttered a sequence of words in

Latin, or Greek, or something older both backwards and forwards, then her hand vanished into the trunk. This time, unlike
in the park, she didn't stick it through the other side, but thrust
her hand invisibly up the trunk until the tree seemed to be
growing out of her elbow.

"Okay?" Gisela said, staring at the brothers, who stared at the
joint where her arm stopped and reality as they knew it vanished
with the rest of her limb.

"So if that part's true, and you can see with your eyes that it
is, then everything else I'm telling you is true as well, right?"

Matt and Danny kept staring at the point where her arm vanished into the bark.

"Maybe you can do that thing where you give yourself a different face," Vish said.

"That hurts to do, Vish, and we don't have time," Gisela said.

"You're right," Vish said. "Not believing me isn't an option,
guys. You know what you're seeing. We don't have time. This
thing used my body, my hands, to rig my dad's car to kill him. If
it gets access to what I saw at the bottom of the lake, it can do
anything."

"Vish has no idea," Gisela said. "There's something we need
to start tonight, and we need extra hands for it. Yours." Gisela
pointed at both Danny and Matt.

"You're asking us to help you beat up some kind of ghoul
monster?" Matt asked.

Gisela pulled her arm out of the maple — it quivered and
twisted toward the three boys for a moment, following the
movement of her arm, like an immense living wand.

"No," Gisela said. That was it, just No. The tone was so bored
and withering that Matt, annoyed, went back into the house

through the sliding door, fast enough that his slight limp looked more like floating. Danny started in after him, but Gisela held up a hand. In his yard, holding up a hand that stopped Danny from walking without magic, just authority, she really did seem centuries old, as assured as an ancient being of myth. Gisela wasn't the girl with the cool boots in the bookstore, except when she wanted to be. She was the woman in the shadows of folk and fairy tales. She was someone that Vish would never know.

"Stop staring, dummy," Gisela said. "Can people see us out here? I guess I should have asked that before I did the tree thing."

Vish came back to himself. The sun was down now, the backyard warm and still glowing with plum-blue light, the near-darkness that would last for about an hour before actual night hit. Anji Maurya had said that the lake held onto the daylight and released it into the air when Vish had asked about this twilight time when he was little. Gisela, and now Danny, were looking at him impatiently.

"No one can see us that we can't see back. Maybe with binoculars from one of the big houses on the hill, but that's it. And unless someone is standing behind those shrubs there, no, no one can hear us unless we yell," Vish said.

"Good," Gisela said. "Your friends believe you now, and that's great. And what we need to do now is get the names that Isla put into you out, so you can go back to your normal, boring life."

"Do we have to keep talking about how boring I am?" Vish said.

"Yes," Gisela said. Danny laughed and then shut up immediately when Gisela looked at him, so he got out one "ha" and then what sounded like a painful choke, as though he'd been winged in his big Adam's apple by a ball.

"Farris is closing in. It's time. We need the names tonight. We need them out of your mind and onto paper. This is the last night the rift is open, the lake magic is here, and Farris knows it."

"What does having the names of these nachzehrers on paper *do*? How does that keep me, or my mom, or my dad, or anyone in this city safe?" Vish asked.

Gisela's authority, her ancientness, seemed to drop away from her suddenly. She pushed her hood back, and rubbed her forehead. There was part of a leaf on the back of the hand that she'd pulled out of the tree, but she didn't notice it. She looked so young and human again that Vish wondered if she had done it on purpose to put him at ease.

"It's not your fault if you don't understand. It's ours, mine and Agastya's. And Isla's, for putting you in this position."

"It sounds like you could have told Vish like, way before, right?" Danny said, as they were walking toward the sliding door. Gisela looked at him, and he smiled. She didn't.

"We've had two days and we're not teachers. Isla was the teacher. She's dead."

"Well don't get mad at me for what you're bad at," Danny said, sliding the door open hard enough that it rattled in its track. Matt was sitting on the couch, the TV tuned to *Die Hard 2* on mute.

"That's good advice," Gisela admitted. "Also something for you to keep in mind in your career as a drummer."

"What's that supposed to mean?" Danny asked.

"Shut up," Vish said, even though he was curious to see what the end of Isla's insult was going to be. "Just tell us the important part, Gisela. I'm sick of this."

Gisela turned off the TV without asking. It was the only interior light in the room, so she told the boys the rest of the story in the fading blue light coming through the big windows.

"The 12,506 names of dead souls that Vish has laid through his synapses aren't just letters and spaces and sounds. Each nachzehrer's name is half of its being in this world. The other half is in the flesh that Mr. Farris ate and made one with his rotten body.

"Names can bring the energy on the other side of the portal into contact with the individual spirits living in Farris, and bring those lives into new human bodies. If we extract the names from Vish's mind, if we time the destruction of the list correctly, we can make sure those dead creatures never make it back into our world."

"'Correct timing'?" Matt asked, with more attitude than was exactly called for. "What's that mean? Is it like baking time for a recipe?"

"It means tonight, when the portal is ready to spill over, when Farris is ready to bring those things into our world. Tonight."

"Wait," Vish said. "What if Farris comes when you're doing whatever it is to get the names out of my head? Will I — will all of us be helpless?"

"I don't know. His body seemed like it was barely hanging together, but putting those teeth into you, getting to your dad . . . he might be so desperate that it's giving him a last bit of terrible strength."

A thunking knock at the front door would have interrupted Gisela if she hadn't already been finished. It was harder than the rap of knuckles on the door's panes of glass. This was a steel-toed boot, tapping into the oak as gently as steel could.

Vish went up the stairs two at a time. He knew who it would be, but he didn't want his neighbours to notice. Agastya had a green army jacket on and looked both sick and alert, his face lean and yellow-brown under the bright hallway bulb as he pushed past Vish, who closed the door quickly. He was carrying an enormous duffle bag strapped across his back. The first thing he did was kneel and gently ease the bag around his torso, then lower it to the ground. There was something heavy in it that clanked, and something lighter that riffled. Agastya stayed on his knees for a moment, out of breath, before straightening up.

"I'm not parked outside, or anything. I walked from the end of the block. Don't worry about anyone ratting us out to your mom."

"I'm not worried. Not about that, I mean," Vish lied. Agastya smiled at him. The smile made him look sicker.

"What's wrong with you?" Vish asked him, just as Gisela came up the stairs with Danny and Matt behind her.

"This is the time," Agastya said, not answering Vish's question. "Right now. Everything happening so fast, the lunar node, the portal. It's a lot to deal with."

"And you're giving your liver a lot to deal with," said Gisela.

"So witty," Agastya said. Vish smelled it then — whisky, sweating through his clothes, coming out in light drifts from beneath the army jacket.

"Did you drive here drunk?" Vish asked, with a cold disgust he'd never managed to summon up when his dad was at his worst.

"I never drive with even a drop in me. Ever. I parked and had a few swigs. Don't talk to me like I'm your child," Agastya said, pushing Vish aside hard enough that he knocked into the banister. Danny, who was as tall as Agastya, steadied Vish and then started to move toward Agastya.

"Oh, relax," Agastya said.

Danny kept moving. It might have gotten worse if Buddy hadn't appeared from the kitchen and started to weave between Agastya and then Danny's feet. It is impossible to have a fistfight if there is a cat winding around your ankles, both for reasons of balance and because it makes you feel ridiculous to make a fist when a cat is rubbing its head on your shin.

"He didn't mean it," Vish said. "Sorry, Agastya."

"It's okay. You were thinking about Dad and his pill collection, I'm sure," Agastya said, shrugging out of the green jacket and tossing it on the hallway chair that Dr. Maurya sat in to put his loafers on at the beginning of the day and his sandals on when he got back from work. Before he could turn back from the toss, Vish had shoved him. Buddy, sensing there was some weight about to descend, bolted, rounding the banister and shooting down the stairs. For an elderly cat, he could really move.

Agastya tripped backwards over the duffle bag and almost clipped his head on the chair by the doorway. He twisted as he fell, and his Carcass shirt rode up slightly, exposing a couple of inches of back. Everyone — Gisela, Matt, Danny — had backed off, and they were standing in an accidental phalanx behind Vish as Agastya stared up.

"I am still worried about my dad, yes, but it wasn't booze that put him in the hospital. It was Mr. Farris. Using me. That makes it your fault. And Isla's fault, and Gisela's. None of this would be happening to me, and Farris would have had no reason to hurt *my* family if I didn't have the names of these monsters in my skull."

"I'm sorry," Agastya said. "And you're right. I meant what I said this afternoon. No one's out tonight."

"We don't have time for this, Vish. Matt, open that bag," Gisela said. Vish was watching Agastya as she spoke, and he could see the man relaxing as she took charge. He still hadn't gotten off the floor, and seemed to be getting more relaxed, until Matt gently lifted his sneakers off the duffle bag and unzipped it.

"Can we use that room?" Gisela was pointing to the upstairs sitting room, which had two enormous windows and contained an almost-never-used furniture set, because Anji said those couches were for guests and Dr. Maurya hated having guests over.

"Yeah," Vish said. "But for what?"

"Danny, get all of the furniture out of the middle and push it up along the sides. Roll up the rug." Gisela guided Danny into the entryway of the sitting room and pointed to the work she wanted done. Like an automaton, or an Igor in a *Frankenstein* movie, Danny just followed the order without asking any of the questions that Vish would have.

"Is this going to make a mess?" Vish asked.

"No. I promise," Gisela said. She was focused now on something that was greater than Vish and certainly greater than the sanctity of his living room carpets. Gisela squeezed his upper arm reassuringly, at the spot just under his t-shirt sleeve where he had a scar from a fall off the swingsets when he was in kindergarten. But she was looking beyond him, at the windows, which were admitting more moonlight than seemed possible. Vish saw that the moon wasn't full. It was a crescent, but despite most of the lights in the house being off, it was almost bright inside with the beams that were coming through the big windows.

Gisela let go of his arm and made her way into the hallway, surveying what Matt was up to. As Danny manhandled the sectional couch into a new spot under the windows, Vish followed Gisela.

Agastya was helping Matt out now. The duffle bag was deflated in the corner, like the discarded, rotting peel of an enormous fruit. On the floor were three large plastic cases, two yellow and one crimson, about the size of Dr. Maurya's brief-case, but oddly shaped. They almost looked beetle-like. Next to each of the humped cases was a stack of paper almost as tall as the case itself. Vish bent to pick up one of the pieces of paper, but realized that it was connected to all the paper beneath it: it was old printer paper, the kind that you had to tear off along the dotted line.

Matt found latches on the side of the red case and undid them, then flipped it open to reveal a beautiful red typewriter with black keys and a logo that read Olivetti. He looked up at Gisela, who was already talking to Agastya.

"Where's the fourth one?"

"No point," Agastya said. For some reason, he'd put his jacket back on and buttoned it up. Probably thinking he looked more dignified that way. Vish was frowning at him, but caught himself and made his expression blank again before Agastya noticed.

"Because you won't be able to use it. Right," Gisela said.

"It's not because I had a couple of drinks, it's because I'm a bad typist." Agastya ignored Gisela's gaze and made his way to the duffle bag, which had, Vish noticed, a remaining lump that kept it from being completely deflated. Agastya pulled out a clear bag of black rocks. It took a second for Vish to recognize these as lumps of coal.

"Like I told these guys, we don't have time to argue," Gisela said. "But I'm going to need you, Agastya. If we're all under, if we're doing this thing — you can at least be our eyes in this world."

Gisela put on her hood, and Vish noticed that her arms were goosebumped. Not because she was nervous, but because the room was getting very cold. Danny hadn't noticed because he was red and sweaty with exertion, now carefully taking the glass panes out of the coffee table before moving it, but it was especially cold in this room. The beams of moonlight came in cool. Vish walked over the now-cleared room's carpet and stood by one of the windows; he could see his own breath, and outside, clouds where the sky had been clear all day. The sliver of moon was untouched by any of them.

Matt stopped fussing with the typewriter he was setting up and walked over to his brother at the coffee table. He didn't even bother to be quiet when he started to speak.

"What the hell are we doing, Danny? We don't know these people."

"We know Vish. And we saw that one put her hand through a maple tree, and she's the singer in our band. So we're helping them."

Danny wasn't much of a debater, but he was a great explainer. As he went back to leaning panes of glass against the couch cushions, Matt thought, nodded, and came back to the typewriters.

Agastya walked up to Vish and handed him a jean jacket: Vish's own, pulled from the hallway closet. Vish put it on and nodded a thank you.

"It's colder outside too," Agastya said. "It's not going to rain, even though it looks like it. But the barometer will be going crazy, and everyone will have noticed that it's about five degrees less than it should be. Because of what's going down in the bottom of the lake. We have to get those names out of you."

"Is Farris doing this?"

"The Nine Spheres are doing this, is what Isla would tell you," Agastya said. "And you'd ask what the Nine Spheres are, and Gisela would say —"

"There's no time to explain," Gisela completed, coming up behind the two guys and pulling them away from the window. She pointed toward the stone fireplace at the side — Vish's parents never used it, but it was too beautiful to take out of the home, so it just sat there, its grey and umber stones glistening clean and the pointless hearth still black with ashes from the previous owner. Agastya sat on the flagstones in front of the fireplace, and Gisela led Vish to the centre of the room.

When he reached it, Gisela gently pushed down on his shoulders. He knelt. She knelt in front of him. Vish looked over her shoulders: Danny and Matt, looking serious but slightly scared, stood on either side of her. Each of the three typewriters had been threaded with a roll of paper, and they were arranged in a triangle formation. Vish could still smell pepperoni from their meal, and almost started laughing at how stupid and familiar and totally out of place the scent of pepperoni was at this moment.

"We do have time for this explanation. And you deserve it. Have you heard of a 'grimoire,' Vish?" Gisela asked. She seemed a hundred years old again, maybe a thousand, her eyes glittering like a cat's from the depths of the cheap cotton hoodie. Buddy had come back from downstairs and was sniffing at one of the beige typewriters.

"You said that's what Farris called his dirty books of magic."

"They're not all dirty, though. A grimoire is a book of magic, personal spells, a storehouse. Isla used to call her notebooks, even the ones she had shopping lists or recipes in, grimoires,"

Gisela said. At the fireplace, Agastya breathed out raggedly, and when he breathed back in, it was a sob. Gisela kept talking.

"She didn't like the mystification of magic. She liked to be clear about how hard and provable the science of it was, and how even the stranger parts were a matter of habit, biology, and the acceptance that physical power can sometimes hide in what look like feelings or thoughts. And she loved books, like you do. Isla noticed you coming into the store time after time, and she decided that you had to be her last grimoire after Agastya gave you that nickname."

"What nickname?" Vish asked. Then he answered himself, just as Agastya said the word out loud.

"Grimmer," Agastya said. There had been no tears after that first sob, but he was quiet, as though he were talking from very far away. "You used to frown — still do — whenever you picked up a book in the shop and started to read the back, and the frown would just get more intense when you opened the book and started to read. So I started calling you 'grimmer,' and that gave Isla the idea, when she realized that she had to store the names somewhere."

"So you're her last notebook, Vish. She put those names in your brain knowing that when the day came, when Farris came for what we'd hidden you would trust us enough to help us," Gisela said. Her voice sounded different — metallic, like the plate reverb setting on the delay pedal that Vish had once tried out for his guitar. And even stranger, the glimmer of the moon off her green eyes had disappeared.

CHAPTER 23

"**Y**ou're probably not going to love this process," Agastya went on.

"I haven't loved any of this," said Vish.

"It's going to save Munish and Anji. It's going to save you and Matt and Danny. And twelve thousand other human beings in this stupid city, even if most of them are jerks," Agastya said. He'd pulled his feet up onto the stones and was hugging his knees. It was colder in the room, almost like winter now. The automatic heaters rumbled to life just as Vish thought this, and the scent of baking dust started to come from the vents in the floors and ceiling.

Vish wasn't looking at Agastya, but deeper into the darkness of Gisela's hoodie.

"You'll love the name of the ceremony," Agastya continued. "'Torment of the metals.' For real. It's an alchemy thing, but it's not just about lead into gold, it's about thought into —"

Gisela's hands rose to peel off the hood. Under it wasn't her head, but a floating blue mask with empty eye-holes. It was a light, natural blue, the colour of the lake in winter. Vish could only recognize Gisela's lips, which started to move as soon as her hands descended to his shoulders. She pushed him down until Vish was lying on the floor and she was standing above him. Her lips moved and the voice that came out was Gisela's, but also Isla's from that graveyard of the dream, and also something deeper and more ancient than Vish could describe.

"Some say a god made the world with words. The world was not made with words. The world *is* words. The beings that seek this world from theirs, that wish to beat back this reality and take bodies from innocents who were born into flesh they call their own: they are words. We will take those words out of you. And tonight, the only night in a cosmic year, in fifteen thousand Copernican revolutions, that we can destroy those names, we will. And the nachzehrers will die as the words burn."

Vish's legs straightened and his arms lay flat at his side. Gisela stepped back from him, and Vish briefly craned his neck up. Matt and Danny were sitting cross-legged, the way they all used to in preschool when the teacher was taking attendance, but their fingers were poised above their typewriters. They were each staring directly at the moon, like deer hypnotized by a cheating hunter's flashlight.

Vish didn't know if Gisela had been muttering the whole time, because he only heard her words when she was right next to him again. He hadn't seen her move, but that blank mask was suddenly directly above his face, the mouth moving quietly and a dozen different voices coming out of it, all saying the same thing at the same time.

"I am the Black of the White and the Red of the White and the Yellow of the Red; I am the herald of the truth and no liar."

Vish had known Matt and Danny since before preschool, but this was the first time he'd ever heard them say nothing for this long. He lay still, and they knelt in front of their typewriters as Gisela continued to move around the room, speaking in her many voices. It was as though there were too many other people speaking at once through her mouth for anyone else to talk. Vish stayed on his back, staring at the wooden beams in the ceiling.

"Dissolve the body," Gisela muttered, stepping over Vish's chest. He looked at where the back of her head, with its dark brown hair and paper-white parting, used to be: now it was just air, and the strangely fleshy but lifeless back of that blue mask that floated in front of what used to be her face.

"Make hard the spirit," Agastya replied, proving that not everyone else had lost the ability to say something. "No one's going to hurt you, Vish, I promise."

Vish heard movement at the fireplace and turned his head to the side. Agastya had gotten up, and Gisela was reaching into the hearth, pulling out great handfuls of ash. Vish was thankful that the rugs had been rolled up and he was lying on cold hardwood when she walked over to him and began to dump the ashes around him.

When he tilted his head up again, Vish realized that "dump" was the wrong word: Gisela's loose handfuls of grey and black ash were surrounding the outline of his body perfectly, including every one of his fingers. He then discovered that he couldn't move any of those fingers. Or his arms, or his legs. When his neck got tired and he lay his head back down, in a growing panic, he found that he couldn't move that again, either.

"I just realized," Agastya said, his face popping into view a couple of feet above Vish's. "Is the chimney blocked? Has it been cleaned?"

"I can't move," Vish said.

"That's normal. Also, you can move your mouth, and your tongue, and your eyelids, so just focus on what you can control, okay. The fireplace, Vish — is it going to work?"

"Mom had it cleaned just before Dad stopped drinking. Back when she thought we were going to sell the house and leave him," Vish said.

"That's great," Agastya said. "That it's clean, I mean. We're going to have a fire going. A very, very hot one." Vish felt cold leaking into the room, as though the glass had been removed from the windows and the still air of outside was stealing every bit of warmth from his body.

"The cold moisture must come out," Gisela said, from a far corner of the room that Vish couldn't see. It was close to her familiar voice, but the words creaked and rasped, as though she had been screaming for hours.

"Do you have it on you? The medal?" Agastya asked Vish.

"My jeans. In the change pocket," Vish said. He tried to wriggle around to make this pocket more accessible, but he felt even more frozen than ever. As Agastya extracted the coin with a thumb and a fingertip, Vish tried a joke.

"It's an amulet, not a medal," Vish said. He wanted the joke to calm him down, to warm him up. It did neither.

"Don't be scared," Agastya replied. "Gisela knows what she's doing. Just like she knows the difference between a medal and an amulet."

Agastya patted Vish on the chest, but he couldn't feel the touch. He couldn't feel anything but the growing cold on his face. Everything else in his body wasn't just numb: it wasn't *there*, at all. Agastya held the amulet above Vish's face, and Vish studied the strange design, the claw with its seven talons. And then Gisela's new, terrifying face appeared, hovering over him with the invisible head behind it.

"Are you sure?" Agastya asked. Vish knew he wasn't talking to him, but Gisela didn't answer either. Agastya took a breath, and then, as though he were feeding the most delicate parking meter in the world, one that would explode if the coin touched the sides, he pushed the amulet into the open slit of mouth in the blue mask floating above Vish. It began to shine. Not shine, but glow, as though it were growing incredibly hot. And it was.

Vish felt the growing blast of heat before anyone else in the room, sweat beginning to pour out of his face, as much as the day in fifth grade when he'd skipped breakfast and lunch then gotten dizzy on the playground, fainting and waking up drenched. Salty water was springing from every pore on his face, and his neck, which he found he could raise and turn again. But he didn't dare draw any closer to the glowing coin that was now filling the place where Gisela's head used to be with yellow light, perfectly shaped to the contours of an invisible human skull. The amulet at the centre of this inferno was no longer visible. Vish turned away from the heat, but was unable to escape it. Facing the fireplace, he saw Agastya stacking the coals from the plastic bag in a perfect pyramid on the metal grate.

Suddenly the heat was farther away from Vish's face; it was as though a miniature sun had passed behind a cloud. But it was just Gisela moving toward the pyramid of clothes, slowly, like a priest in a funeral scene on television, a comparison that leapt into Vish's mind to prevent him from going insane at what he was seeing.

Gisela crouched in front of the fireplace stones. Her glowing forehead touched the stones as she bowed. Agastya stood well back from her, his jacket discarded now, his black hair so drenched in sweat that it was hanging in front of his face, hiding his eyes.

Without any sound, Gisela lifted her flaming head and spat the amulet into the centre of the coal pyramid. All of the light and heat transferred in an instant, and the coals glowed first orange, then red, then white. The room became hot, infernally hot. Vish breathed air that singed his nostrils. Gisela turned around.

"You're back," Vish said. If he was crying, he wouldn't know it; his whole face was slick with salty moisture. Gisela — her face, her nose piercing, her hair, her green eyes glowing with concern and purpose, not creepy alien fire — looked back at him.

"Don't move," she said. "Your body is your own again, but the torment of the metals isn't finished yet."

"I don't want to be tormented," Vish said, twitching the fingers on his left hand to test the truth of what she'd said. They moved, and he could feel the light ash that had been piled around him, as well as the slickness of his sweat and the gritty crystals of salt that were coming out of him. Vish felt pounds lighter, and weak. He craned his neck up for a second and saw Danny and Matt, staring straight ahead and sitting in front of their typewriters as before.

"I said 'don't move,'" Gisela said. "Please. The cold moisture that left you was the lunar body. Now it's the chalk coming out, the solar body, all that salt in your sweat and more. We're so close to unthreading what Isla put into you, but you need to be still and let it all come forth."

Gisela sat in front of the red typewriter and Vish laid his head back down. He hadn't seen Agastya and was too exhausted to lift his head again even if he did want to look for him. The last thing he saw in the minutes he lay on the floor, trying his best to keep breathing, was from the corner of his eye: the pile of ash was now topped with a layer of crystals, white and blue and red, now as high as his ears.

Vish started to speak. Or rather, his mouth started to speak.

"Erluin," said the voice that had opened Vish's mouth. And the word became form, as Gisela's fingers moved over the keys of her red Olivetti typewriter. As the sound left Vish's cracked, dry lips, it lived for a second as a tiny shred of flesh, something that looked like a rotten steak hanging in mid-air, vanished into the typewriter, and emerged as black marks on a white page: Zabulon.

Vish realized that he was watching this happen. Not from inside his body, but from a point near the ceiling, hovering between criss-crossed beams of the pale brown wood that he could now see every knothole and grain line in. He could see his own still body on the ground, and its mouth moving too quickly for the names to be heard over the furious clatter of the three typewriters in the room below. Danny, who had gotten a C minus in the typing unit of their Computer Science course, was typing one hundred, two hundred words a minute, as fast as the mechanical keys could go. Matt and Gisela were even faster, but their rhythm was perfect: each of them in turn catching a name, catching the wisping essence of a nachzehrer that vanished onto the spooling roll of paper, the endless scroll, that was shooting up and out of their typewriters.

Vish watched all of this, then watched his own still body with its babbling mouth, and decided he didn't want to be floating near the ceiling anymore. Seeing a ghost would be scary, but being one was worse.

CHAPTER 24

Vish couldn't stand to look at himself for another second. If disembodied spirits could throw up, the sight of his unconscious body speaking names from a hundred languages he didn't know would be exactly the thing to make him spew. So Vish turned away and found himself drifting along with his vision. Buddy was walking the other way, in from the kitchen to sniff at the typewriters now, or perhaps to investigate their furious clacking sound. The cat looked up at Vish's drifting shade, and absolutely saw him, mewing suspiciously. Vish kept moving. Through the wall in the living room, and into the hallway.

At first, Vish thought the limp duffle bag was somehow snaking along the hallway, perhaps blown by the cold breeze coming from the front door.

The door was open. No one had locked it after Agastya came in, but it had been closed. It must have been. And Vish saw the actual duffle bag, lying still and boring as an empty bag will. He looked closer at the moving, flattish thing worming up the hallway carpet.

And he saw that it was Mr. Farris.

Farris had looked almost healthy in the graveyard, spry in the world of dreams, but here in the world, the grey flesh he'd come into the bookstore with was not even grey any longer. It was a rotten shade. Not the healthy brown of Vish's family, not even the sometimes yellowish-brown of Agastya, but a subterranean brown-green that looked like pure rot, and had stained Mr. Farris's silly tourist clothes the same colour. Vish did see the snowboard company logo on the back of a shirt that had once been light blue.

The clattering of the typewriters continued without a pause, a mechanical thunder that had disguised the opening of the door and now the creature's slow creeping toward the ritual in the sitting room. Vish tried to call out, but his voice was stuck in his body, down there on the floor.

But Mr. Farris heard him. The neck on the creature below twisted, and that terrible white mask that Vish remembered from his yard, the eyeless toothless screaming paleness that he now recognized as the flesh of a being from beyond this dimension, shone upward at him with an ancient hate.

"Thank you for leaving your body, Vish," the creature said, the words drifting directly into Vish's mind even though the mask didn't seem to move its lips. "It will make it so much easier to slip into and live in for the next hundred or so years. I'm going to pick up that list of names with your hands, you know. But they'll be my hands by then."

The creature rose up from its squirming progress to walk the final few steps into the sitting room. Agastya was nowhere to be seen, and Danny, Matt, and Gisela were absorbed in their typing, capturing the names and shapes that came issuing from the chanted words that filled the air in the room.

Farris's voice echoed in Vish's mind again.

"Your sweet mother and your damaged father will belong to me. Every nachzehrer in my army will be a slave, every body they occupy will belong to me. I'm going to own everything you love, you disgusting, ugly child."

Vish looked for the cat and realized that it was gone. He called Buddy's name before realizing that he had no voice. As Farris kept crawling, Vish passed through the wall behind Gisela, looking for Buddy.

He found him on his parents' bed, somehow instantly asleep. The silver and black curl of his body on the white sheets breathed placidly as Vish tried, once again, to scream. Nothing came out.

Vish remembered what Gisela could do to her own, physical face. Twist it, make it move. She could put her hand through a tree. She'd pushed him out of his own body. And if he was a ghost now, that meant that even if he couldn't do magic, he was part of magic. And ghosts can make themselves felt.

Concentrating all he could on making his arms solid, Vish pushed his ghostly hands into Buddy's solid fur and felt it give under his touch. The cat's green eyes snapped open, and he was instantly alert, leaping off the bed onto the floor.

And then Buddy yowled, the unearthly echoing cry of a cat warning that he's about to do some serious damage. He ran out of the bedroom, as Vish passed through the wall again.

Farris was now only a few steps from Matt, reaching for those blur-fast fingers moving over the keyboard —

Agastya's footsteps came thundering up the stairs, rounding the banister. He screamed, "FARRIS!"

Mr. Farris's head was still backward, the empty white mask drooping over the loose flesh beneath it as the body kept staggering toward Matt. Matt kept typing as Farris's melting green hand clamped gently onto his shoulder. Vish could see the slippery fingers trying to close into a gripping claw.

But Agastya was there. For the first time since he'd met the man, Vish saw him move fast, picking up the melting beast that was Farris and embracing it in a violent hug. Agastya kept running, and Vish realized he was heading straight for the massive windows that were letting in the cold light of the slivered moon.

No, Vish thought, and tried to scream. No. No.

Agastya, still holding Farris, leapt over Vish's uttering, still body on the ground, and was almost at the windows when he collapsed on his knees. Vish heard Farris's voice in his mind, just as he knew Agastya had.

YOU TOUCHED ME. YOU'RE MINE.

First, Farris's hand, now a claw with the white bones shining through the useless skin, clamped around Agastya's left arm at the bicep. Agastya screamed, but didn't let go of the thing. Horrified, Vish watched the skeletal fingers sink into Agastya's arm, which began to blaze, char, until what projected from his sleeve was a dark column of ash.

Farris's other hand was plunged into the centre of Agastya's chest, tearing right through the logo on his t-shirt.

As Vish watched, Farris's green flesh began to liquefy, until the kneeling Agastya was clinging to a dark skeleton that was also clinging to him. And then the mask, the demonic essence of Mr. Farris, began to peel off the meatless skull: and it latched onto Agastya's face. Tiny, flickering, pale tendrils cast Agastya's lank, hanging hair away from his face as the mask began to graft itself to him.

Agastya screamed as quietly as Vish had ever heard anyone scream. He sounded like a child in a vanishingly deep tunnel, a child who knew he would never be found.

And that is when the typing stopped. Vish saw Gisela rising from behind the typewriter, holding something dark and heavy.

It was Buddy, in the same kind of trance as Matt and Danny were, staring into nothingness, with Gisela cradling him carefully, one hand under him and one on his back.

"Let him go, Farris," Gisela said.

The Farris-mask, halfway on the skull and halfway on Agastya's face, shifted, an empty eyehole looking straight at Gisela. The empty mouth began to smile, and perhaps was going to say something.

It was Agastya's mouth that moved to answer, with Farris's voice.

"There had to be a cost, you know. You're not going to win all the way. I've taken this one with me, even when you thought I was at my weakest. If you want him back, if you want him alive, you'll have to speak to me. We can make an arrangement, Gisela."

Agastya's left hand, the one that wasn't a hunk of ash, came up to his own throat and started to squeeze. The words stopped.

Gisela lifted her hand off Buddy's back, pulling from it a beam of light, a light somehow as dense as a bar of iron, glowing white from a fire hotter than anything on this Earth.

The light left the cat, drawn by Gisela's hand, and shot directly into the Farris mask.

Vish heard a scream in his mind, as loud as Agastya's had been quiet. The sound of something that should have died long ago finally being erased.

Agastya, his face tired but unmarked, staggered to one of the couches that had been pushed into the wall and collapsed. Gisela knelt and placed Buddy on the ground. He didn't move, and Vish was terrified that he was dead, that he would have to tell Rita Goodis that he had killed her cat on the first night he'd had it. But Buddy sprang up the next second with a twitch, running toward the kitchen. And at that moment, Vish's body began to speak in its hundred tongues once again.

"d'Aubigny. Giffard. Ranulf d'Avranches."

Matt and Danny resumed their typing. Agastya nodded at Gisela, and she knelt and started typing again as well.

And in half an hour, the 12,506 names were committed to paper. Agastya was asleep on the couch, the right sleeve of his t-shirt dangling empty, his face covered with sweat. His breathing sounded strange, a wheezing whistle. The hole in the centre of his shirt didn't reveal brown skin, but burnt-black skin: there wasn't a hole, not exactly, but a dark covering over immense damage within.

Vish suddenly stopped seeing everyone from the ceiling, and opened the eyes of his own, his very own, body, and sat up. Buddy leapt into his lap and licked his eyebrow. A cat's tongue is very rough, but Vish felt revived by the rasp.

"Now what?" he asked.

"I need to put my hands in your freezer for an hour," Danny said, staring in awe at his own red, swollen hands. Matt, next to him, was shaking his hands as though he'd just grabbed a hot lasagne pan.

"This is going to be amazing for my calluses," Matt said.

Gisela was smiling at Vish, but her lips were trembling, and soon her whole face relaxed, with even her eyes shutting.

"Now you put on the coffee machine and I do the part with the gold. After the part with the coffee."

"What's the part with the coffee?"

"Me drinking it, idiot." Gisela tried to smile again, but instead, she very gently collapsed backwards, not even a bit conscious.

CHAPTER 25

A few minutes after she woke up, Gisela asked Vish to open two tins of tuna.

"We don't eat that," Vish said.

"Salmon," Agastya offered, before moving toward the dish cabinet. Gisela stopped him.

"Agastya, the only reason you're still conscious is magic. Your arm is gone. At least one of your lungs is collapsed. You're in deep shock. Please, just sit down."

Agastya waggled his empty sleeve and laughed.

"There's not much time left for this to bother me," he said, trying to laugh. But he saw Vish staring at him and smiled instead. "It's okay, man. I'm fine."

"We need to get him to the hospital," Vish said. "We'll say he was in an accident, something like that."

"No," Agastya said. "I'm not going to any hospital. This is perfect. Farris just resolved an argument that Gisela and I have been having for years."

Gisela filled up two large white plastic bowls, ones that the family usually used for popcorn, with ice. Danny and Matt plunged their hands in, apparently finding some relief.

Vish got two tins of salmon open and dumped the fish on a plate on the counter, then looked at Gisela. She was gently flexing her fingers.

"You want a go on the ice bath?" Danny asked. "Feels stellar."

"I think it hit you guys harder than it hit me," Gisela said. "I'm okay."

She noticed Vish staring at her over the plate of fish.

"It's not for me," she said, just as Buddy jumped onto the counter and began eating faster than Vish had ever seen any animal or human eat.

Vish felt suddenly queasy, not at the sight of the tabby delighting in his meal, but because he felt like he was still about two inches outside of his own body. Backing up toward the kitchen table, he jostled Matt and then sat down heavily on one of the padded chairs. Matt pulled a freezing, wet hand out of his ice bowl to steady Vish, and the chilly fingers on his arm jolted Vish back together.

"Where on earth did you get this cat?" Gisela asked, when Vish looked back up at her.

"It's my therapist's," Vish said. "I thought that if Farris was scared of Moby, he might be scared of Buddy."

"Cats are useful," Agastya said, slumped deep in a chair. His voice sounded as dry and wispy as the ashes Mr. Farris had turned his arm into.

"You can borrow cats from a therapist?" Matt asked.

"This one," Vish said.

"Is that why you don't just go to your dad for free?" Danny asked.

"Why would he use his own dad as a therapist? His dad was most of his problem," Matt said. "Sorry, Vish."

"It's okay."

"Farris wasn't afraid," Gisela said. "By the time he came into this house he was too close to the end to be following any rules at all. His body was completely falling apart. Maybe he knew he wasn't going to be able to free all his nachzehrers, but he was at least going to try to take us all into death with him."

"He did a decent job with me, at least," Agastya said, smiling.

"Stop talking like that," Vish said.

Buddy was finishing his salmon, licking flecks that had danced off the saucer and onto the counter. Gisela got some paper towel and petted the cat as she cleaned up his mess.

"What did the cat have in him?" Vish said. "I saw you use him as, like, some sort of furred ray gun."

"I cannot believe I missed this," Matt said. His hands were out of the bowl now, and he pushed them through his hair before drying them off on his jeans.

"You didn't," Agastya said. "You were right there."

"You know what I mean," Matt said.

"Shut up," said Gisela. "I'm too exhausted to talk over people." The guys obeyed.

"Cats collect vibrational frequencies. The electric translation of psychic impulses. There's a vibrational level of magic in extreme emotion — sort of like how a house can hold on to the atmosphere of a murder, or some moment of extreme joy —"

"Or a weird triple-typing exorcism thing," Agastya said, waving toward the living room. Gisela stared at him. "Sorry, sorry."

"Cats harbour and store these vibrations, just like they can suck in Earth magic. It's unique to the species. Dogs don't do it.

Tonight, I took every bit of human agony, fear, rage, and joy that had passed into Buddy from the people around him, which must be years of his owner's patients, and I turned it on Mr. Farris. That was enough to finish him off."

Buddy leapt up from the counter onto Gisela's shoulders. She yelped, startled, then laughed as he settled around her neck like a living tabby scarf.

"He probably feels about two hundred pounds lighter with that psychic mess taken out of him," Gisela said. "Are your hands feeling better, everyone?"

"I do not feel better," Agastya said. "But I do feel sober."

He smiled at this, but Gisela didn't smile back.

"Can you drive?" she asked. "I really should have gotten my licence by now."

"There's no pain, for real," Agastya said. "And the car's not a stick shift. I can do this."

"Where are we going?" Vish asked.

"We need to take the names and Farris to the rift," Gisela said. "We have to get them onto the other side and out of our world forever."

CHAPTER 26

A gastya put on one of Dr. Maurya's jackets and left to collect his car. Matt, Danny, and Vish followed Gisela's careful instructions in the sitting room. They extracted the three long rolls of paper from the typewriters and rolled them as tightly as possible, forming dense, bright-white logs of paper.

The pile of coals was still glowing in the fireplace grating, a bit more dimly than before. The moon outside had dimmed, looking more like a normal one, and it gave the only light besides the orange radiating from the hearth. Gisela flicked on the ugly overhead fluorescents.

Vish gasped. The floor, and the carpet in the hallway, were an unholy stained mess, the trail left by the decomposing Farris ending with the awful puddle near the base of the couch at the window.

"At least it didn't touch the furniture," Matt said.

"Get a dustpan," Gisela said. Vish ran for one from the hall closet, and when he came back, Gisela used her bare hand to push the liquid remains of Mr. Farris into it. She then poured the liquid onto the fire as Matt and Danny stared into the flames.

"We'll worry about most of the housekeeping later," Gisela said. "Do you guys have every bit of those scrolls wrapped up? Every single name? Then give them here."

Danny carried the three logs of paper to Gisela, who was kneeling in front of the fire. She used the tongs to take something off the coals while Danny waited: it was the medal, the amulet, still intact, now brilliantly golden. Gisela took the rolls of names from Danny and arranged them, moving quickly, into a sort of tent-structure over the coals. She blew on the coals, and their glow intensified: the smouldering paper quickly began to catch fire, and soon a healthy, bright blaze was burning. Gisela walked back toward the lightswitch and turned it off. The boys stared into the fireplace, and Gisela took the amulet into her mouth, closing her eyes, whispering something without moving her tongue, words that Vish felt must have passed directly into the coin.

And then, just as she had when Vish had first seen Mr. Farris in the store, Gisela craned forward and spat: the amulet came arcing out, flipping in the air, to land exactly where the three tented logs of paper met, at the peak of the flames.

The golden coin began to glow and melt, to spread and embrace. Danny started to say something but Matt clapped him hard on the shoulder, then winced and shook off his sore hand. The amulet had turned into a dripping dome, encasing everything in the fireplace: the papers, the coals. And then it began to contract. In less than five minutes, there was a glowing gold sphere the size of a tennis ball in the fireplace.

Danny walked over and reached out a hand. Gisela cleared her throat. "You realize that it's not a great idea to touch metal that's just been in a fire, right? Fire hot, hand burn? Yeah?"

"Be nice," Vish whispered. He knelt and stared at the ball. "Is this alchemy, Gisela? Is all of this magic and science about making lead into gold?"

"No. Alchemy is the kiddie version. But what it got right is that gold has a purity — well, all the elements do, but gold has a particular quality — that is great at containing answers. Or sealing them off forever. Those names are close to never existing again in this dimension, or in the one across the portal."

A metallic clinking sound behind the little group clustered around the fireplace made everyone jump. Vish knocked the tongs over, creating a much louder clank of iron on flagstone.

Agastya was standing in the hallway, shaking a key ring. "Lakeside cruise?"

It took Agastya almost a minute to twist the keys in the ignition with his left hand, but he gave Gisela a very unkind look when she reached over to try to help. The ride to the lake was quiet, except for the two seconds of "A Spiral Architect" by Black Sabbath that blasted out of the stereo before Agastya could turn it off.

"Sorry," he said.

"Never apologize for Sabbath," Danny answered, and tried a smile. Agastya just reversed out of the driveway and started driving, having some trouble with the left turn at the end of the street due to his single-arm situation, but pulling it off nicely.

Vish sat in the middle of the backseat of the Buick. Danny and Matt were on either side of him, and Gisela was in the front passenger seat, holding the golden ball wrapped in one of Vish's jackets from the hallway closet. No one spoke, and there was so little movement that when Gisela reached a hand out to squeeze Agastya's, on the wheel, the boys could almost hear the gesture.

The streets were quiet, even downtown, everyone driven inside by the temperature drop: it was at least fifteen degrees cooler than it had been in the afternoon.

Somehow, Vish knew where the car would be stopping. It was the little parking lot closest to the part of the beach where he'd plunged in the night before to give Mr. Farris's teeth back to the portal. There was only one other vehicle parked there, a City Parks vehicle. It had a parking ticket tucked under the windshield, which Vish found very funny. He chuckled as Agastya turned the key in the ignition.

"What's funny?" Matt asked.

"Nothing. Tell you later. Maybe," Vish said.

Agastya got out first and started walking fast, Gisela following behind him.

"Let's go!" Vish said, prodding Danny in the arm.

"Go where?"

"The beach."

When they were all standing at the shore, the silence got to be too much for Vish. Agastya was staring at the gentle lap of the waves, and Gisela had her hand on his back. It was still cool outside, and the lake was moving strangely: waves seemed to be splitting apart from each other, as though something beneath was trying to rise up.

"Well?" Vish asked. "Can we throw it in and go home now? I have to vacuum a dead ghoul out of the carpet."

The joke fell flat. Not even Danny laughed. But Agastya did look up from the waves, grinning.

"We're almost finished," Agastya said. "Gisela, can you — I want to go in with my face, okay? Not like this."

Gisela nodded.

"Just put your face in the water," she said. "The lake is so charged now, its atoms have more magic left in them than I can work up tonight. The waves will undo Isla's work."

Not even bothering to answer, Agastya walked a few steps closer to the lake and took a knee, then planted his face in the waves, as though he were praying to some watery god. He stayed still for almost a full minute, then came up, breathed in deeply, and turned around.

It was dark on the beach, but the walkway streetlamps thirty feet behind them gave off enough light for the boys to see Agastya as he came closer.

"Hey, Vish," Agastya said. His voice was different. So were his nose, his eyes, his jawline, his cheekbones.

"Oh my God," said Matt. Vish said nothing at all.

He just kept staring at the face in front of him.

It was his own face, as it would be in a little over twenty years. Vish stared at Vish, and Vish stared back, smiling.

Gisela started speaking first.

"I told you that Isla and I bounced around through time after we left the place where she found me, Vish. Mostly we spent time in the sixteenth century, sometimes skipping into nineteenth-century London, and even a bit of time in India in the 1900s. But we also spent about a year in Vancouver in 2010."

"Why?" Vish, the young Vish, managed to croak out.

The man he'd known as Agastya until two minutes ago answered. "Because Isla had to find where the portal would surface. Even quantum physics has its uncertainties, and she was off by a few hundred clicks and a couple of decades. Isla came into the record store where I'd been working for five years, and we talked, and fell in love."

"I work at a record store for five years in my thirties?" Vish asked. Gisela laughed. Vish couldn't think of many jobs he'd want more, really, other than playing on the records themselves.

"I don't know what happens to you," the older Vish said, straightening up and touching his lower back where it pained him. The younger Vish touched his own, pain-free back, and waited to hear what his older reflection would say next.

"I'm not you. I'm you-with-mistakes. To start with, I never had the guts to be friends with Matt and Danny after I got back from boarding school. I never joined their band, never really hung out with them again. That was the first time I ran from something good. I kept running from good things over and over again, for the next twenty years. I stopped having anything like what you have now, in you."

Agastya-Vish smiled at Matt and Danny, who were much too stunned to smile back. He kept talking to Vish.

"I started drinking and never stopped. Sometime after college. But I couldn't have lost everything, not quite. There was still enough of me left to be interested in when Isla found me, but we soon understood that it was magic that had brought us together. I wasn't the kind of person that someone like her could love, not for very long. I quit everything I ever tried except drinking, Vish. By the time she died, she mostly just felt sorry for me. She still loved me, maybe, but that's because of the kind of person she was. Not because of who I was anymore.

"So just promise not to become me."

"I can't," Vish said. "I can't promise that. I don't want to not be like you."

Agastya-Vish knelt in front of Vish and whispered to him, making sure that no one else on the beach could hear. "Then just avoid the bad parts, okay?"

Before Vish could answer, Agastya-Vish stood up. He grabbed the wadded-up jacket from Gisela and turned and started walking to the shore. Gisela barely had a chance to catch him before he stepped into the waves.

"Stop, Vish," she said to the older man, who was trying to keep smiling, trying not to let what he was holding shake in his hands. She pulled the jacket off the golden orb.

Agastya-Vish took the car keys out of his jeans pocket and handed those to her. "Car's not much good without these. You have the store key on you tonight? Your ownership papers are all in the apartment. Take care of Moby. Extra good care."

"I said stop, Vish," Gisela said to Agastya-Vish. Farther back on the shore, the younger Vish had taken a hard seat in the sand, unable to think, but trying to record everything he was seeing and hearing so he could work on understanding it later.

Gisela looked at Agastya-Vish, putting her hands around the hands that clung to the golden orb. "Isla did love you. It never became pity."

The man looked at her. "I don't believe you, but I do think you believe what you're saying. Thank you. And thanks for sticking around me when Isla left instead of holing up in your cabin and waiting for Farris. And I guess I should thank him too."

"For what?"

"Messing my insides up enough that I won't live through the night anyway. So you're not going to fight me on who carries this thing to the bottom of the lake."

He hefted the golden orb, kissed Gisela's forehead, and turned to walk into the waves. When he was in as deep as his waist, he turned back.

"Bye, guys. It was great seeing you again, Danny, Matt. You have no idea how great. I got to do something useful with my old best pals. And we did such a good job that none of the idiots in this crappy town are ever going to know about it!" Agastya-Vish started laughing at this, backing farther into the split waves of the lake, chest-deep now.

"Do I get to work in a record store too?" asked Danny. Matt gave him a disappointed look that somehow burned through the darkness.

"You do better than that," Agastya-Vish called. "Much better. Goodbye."

"Be careful," Vish called out from the beach, knowing it made no sense, and knowing that he was crying in the dark.

Out in the waves, the man stopped, in as deep as his neck. But he didn't turn back or call out. No one on the shore could think of anything to say. In another second, he started moving again. The lake closed over his head. After a few minutes, Gisela helped Vish up, and Matt and Danny each put a hand on his shoulders as they led him back to the car, where they discovered that Gisela could drive, licence or not.

Vish slept most of that night, while Gisela and the boys cleaned the house. He woke up at about three and tried to help, but Danny marched him back downstairs. Above him were the sounds of the vacuum and the strange slurp-suck of the carpet shampooer that

Gisela had gotten from the bookstore. Agastya had bought it a month ago, saying they would need it. He didn't know magic, but he'd seen enough rituals to know that a mess was likely, and also knew from first-hand experience that Anji Maurya would kill first and ask questions later if she saw that mess.

Vish surfaced at eight in the morning, to a call from his mother. After he fumbled his cheap *Time Magazine* phone off the table and fell on top of it, breaking it, he ran into his father's study, where the nearest phone was. Vish could tell the house was empty, just by feel.

"He's awake," Anji Maurya said. "He's awake and he's talking. He's fine, Vish. Can you take a taxi here, now? Please?"

Vish talked to his mother for another few minutes, but couldn't remember any of it. After showering and getting dressed, he took a deep, terrified breath and walked upstairs and into the sitting room.

It was immaculate. All the furniture was exactly where it should be, there were no slime trails or human puddles, and the only odd smell in the air was the perfumed scent of carpet shampoo, which Vish could only smell because he had a particularly sensitive nose. He went into the kitchen and ate a banana. Buddy was sleeping on a blanket beneath the kitchen table, a bowl with another half can of salmon near him. Vish called Kelowna Taxi and waited for the car that would take him to his parents.

CHAPTER 27

V ish talked to Matt and Danny plenty in the following week, but they didn't ruin either surprise that was waiting for him at the bookstore when he turned up for his next shift. Dr. Maurya, his face bruised and his arm in a cast, had insisted on driving Vish himself. Because he was very, very bored.

"I know I can work, but these neurologists — well, it would be hypocritical of me to ignore medical advice, and the gossip would spread, so you know, I have to be obedient," Dr. Maurya said. "I'm not officially supposed to drive, either, but I feel fine, I must say. Now I know how you feel when we give you unreasonable orders."

Vish's hand went for the radio dial and Dr. Maurya didn't stop him. The tuner found a Neil Young song, a bit soft but quite good. Anji Maurya had been singing a Whitney Houston song in full voice when they left the house; she'd closed two listings, earning commission on two mansions in Mission, her best week yet. Anji called it luck, but Vish had overheard his father, through the kitchen door, telling her that she sold those houses because she was the best — he used an emphatic swear — real estate agent in the city, ten times the worker that Marissa Bingham was. Then Vish had heard them kissing and headed very quickly for the stairs.

Vish kept the radio quiet so he could listen to his father talk, which he now loved doing, and promised himself he would always love doing, even when he hated what Dr. Maurya had to say. He'd started in on Buddy now.

"And Rita — she cannot stop talking about the cat, the cat, the cat. What did your son do for him, she says. Prepare to be bugged about it in your next session. She says he's acting like he did when he was a kitten, that he seems years younger. What did you do?"

"I gave him salmon because I forgot where I put the dry food he usually eats. I guess that was it."

Dr. Maurya gave Vish a look, one that seemed menacing because of the bruising around his right eye. But then he pulled up in front of Greycat Books and told him to get to work.

"I'll call if I need a ride," Vish said. "Might hang out with Matt and Danny after my shift, though."

"Whatever you want," Dr. Maurya said. "Enjoy your summer."

Vish stood on the sidewalk as his dad pulled away in Anji Maurya's car. On Monday, the family would pick out a replacement for Dr. Maurya's totalled Camry, hopefully something more exciting that Vish could start driving himself next year. Downtown was sweltering and busy again, and Vish could feel the sweat in the pits of the *Appetite for Destruction* t-shirt he had on. He couldn't remember if he'd put on deodorant that morning, but was sure it would be obvious soon enough.

Vish walked past a few people on the sidewalk, all of them potential tenants of the nachzehrers, and entered Greycat Books, proprietor Gisela Telemann. It wasn't her real last name, but it was what Agastya-Vish had used for the paperwork when he transferred the business.

Moby was sitting on top of the cash register, and two college-aged girls wearing hippie clothes were buying orange-spined Penguin Classics — Vish couldn't see the titles — from Gisela, who was behind the counter. Vish was annoyed he hadn't gotten to ring them out, but it was his fault for being a few minutes late.

When the girls left, Gisela gave Vish a worried look, the one that made the shadow under her septum ring thicken slightly.

"Did Matt tell you what Danny did?"

"No," Vish said. "What?"

Gisela put a torn white thing on the counter. From his perch, Moby extended a paw toward it, but Gisela gently pushed the furry limb aside.

For a second, Vish was terrified that it was a piece of Farris's mask, but then he came closer. It was a white scrap of paper, with black letters typed on it.

Haziga

Gaveston

Luisa Margarida

Balka Kalji

Samdup

Ommony

"Oh, no," Vish said. "Oh, no."

"Yeah, oh no," Gisela said. "That idiot found it in his shoe, after we'd finished the cleanup. Admitted to Matt that he had heard a small tearing sound when he was rolling up his scroll."

"So it was all pointless," Vish said. "The ceremony. Agastya being gone. All of it. Farris is gone but the nachzehrers are here anyway. It was pointless."

"Hey." Gisela came around the counter, and Vish stopped babbling, because he was pretty sure she was going to slap him if he didn't. "Don't you ever say that any of this was pointless. Ever. I lost two people stopping what Farris was trying to do, and we did it. We did. There is a big difference between six of these things maybe, possibly, having got through the portal and into hosts up here, and *twelve thousand* of them. So don't panic. If we need to handle this, we will. That's why Agastya and I always planned to have me stick around town for a couple of years. Just to make sure."

Gisela walked past Vish and started sorting the Biography shelf.

"You're worried," Vish said.

"Of course I am. I'm not stupid. I'm going to see what I can find out, but we may just have to wait and see if one of these things turns up," Gisela said. She kept on working. "Can you go upstairs and leave me alone for a second? Matt and Danny are up there."

"What? Why?"

"Just go."

Vish obeyed, thinking of escaped monsters as he opened the door to the apartment he had once known as Agastya's. The Conan poster was still up at the top of the stairwell. He'd thought that Gisela was going to move in, but she liked her little cabin across the lake and had no intention of giving it up. Vish walked upstairs.

Danny's drum kit was set up with a big, ugly piece of carpet below it to prevent the kick drum from sliding all over the place. There was a pillowcase draped over the front of it. Matt's bass was plugged into a Traynor amp, and — Vish's guitar was there, along with a Fender Twin-Reverb amp he had never seen before.

"Did you guys steal this?" Vish asked, forgetting to scream at Danny about the forgotten scrap of paper.

"We told your parents we were taking the guitar as a surprise. We have a full-on jam space now, man. This is huge. And the amp — the guy left it behind for you," Matt said. "I mean, you left it behind for you. You get it."

"Dude, look. Just for a second. Look at this," Danny said. He whipped the pillowcase off the front of the drum kit.

Carefully stencilled in red and black Sharpie, in a font somewhere between the Megadeth logo and the Metallica logo, were the words *The Grimmer*.

"Epic band name," Danny said. "You know it. I couldn't get it out of my head."

"He's right, don't you think?" Matt said.

Matt kept talking as Vish ran his fingers over the bristly silverface cover in front of his new amp's speakers. He'd always think of Agastya as another person, as *him*, but he had accepted that he'd met a version of himself. Someone he didn't quite ever want to be, but who he really liked. He plugged the guitar in, and along with the other guys, started jamming.

It lasted five minutes before Gisela came upstairs and started yelling. They didn't notice her at first, but when Danny did, he didn't just stop playing, he dropped his sticks.

"She *really* yelled at me about the paper thing," he whispered to Vish, whose ears were ringing slightly from the noise he had played a part in creating.

"Guys," Gisela said. "This is a business. It's a jam space after hours, not right now. Clear?"

"Clear," said Matt. The other boys repeated him.

Gisela started to go, then turned back.

"Also, we are going to have to practise at least four times a week when I get my keyboard up here. Because right now you truly, truly suck."

Gisela went back to the store. Danny started laughing first, and the others joined him. They left their instruments behind and walked downstairs to join their friend.

ACKNOWLEDGEMENTS

My family, quite different from the family in this book, but just as encouraging of reading and the viewing of Westerns.

Kris Bertin, Ashley MacCuish, George and Harry Bertin
Alexander Forbes
Seamus Weisgerber and Sammy Weisgerber
Vindhya Rathore, Raj Rathore
Michael Kelly, Carolyn Macdonell
Patrick Tarr, Owen Tarr, Elisabeth Brückmann
Sam Wiebe, Carly Reemeyer, Saelan Twerdy, Graeme Desrosiers, Lindsay Clarke
Andrew F. Sullivan, Amy Jones, Michael LaPointe, David Bertrand, Jennifer Idems-Bertrand, Waubgeshig Rice, David Demchuk, Pasha Malla, Craig Davidson, Andrew Pyper
Jamal Severin-Watson, Lynne Parker, Charlotte Dykes
John Bellairs, Robert Westall
Samantha Haywood, Laura Cameron, Megan Phillip, Barbara Miller
Jen Albert, Jessica Albert, Jen Knoch, Jen Sookfong Lee, Claire Pokorchak, Lisa Pompillo, Shannon Parr
Bert Ainsley

This book is also available as a Global Certified Accessible™ (GCA) ebook. ECW Press's ebooks are screen reader friendly and are built to meet the needs of those who are unable to read standard print due to blindness, low vision, dyslexia, or a physical disability.

At ECW Press, we want you to enjoy our books in whatever format you like. If you've bought a print copy just send an email to ebook@ecwpress.com and include:

Get the ebook free!*
*proof of purchase required

- the book title
- the name of the store where you purchased it
- a screenshot or picture of your order / receipt number and your name
- your preference of file type: PDF (for desktop reading), ePub (for a phone / tablet, Kobo, or Nook), mobi (for Kindle)

A real person will respond to your email with your ebook attached. Please note this offer is only for copies bought for personal use and does not apply to school or library copies.

Thank you for supporting an independently owned Canadian publisher with your purchase!

This book is made of paper from well-managed FSC® - certified forests, recycled materials, and other controlled sources.